D0663219

PERFECTLY MESSY

LIZZY CHARLES

PERFECTLY MESSY

LIZZY CHARLES

This book is a work of fiction. Names, characters, places, and incidents are either products of the author's imagination or are used fictitiously. Any resemblance to actual persons, living or dead, business establishments, events, or locales is entirely coincidental. The author makes no claims to, but instead acknowledges the trademarked status and trademark owners of the word marks mentioned in this work of fiction.

Copyright © 2014 by Lizzy Charles
PERFECTLY MESSY by Lizzy Charles
All rights reserved. Published in the United States of America by Swoon Romance. Swoon Romance and its related logo are registered trademarks of Georgia McBride Media Group, LLC. No part of this book may be used or reproduced in any manner whatsoever without written permission of the publisher, except in the case of brief quotations embodied in critical articles and reviews.

Published by Swoon Romance
Cover designed by Victoria Faye
Cover Copyright © 2014 Swoon Romance

PRAISE FOR LIZZY CHARLES

"*Perfectly Messy* is Young Adult Romance to a kissable "T." Lizzy Charles nails the butterflies, doubt, mistakes, and beauty of first love with exquisite ease in what is certainly a worthy sequel to *Effortless With You!*"

—Rebecca Yarros, bestselling author of *Full Measures*

"A definite MUST READ! *Effortless With You* left me smiling like a doofus and hugging my Kindle."

—Cassie Mae, bestselling author of *Reasons I Fell For the Funny Fat Friend* and *How to Date a Nerd*

To my son, for being with me through all of this.

To my husband, for keeping things messy.

CHAPTER ONE

Lucy

A mousy-haired freshman darts out of my way as I take my first step out of French. I stop in the doorway. "Thanks, but you go ahead." He blushes as I wave him forward. People behind me groan. They'll just have to wait. He looks weary so I smile. There's no reason he has to get out of my way. I'll wait for the person in front of me just like every other human being should in this school.

Being on top is so different. *Strange*, really. Becoming Justin's girlfriend placed me into high-school royalty, which makes sense, as he was just crowned Homecoming King. Immediate popularity is a nice perk, but I don't know if I'll ever get used to this sort of treatment. It's almost sickening how fast I went from the kid hiding in the janitor's closet to the girl who clears a path with a glance.

1

The guy finally takes a step from the wall, glancing back with a wave as he makes his way down the hallway. Good. Normalcy.

Laura taps on my back while clearing her throat. *"Maaa belle, s'il vous plaît."* Long drawl, pronounced "s" and "t." I stifle a laugh. When she combines her French with an accentuated southern accent, it's nothing less than awesome. And horrible. That too.

She gives me a little shove, and I stumble into the hallway. "All right, all right. I'm moving."

"So, what does Justin have on the agenda tonight?" she says, twirling a pencil around her curled blond hair and locking it in a top bun.

"Another surprise." It takes everything in me to not squeal with delight. He's so amazing with surprises. Last time it was ice cream while walking around the state capitol. The time before? A twilight game of one-on-one basketball, the winner choosing the type of kiss they'd like. I totally let him win, dying to know what way he likes me kissing him most. It's crazy passionate kissing, melting into a long, careful kiss, where we start standing but I end up on his lap. Not that he told me this, but he basically showed me. I just can't get enough of the way he—

"Earth to Lucy." Laura pops up in front of me, fingers twitching like Martian antennas. "Man, you've got it bad. I don't know if I ever got so lost over Luke."

Shaking my head, I desperately try to rid myself of Justin-like thoughts. I don't know why I try though. It's impossible.

"It's just, he's so amazing, Laura. He's beyond any guy I ever imagined possible..."

Laura rolls her eyes, placing her hand against my

forehead. "Yeah, you're definitely lovesick. Let me get you home before I have to take you to the ICU."

"About that ride home…"

"Let me guess. Justin?"

"He wants to pick me up. We haven't seen each other for a couple of days. We need time to reconnect."

"Riiight." Laura turns from me, wrapping her arms around her body and moving them up and down so it looks like she's making out with someone in the corner. Some guy wolf whistles as he passes us. Nicely played.

I spin her out of the self make out session. "No, really. With Justin, it's not only that. Talking to him is incredible. I could go on forever, he makes me so relaxed."

"And?"

"And what?"

"AND?"

I throw my hands in the air. "Okay, and I like the kissing part too."

"There we go!" Laura says as she wraps her arm around my shoulder and gives it a squeeze. "That's nothing to be ashamed of, Luce. Let's enjoy the hormone-driven roller coaster while we can."

I pull her into a quick hug. "I'll call you, all right?"

"Text. I'll probably be getting my own make out session on with Lukester tonight."

"*Okay*, never mind. Let's catch up tomorrow, cool?"

"Great." She winks as she walks away with the perfect amount of minimal, but classy, hip sway. Lucky. She owns her southern charm. If I tried that, I'd look like a penguin. A flash of blond from across the locker bay catches my eye. Marissa glares at me. My eyes dart away, refusing to allow myself to go down that hate road right now.

I stop for a moment, opening the door to the closet where I used to hide from my brutal teammates during my freshman year. Now that I'm finally a junior, I make sure to check it regularly. I'm keeping my promise to check in there often, in case someone needs help. I never want someone to have to use it as a shelter from torture again.

Only brooms, brushes, and toxic chemicals this time. Good. Maybe our school is changing.

I turn into the locker bay for upperclassmen. They're larger, and near the snack bar. I fiddle with the combination before opening the door. It's ridiculous that they've banned cell phones from everywhere but the locker. I used to keep the combination in my note app. Seriously, how do teachers expect us to remember all the passwords and stuff required to survive a school day without a phone?

The lock finally gives and, with a swift kick to the bottom left corner, the door pops open. A note flutters to the floor.

Hey, Lady. I'll meet you in about forty-five seconds. Can't believe I have to wait so long to hold you. Love, Justin.

I glance around at the empty hallway. There's no way he's got this timed that precisely. I laugh. The guy's got to have limits, right?

With my French book slid in place on the shelf, I pull out my AP English homework and *Emma*. Mr. Tatem is giving me the chance to rewrite my *Emma* essay from last year to boost my GPA for college applications. Initially I refused, but he insisted. So here I am, facing a giant twelve-page rewrite plus the AP reading and a small three-page essay for the weekend. Hopefully, this is the only essay he wants rewritten. Redoing tenth grade Advanced English while dealing with AP English would end me via an agonizing, literary death.

A warm palm wraps around my hip and gives it a slow squeeze. I yelp, dropping the book as Justin's laugh rolls through my heart.

"Hey, Lady," he says, spinning me around and taking a step closer. He pins me against the locker, playfully touching his lips to mine.

"Sixty-two seconds," I say when his lips pull away. Actually, I have no idea, but it's Justin. Who am I kidding? It's probably been exactly forty-five seconds since the note dropped.

Justin chuckles as he takes a step back, doing his signature hand pull through his gorgeous dark hair. His biceps pop and I bite my tongue. Holy crap. I can't believe I used to hate when he did that.

"Can you please do that all the time?" I beg with a step forward.

"The kissing? Yes."

"Well, that and the flexing."

"For you? I suppose." He bends down and scoops my bag up over his shoulder as we walk out toward his car.

"So, what's the plan tonight?"

He hands me the purple flyer I've been avoiding for the last two weeks. I don't even need to open it to know what it says. *October fourth, three-fifteen, girls' basketball tryouts, south gym. Sign up online.*

One week.

"I don't know, Justin."

"Just take it." He places the purple sheet in my palm. "You get distracted every time you see this thing on a wall. Please, keep it. If anything, so I don't have to steer you through the sea of students every morning."

"Fine." I groan, folding the flyer and slipping it into my back pocket. "Better?"

Justin admires my placement of the paper. "I don't know. Why don't you bend over a bit more so I can make a further *ass*essment?"

I yank out the flyer and swat him on the chest. "For real?"

"What? I can't help it around you." He clicks his key fob. The engine roars to life as he opens my door.

"So, we're playing ball tonight?" I touch my phone's screen. "I should probably let my parents know."

"Nope. I've got something completely different planned."

"Okay? What's up your sleeve?"

"Don't worry about it. I called your parents already, even stopped in to get everything you'll need," he says, gesturing toward the back seat as he shuts my door. Mom's old garment bag hangs from a hook. My red pumps lie on the seat.

Oh my God. My stomach plummets. My room's a mess. I haven't picked up laundry in a week. There's got to be underwear on my closet floor. And not just any underwear, period underwear, the cotton rejects that you don't care if you destroy. Crap. What if he saw my period stains? My stained granny panties!

"You were in my room?" I squeak out as he slides into the driver's seat. He doesn't answer immediately. Holy hell. He totally saw my period stains! "Please, tell me you weren't in my room."

He shrugs.

"Justin. Seriously. I need to know." I cover my mouth. This can't be happening. One month of dating, no matter how comfortable I am with him, is way too early for this sort of exposure.

Justin takes my hand. "Relax, Lucy. Your mom went up there." He rubs my arm. "The only time I've been in your room was the night Marissa cheated with Zach. Stupid guy to go for that. Even then," he squeezes my palm, "I don't remember anything except how pretty you looked, even crying."

"That's kind of pathetic."

"Whatever. I took every glimpse of you I could get."

I shift in my seat a bit, not yet knowing how to handle all of his compliments. They're never ending and it's hard to understand why. With another squeeze of my palm, he eases up on me. I love how he knows exactly what I'm thinking.

"So, where are we going?"

"My place."

My heart jolts. I've never been in his house. We've driven by it, but his parents were never home and his dad's staff uses his living room as campaign headquarters. In the last weeks, it's gotten out of control. Thankfully, Justin's post-secondary Psych class ends at one fifteen every other day, so he's home helping out his dad way before the actual school day is over.

"Wait, so like, meeting your parents?"

"Not now. They're out. Just you and me."

Alone with Justin in his house? For real? This is his best surprise ever.

"So, I'll get to see where you eat?"

"Eat, sleep, and shower," he says as he pulls into his neighborhood development.

My face warms, but I don't even try to get rid of the

tomato shade. Instead I toss him a sideways glance. "Sleep and shower? What exactly do you have in mind, sir?"

Justin playfully shrugs as he pulls into his driveway. Butterflies *ping pong* through my gut. Making out on his bed would be heaven, but seeing his bed will be a new side of Justin. Way more intimate.

Justin pulls around the main garage to a small, non-attached two-car garage in back. The garage door raises and there sits his old rusty painting truck, tarp drawn over it. Dead.

"I can't get rid of her yet. Still hoping I can get her fixed. Plus, she makes a great storage vehicle for the painting supplies." I open my door before Justin can, stepping over random gallons of paint that are pushed flush with the walls. Varying sized ladders hang from nearly every wall or ceiling beam.

"Oh really?" I laugh when Justin accidentally knocks the end of a ladder as he squeezes out from the tight fit on his side of the car.

"Hush, you." He vaults the hood of his car, sweeping me up in his arms with a kiss.

Suddenly, a towel hits us in the face. "Too much PDA, guys!" A head full of light brown hair pops up from inside the truck bed and I scream. I hate how easily I startle.

"Alex!" I squeal. "I've missed you!" Our school's so massive that the few times I've crossed him in the hallway isn't enough compared to the hundreds of hours we spent painting together last summer.

"Dude. Were you hiding in there waiting for us?" Justin tosses up his hands.

Alex tosses a paint roller at Justin. "No. I have a life." He winks at me while he jumps out of the truck. "Lucy, how are you? I've missed you too." After Justin puts me down, he wraps me in a perfect Alex-hug, the type that always brings a smile no matter how awkward the situation is.

"Why are you here, Alex?" Justin lays into him with an underlying tone that says *leave us alone*. I can't help but giggle. It's still amazing to me that Justin wants to be alone with me. Me!

"What? Can't a guy just show up to haunt his favorite cousin's garage? Especially on a day where that cousin is bringing home his girlfriend to an empty house. Feels like the perfect time to drop in."

"Dude." Justin eyes him while Alex tosses an arm over my shoulder and gives it a squeeze. I love watching them banter like brothers. They're that type of cousins, real family rather than only a link by blood.

"All right. I get the hint." Alex says with a laugh. He reaches over the truck bed and pulls out a brush and a can of primer. "I'm finishing up the front window trim on the rambler down the block, remember?"

"That's right. It chipped in the last storm."

"Do you also remember that you said you'd pay me double for doing it tonight?"

Justin's eyes bulge. "Double?" Alex's face is stone as he nods.

"Oh, Justin. That's so sweet of you." I nudge Alex. If Alex is serious, there's a joke behind it. I'll never forget that Alex was my first friend when I had to work for Justin's painting business last summer. I may be dating Justin, but I'll always stand by Alex in all Justin targeted pranks and jokes.

Justin steps toward Alex. "Double?" he asks again.

"Yup."

"You sure I said double?"

"Absolutely."

"All right then." He pulls Alex in close and throws two stunt punches in his gut. Alex's response correlates perfectly, crunching over in feigned agony.

"Thanks, boss," Alex says in a moan.

"I aim to please." Justin smirks. Alex reaches up, trying to grab Justin's head and pull it into a headlock. Justin bows out though, slapping Alex on the back with a laugh.

"You around to play ball tomorrow?" Alex asks while they scuffle.

"Can't. I've got two papers to write and a post fundraiser meeting with Dad." Justin takes a fake punch to the face.

"Next week?"

"Text me, man. We'll work something out." Justin wraps his arm around Alex's neck, catching him in headlock. He gives him a quick noogie before release. Alex rubs his head before taking a seat on the bumper of the truck. Justin grunts. "Maybe you should get going on that rambler's trim before it rains."

"I was actually thinking of staying. Did you know that acid rain is a real thing? It's not worth the risk."

Justin grabs a cart, tossing in the primer and paint brush. "One. Two…" Justin starts counting. "Three. Four."

Alex stretches his arm overhead with a fake yawn. "Do you mind if I take a nap on your basement couch? I'm exhausted. I won't be a bother. Promise."

"Five. Six. Seven."

"Or we could play Yahtzee?"

"Eight." Justin's voice is stern. "Nine." He reaches for Alex as he says "TEN."

Alex bolts from the bumper, grabbing the cart and running from the garage. "Bye Lucy!"

"Bye!" I wave as Alex jogs away. "Justin, what happens when you get to ten?"

He rubs his jaw, making my stomach flip in delight. "I don't know. He's never been brave enough to find out."

"He's a good kid."

"Yeah. So far freshman year has been good to him. Hope it continues."

"Me too," I say quietly, trying to block the memories of my own bullied freshman year.

Justin wraps his arms around me, kissing my neck. "So?"

"So?"

"Want to see where I live?"

***

I run my finger over the smooth granite countertop as Justin grabs apples from the woven fruit basket sitting on the antique farm table. "It's gorgeous here," I say, admiring the rich dark wood of the kitchen.

"My mom loves interior design."

"It's like a magazine. Flawless."

"Yeah, she's kind of a clean freak. But," he opens some cabinets along the wall, "she just knows how to hide the mess." The cabinets are lined with cork, random papers pinned disorderly to the doors. Crumpled paper sticks out from the overfilled drawers. Much better.

"Now, this makes me feel more at home."

He moves behind me, sweeping away my hair from my ear. "Good, I always want you to feel at home here," he whispers, then nibbles my neck. Goosebumps run over my skin and my knees nearly give with the touch of his lips. He only stops kissing my neck and shoulders when the phone rings.

"Don't move," he says as he takes a step away to grab the phone, one hand still on my hip.

Me, move? *Never.* There's no other place for me. As he scribbles something down on a Post-It, I check out the gray wooden-framed photos on the nearest wall. There's one of Justin with his arm wrapped around the shoulder of a redhead with flawless skin, and Justin's green eyes.

"That's Tonya, my sister," Justin says as he gets off the phone.

"She's beautiful."

"Ha. You tell her that immediately, and she'll love you. Trust me."

"I'd love to meet her someday."

"Well, now that you mention it…" He nods to the garment bag and my shoes he put to rest on the table. "That's kind of the surprise."

"Meeting your sister?" That'd be cool. I could handle that, as long as Justin was there. Honestly, sometimes I think I can handle anything with Justin at my side.

"Actually," he bites his lower lip. "Don't hate me, but kind of my entire family."

My stomach drops through the floor. He immediately steps closer, rubbing my lower back.

"Your parents and sister? Like, tonight?" I choke out.

He nods. "And Grandma…At a campaign fundraiser."

"You're kidding me, right?"

"No."

I reach out for a chair. All in one night? Crap. What's in

the garment bag? I don't have anything on earth that would fit this occasion. I grab it, unzipping it like a mad woman. A dress with a white lace overlay rests on the hanger, a Nordstrom's tag still attached.

"Did you buy this?"

He pulls up the chair next to me and takes my hand. "Yes."

I stare stupidly at the dress. What if it doesn't fit? I have a hard enough time finding stuff that works on my body. He's got to be kidding me. If I put this on and it doesn't fit… What will I say to him?

"You okay?"

"Umm, this is a lot." Too much. Too risky.

He takes the dress in his hands. "You're right. I'm sorry. I shouldn't have sprung this on you. My goal was that you wouldn't worry for days before meeting my family." He takes out his cell. "Listen, I'll call them and let them know I was an idiot and that we need to reschedule."

Yes, reschedule. That way I can go buy a new dress that will fit, practice my greeting, and at least have clean hair. Definitely.

With my hand free from his, I slide the lace overlay of the dress between my fingertips. It's so beautiful. I'm nuts. Yeah, it's a majorly dumb move to buy a girl clothing and surprise her with meeting the family, but at least Justin's trying. Hell, chick flicks are filled with that scene where the girl opens a beautiful box and her dream dress lies nestled in tissue paper. This is totally romantic. If the dress doesn't fit, we'll swing by my house, and I'll wear one from the summer. If I'm dressed too casually, I'll still survive.

"Don't cancel." I reach out and take his phone. "This is amazing. I just needed time to wrap my mind around it."

I squeeze his palm. "I want to meet your family, and the dress… It's gorgeous."

"Really? You like it?"

"I love it. But, I can't guarantee it'll fit me."

"Well, let's find out," he says as he pulls me up from the chair. His palm rests again on the small of my back as he leads me through the hall to the basement door. "My room's down here."

My fingertips tingle. His room? Okay, it's just where he sleeps. No big deal… Except it is. *Huge.*

We pass through a sitting area with a large flat-screen TV and sectional couches, surrounded by blurred French doors. He opens one set, letting me step into his room alone. "I'll wait out here while you change."

I nod like an idiot as he closes the door behind me.

Holy crap. I finally take a deep breath, welcomed with the fresh scent that normally clings to Justin's clothes. A queen-sized bed, made up with a hunter-green comforter, is positioned under the window. I scan the walls for posters of hot naked girls. None. Okay, good. His hamper is slightly overfilled in the corner of the room and random pens and notepads clutter the top of his dresser. I pick up a five-by-seven photo of Justin as a little boy with his brother and sister cooking s'mores around a campfire. His brother's hair is gone, probably halfway through his leukemia battle. Tonya and Jackson's arms are wrapped around Justin. He's beaming.

My eyes sting and I quickly put the photo down. This is not the time to cry.

I eye the bed again and my tummy flips. As far as I'm concerned, that's one of the most intimate places I can imagine Justin. My face warms, and I sneak a look at myself in the mirror. Crazy eyes with flushed cheeks. I pull my fingers through my hair, trying to keep the loony troll look at bay.

I pull off my jeans and my shirt. It's weird to only be in my underwear and bra in here. The dress slides easily over my head, sitting nicely on the hips. It even fits over my chest without pulling at the fabric. I turn in the mirror. What is this miracle dress?

Taking a deep breath, I open the door. Justin flips off the TV as he turns around.

"Lady, you look beautiful."

"You didn't actually pick this out, did you?" There's no way a guy would be able to guarantee a perfect fit like this.

"I said I bought it…"

I turn and the dress twirls out just enough to expose my lower thigh, nothing too high. It'll be awesome on a dance floor. Not that I dance, but still.

"Laura?" This isn't her style, but she's definitely been shopping with me a few times to know my size and what not to buy.

"Nope."

"My mom?" I ask in disbelief. There's no way I can picture her in a store with nice dresses like this. Especially with Justin. It just doesn't mesh.

He runs his hand down the lace on my back.

"Tonya."

"But, she's never seen me."

"Her business is fashion. I gave her some photos of you, she sized you, and dragged me to the right dress. The only input I got was the color, and barely even that. She's pretty controlling about that stuff."

"Well, at least I know I'll be wearing something she approves of."

"Don't ever worry about that, okay? Most of the time Tonya trots around town in workout pants and a tank top."

"Okay, cool." I tug at the dress. "Do you mind if we swing by my house so I can do my hair and makeup?"

Justin picks up a backpack. "That's where your mom came in." My makeup bag, hairdryer, shampoo, conditioner, and hair wand are all within. If there was ever a time she needed to come through, this was it. And, score, she did it well.

"So," he nods back toward his room, "you want to wash up?"

"You don't mind?"

He laughs, opening the door to his bathroom. "Well, it is inconvenient to know the most beautiful girl in the world is taking a shower in *my* shower, but I'll survive." He kisses the back of my neck. Tingles of awesome shoot down my spine. "Can you be ready in forty minutes? We're due at the fundraiser by five-thirty."

"Fundraiser?"

"Yeah, it's one of those pay-for-a-plate dinner things to fuel the last month of the governor campaign." He wraps me in his arms. "Don't worry. We aren't staying long. At eight thousand dollars a plate, it's pretty standard that the family shows up for the appetizers and then splits before the dinner and speeches. I was thinking we'd do Chipotle after?"

I breathe out a huge sigh of relief. Appetizers with his family is totally doable. It's way less pressure than a whole dinner. "That sounds great."

"All right, now go make my dream come true."

"Your dream?"

"Just get your butt in my shower." He tosses me a towel.

I lock the door before turning on the water, instantly spraying hot. I carefully hang up the dress before taking the quickest shower imaginable. He knows I'm naked in here and it's totally crazy knowing I'm naked in the same space he's naked in every day. Not that we're naked together. It's just bizarre. My brain can't separate it, and my heart races every time my mind drifts that way.

I hop out of the shower quickly. I don't have time for those distractions right now. I've got to focus on the challenge ahead: meeting Justin's family without making a total fool of myself.

CHAPTER TWO

Justin

Pushing every button on the controller is useless. Not even the Twins versus the Brewers can keep my mind from picturing Lucy on the other side of that wall. *Showering.* Water-falling-over-her-body-and-pooling-on-the-tile type showering.

Crap. I pull on my crotch to readjust for more room. This was not a good idea. I flip off the television. I need to get out of this basement. Now.

Upstairs, I grab water and open up my calendar app. My to-do list glares back at me. Perfect. There's nothing sexy about this chaos. Captain's basketball practice, post-secondary Psych, English, and Calc II, a meeting with Dad and Paul—Dad's political image adviser, two phone conferences with the Leukemia society, a King and Queen visit to Northland Elementary with Jen, and prepping for the James. J. Hill House's board meeting. All before Tuesday.

My eyes flicker up to the framed kid's art on the wall. Four baseball bats surrounding an infield, expertly sketched by Jackson in the hospital. He lived for baseball. He would've gone major league, for sure. Even at eight, he had his whole life planned.

I yank on my hair and glare at this epic list. How would an older Jackson deal with this? He wouldn't piss or moan. He'd tackle it straight on. I eye the hour slots on my calendar and make my game plan. Everyday needs an hour block for basketball with Lucy, just in case she wants to practice. I've seen the light in her eyes when she plays. There's no way she'll pass up tryouts. Being ready to help her the day she decides to make that leap again is important.

The sound of running water from below halts. *Thank God*. I snap my pencil as I strain to not picture her wrapping up in a towel. Frick.

The minute hand on the clock goes around three more times. All right, that dress has to be on by now. I fill up an extra glass of water for her and head back downstairs, choosing to sink into the couch rather than my man chair. I listen to her hairdryer buzz from behind my door as I Instagram a photo of us. Whoa, that last one got three-hundred and forty-one favorites. I click over to my profile. Five-hundred some followers? When did that happen?

The door clicks open and I drop my phone as Lucy enters. Holy crap. Every curve begs to be touched. I reach out, wrapping my arms around her. "You look beautiful."

"Your sister has good taste." She quickly glances away, covering up her discomfort with a quick brush of her bangs.

I cup her chin and lift her gaze to mine. "Lucy, you've got to understand… you're so hot."

Her skin flushes pink, making her blue eyes crystal.

"You," I lean in and kiss her, slipping my fingers through that silky hair, "are torturing me. I hope you know that."

"I can change back?"

"Only if I get to watch." My gut somersaults as the words slip out. Now I'm picturing her sliding that dress over her head again. *Get control.* She rolls her eyes with a sly grin. Would I have the strength to look away if she was totally cool with changing in front of me? Or the strength to hold back everything else my body wants to do if she said yes?

I shift in my jeans, coughing to cover and calm the answer that's in my pants. "All right, I'll be back. Can't show up tonight in this." Everything about her is tantalizing in a way that drives me wild, from that look in her eyes to the way her hair falls on her shoulders and touches her chest… frick. I fumble with the door handle, finally ducking into the bedroom. With a yank, I'm down to my boxers. *Whoa. Settle down!* It's a good thing we're leaving or my body is going to flip. I've got to learn how to control this around her.

I pull on my gray Dockers and a green-and-white striped dress shirt. Paul hates the combo, wanting me to wear *more purple hues*, but screw him. This is what I like. I swing open the door to find Lucy turned away from me, thumbing through the Blu-rays along the wall.

My heart sputters like my old truck. What I wouldn't give to have that view every time I open this thing.

"You ready?" she asks.

I pull her close. "The question is, are you?" The corner

of her lip twitches. Clearly, she's not. "We don't have to do this tonight, Lucy. We can wait for you to meet my family later."

"No, I want to meet them. Now is good." She's good at covering up her nerves from everyone, but she has an easy tell that she's freaking out inside. Yup, there's that lip twitch again. She pushes through though, confidently saying, "It'll be good for me."

"They'll love you. I promise." I squeeze her hand.

"We'll see."

***

Lucy shifts again in the chair, occasionally rubbing the tablecloth between her fingers. I take her cool hand in mine. It's so small compared to my own. I enclose it in both hands, warming her skin in a pathetic attempt of helping her relax. A blond waiter nods at me, wearing hipster glasses that I could never pull off. A Fender guitar shirt flashes in my mind, replacing his button up white shirt. Ah! It's Ian, that musical homeschooled guy I sit next to in post-secondary Psych.

I stand. Campaign family rule: we always stand when greeting. "Hey, Ian. Awesome to see you."

"You too. Didn't know you were the governor's son."

I shake his hand. "Not the governor yet. But let's hope so."

"I hope so too. Your dad is fantastic. Standing up for everything our congress is too chicken to face." He holds out the tray. "Bacon-wrapped scallops?"

"Thanks." I take two, passing one over to Lucy.

"Ian, this is my girlfriend, Lucy."

He shifts a step back, focusing in on her eyes. Nice move, very polite dude. "Great to meet you. Justin and I are in Psych together. Here," he nods down to the tray, "take another two."

"Thanks," Lucy says as she takes them. "It's nice to meet you. Are you enjoying post-secondary?"

"Yes. Best addition to homeschool, ever."

"Homeschool, really? I've never met anyone who's homeschooled."

He winks at her, but in a forced, dorky way. "Well, here's a secret. We're all pretty weird. Not concerned about what the crowd thinks. You know?"

I point to his hipster glasses. "Oh really?"

"I had these way before they were *in*."

"Riiight." Lucy laughs. God, I love that soft rolling tone. She begins another thought but a bald dude calling for scallops overpowers her voice.

"Well, the people need to eat. It was nice to meet you. I'll see you Monday, Justin," Ian says as he swerves through the tables toward that shiny-headed man.

Lucy sits back down with her legs crossed, hands actually visible on the table. She's much less rigid now. I'll have to thank Ian for his help next week. She's fine for a bit as we chat about bacon but then her left hand drops, picking again at the tablecloth. Crap. I should have chosen a night when Alex was here as well.

"So, when do I get to meet these amazing parents of yours?"

"Soon. He's almost done over there." Dad's shaking the hand of that donkey-like house rep with the straggly hair. He asked me to intern with him last summer, but his voice struck me wrong. Plus, no political internship could take me away from painting with the guys.

Mom catches my eye. I squeeze Lucy's shoulder. Her lip twitches again. She's gnawing a hole into the side of her cheek.

Mom waves as she approaches us.

"Here we go." I give Lucy's hand a solid squeeze. This was a horrible idea. What was I thinking?

"Don't worry about me. I'll be fine." Lucy smiles and waves back to Mom. She lets go of my palm, probably out of respect, linking her own fingers together in front of her.

"Hi, you must be Lucy." They shake hands. I study Lucy's smile as she responds. Not even a twitch.

"It's wonderful to meet you, Mrs. Marshall."

"Likewise. Beautiful dress."

"Thank you. Your son gave it to me."

Mom eyes me. "Ah ha. That explains why he went shopping with Tonya. I thought you were up to something."

"Well, you did want to meet Lucy."

"Yes, very much. But honey, I would have been happy to meet her wearing jeans and a t-shirt."

"Ah, but then we couldn't be here, could we?" I eye Mom's blue, shiny dress.

"Good point." She turns back to Lucy. "Well, please let me reassure you that I'm not this formal. This is all for show." She waves at Dad, who's finally stepping away from donkey-man. "Jeff, come meet Lucy," she calls over the crowd.

Tonya's head pops up from a nearby table and she immediately makes her way towards us, meeting Dad as he maneuvers our way too. All eyes turn on us. I grind my teeth at my own stupidity. Talk about the fakest way to meet my parents ever. My pinky finger finds Lucy's; I briefly lock and squeeze before pulling back. Lucy stands up straight as she takes a step forward to shake Dad's hand.

"Lucy, right? It's so wonderful to meet you. I'm happy you could make it tonight."

"It's great to be here. Thank you for having me, Mr. Marshall."

"Oh, you can call me Jeff."

"And me Christy," Mom adds.

"Tonya," my sister chimes in as she gives Lucy a hug, winking at me over her shoulder. When she pulls away, she turns Lucy around. "A perfect fit."

"Thanks. You made a great choice. I'd love to pick your brain about shopping someday. I'm pretty clueless."

"I would love that." Tonya says, her eyes squinting and making that folding crease she does after a good fashion show. Score. That look means Lucy's been Tonya approved. I close the gap on Lucy as Tonya steps away, shielding her from the three hundred people staring at us.

A strong flash of hot pink joins the group. She's hunched over a bit as she reaches for Lucy's hand. "And I'm Grandma. Call me Dots."

"I love that name," Lucy says.

"Me too. It's not mine though, my given name is Irene. But ever since I was a baby my brother called me Dots. It stuck. As far as I'm concerned, they named me wrong." Grandma reaches out, bopping Lucy's nose. "You're right, Justin. She is cute."

Lucy laughs then as Grandma pulls her into a hug. A real laugh and I know we're solid. Even in front of three hundred strangers. Then suddenly a smoker's cough interrupts her gorgeous laughter. That scallop-demanding bald man in a pinstriped suit steps forward, right into our family circle. Paul immediately follows, which means this guy is important. When Paul steps up, it's Dad's cue to browse his memorized list of names and associated issues. Recognition quickly sparks in his eyes. *Here we go.*

"Carl," Dad reaches out to shake that plump sweaty hand, "it's wonderful to see you." Dad's gaze flickers toward the family, his eyes lingering over me. What? Am I supposed to know this dude? "This is our wonderful donor, Carl, the entertainment executive who's supporting my public television stance. He's been a great contributor to my campaign."

"We're in it together, right, Jeff? No need for formal introductions." Carl shakes everyone's hand, except for Lucy's. It takes incredible control not to wipe the sweat from his palms on my jeans. Lucy takes a small step back, taking the hint that she's invisible to him. I pull her forward again, there's no way I'm letting Carl get away with that.

"Justin," Carl pops a bacon-wrapped scallop into his mouth. Where did that come from? He reaches into his pocket for another one. Nasty. "I'm thrilled to meet you. I've read so much, feel like I already know you. Maybe we could have a chat soon? Remember that email I had your dad pass along to you last spring?"

My trained grin takes over as I panic, racking my brain for clues.

"You turn eighteen in a few months, correct?"

"I do. December." I buy myself time with my answer. Eighteen. Why does he care about my eighteen birthday?

Wait. There's no way. I eye Dad, who nods just slightly. Is he kidding me?

This is that same maniac who wants me on his college-aged bachelor reality show? Dad can't be serious. Hell. No.

"Have you given my proposal any thought?"

Absolutely I have and it's not happening, but Paul's bulging eyes caution me. Cushion that truth. So I pull out a plush political answer. "I have. I'm sorry I haven't gotten back to you yet. I've been finishing up a season with my business and have been involved in the campaign and school."

Carl claps me on the back. "Right, school. Keep those grades sharp. I'm counting on you getting that GPA just right so you can make the top of the list."

"I'll do that." I toss my dad a look. Really? You're taking money from this guy? This is the side of politics I hate.

"And who's this?"

Carl's eyes have landed on Lucy, only because she's at my side. He rudely directs his question towards me, as if she can't speak.

"Lucy," she says, stepping forward, answering him with confidence I admire. Carl laughs and glances at Dad, surprised at her forwardness, acting like she was out of play. Umm, it's called having integrity and courage. I love her for it and totally want to rip his head off for turning this conversation into a caste system.

Dad steps in, recognizing my glare. "Lucy is Justin's *special friend.*"

Special friend? What? My jaw drops, but Tonya glares at me. That damn sister look. I close my mouth, seething. They know I adore Lucy. They know she's my girlfriend. What the hell is this "special friend" crap?

"Oh? Just a friend. Good." Carl steps back and pats my shoulder. "Wonderful food. Let me know about the show when you can, Mr. Marshall."

No way. Never going to happen after that absurd

display of character.

"We will." Dad answers for us both. "Enjoy the rest of the dinner, Carl." We all wait as he leaves, smiling stupid smiles at one another.

Grandma throws up her hands, breaking off the show. "What's next? Or, better, who's up next?" She eyes Dad, clearly not pleased with his dumb ass move to be so politically correct to a creep. I agree. Dad's never dropped to a scuz level before. He usually calls it as it is. Grandma reaches out and squeezes Lucy's arm. "Don't worry. I was a 'special friend' for four years, when Justin's great grandfather was a senator."

Mom clears her throat, continuing the show, deliberately stopping Grandma from getting too real. "It was wonderful to meet you, Lucy."

Dad takes a deep breath, his eyes meeting Grandma's and communicating something in their mother/son language. He smiles, a bit fakely, looking back at Lucy and me. "You'll have to excuse me, I need to greet the other guests. I hope you have a fun evening."

I'm stunned. I mean, I never dragged Jennifer to a political event before, but that was because I didn't want to bore her. Not because I thought she'd be treated like that.

"Thank you, Mr. Marshall. You too," Lucy answers for me. She tugs on my arm, ready to escape. Her arm wraps easily through my own, and I rest my other hand on top of it. I keep it there, praying Carl the Creep sees it and gets his answer.

"So, how about some Chipotle?"

"I'm game," she says.

Hell, yes. She's always game and that's exactly why she's incredible. This girl can take anything life throws, but I'm going to make sure life doesn't throw crap at her anymore. It's not happening, not while I'm around. Lucy deserves all awesomeness, and I'm going to give her that. Even if it's not politically correct.

CHAPTER THREE

Lucy

The salt from these chips is so addicting. Justin chuckles as I lick my fingers. "Here. Take the last one. I'm full." Yeah right. The niblets of what's left of his steak tacos have been picked clean. Taking the chip, I break it in half and hand part back to him.

"How about this?"

"Well, now that you've ruined the chip, it'd be a shame not to." We take turns circling our bit around the guacamole, making sure to scrape every remnant of it clean. It's too precious to waste.

"You know why you're impressive?" Justin leans in, and my insides flip flop. Even after a month of dating, I'm a jumble of butterflies every time he moves near me.

"Why?" I ask, trying to be a little snarky and flirty. It's

a lame attempt, and his laugh proves I failed.

"Because you eat an entire barbacoa burrito bowl on a date."

"Well, there's no use hiding my appetite from you. You saw me eat long before we dated. And this," I nod down to the empty paper in the basket below, "is not worth skipping to impress a guy."

"Would you not eat to impress a guy?"

"Not anymore. But once, yeah, I would. Back when I followed the rules."

"For the record, guys think it's cool when girls eat." Justin holds out his hand for my trash. "And, you never need to follow the social rules with me, you know that, right?" His gaze holds mine for a moment longer. Is he flirting, or talking about what just happened with his parents? I don't know how to answer, so I hand him my red Chipotle basket like an idiot. I may not need to follow the rules with him, but it's obviously different with his family.

The whole situation was so foreign. I never imagined I'd meet them in a banquet hall dressed in lace with all of these random big wigs watching us. Then being tossed to the friendship category by Mr. Marshall the moment some contributor notices me? I must have done something, but I can't figure out where I made a misstep. Holding myself together was hard, but I thought I did okay. Tonya, Dot, and Mrs. Marshall seemed to get me. But then the moment the world turned to watch, it felt so fabricated—so unlike Justin. It sucks that he has to dive in and out of that environment so often.

Justin returns from the trash, taking my hand on the way to the car. Normally, he has a stronger grasp so I give his hand a little squeeze. He smiles, but doesn't say anything as he holds open the door. Maybe I should bring up what happened. Did he even notice how weird it was? Crap, what if that's normal for him and he thinks everything went well.

He drives us a few blocks before pulling over into a grocery store parking lot.

"Are you out of milk? Eggs? Sugar?" I force my British accent, which may as well be Canadian, but I know he loves the absurdity. He cracks a smile. There. Good.

"Sorry," he shakes his head. "Tonight sucked. I put you in a crappy situation—a total freak show. I never expected that. My parents are good people, but unfortunately that didn't show well tonight. That guy stepping in, with his crazy ideas and huge bank account, ruined everything."

I take a moment, letting his words sink in. My muscles loosen and, for the first time tonight, I don't feel like a horse jammed into a snail's shell. He gets how *off* the evening was.

"Thank God," I finally let out with a breath.

"Were you that desperate for my apology?" His green eyes narrow in concern.

"No, I'm thankful you felt something was weird too. Everything was fine. I mean, I thought it was fine, but then I worried I messed up."

"You were great. It's this complex situation with that Carl guy. He wants something from our family that we won't give him, but he's willing to pursue it by pouring money into my dad's campaign fund until we say no."

"What does he want?"

Justin takes one hand away from mine, rubbing his perfect jaw. His stubble's already thick, even after this morning's shave. "It's really embarrassing," he finally says.

I nod, not wanting to push. I have no claim on any

information about his life that he doesn't want to share. "It's okay. I get wanting to keep embarrassing moments to yourself. Unfortunately, you've already witnessed many of my own."

He chuckles. "Okay, brace yourself. That bald guy? He wants me to be part of this college bachelor thing, dedicating my next year, as a freshman in college, to a reality show. He's a producer."

My mouth flies open, and I gaze at his waiting expression. *Do. Not. Laugh.*

"We're talking calendars, photo shoots, interviews, Us Weekly." He bites his lip, giving me his playful grin. "Not to mention the weekly show."

Then I burst out laughing. Whoops!

"I'm sorry," I gasp between breaths, covering up my mouth. "I'm not laughing."

"Yes, you are." He fakes seriousness.

"Well, come on? I mean, I get why they'd want you on a magazine cover because," I tug at his shirt and he moves in closer, "well, you're the hottest thing I've ever seen."

His eyes do that smoldering thing that I can't figure out how to do back.

"See, sexy, just like that!" I push back playfully. "No wonder your dad pounced on the special friend category. He wants you to be the next big Bachelor," I tease.

Justin reaches over, quickly pulling me across to his lap. His eyes grow more intense. "It never occurred to me that my dad took that guy's proposal seriously. I forgot all about it because, one, I'd never do the show, and two, I have you." He kisses the tip of my nose. "And from here on, I'm not letting anyone treat you like that. Dad doesn't want me to do the show. And, more importantly, I don't want to. I'll talk with my dad about that *special friend* comment. What a load of crap."

My stomach turns. "But his campaign?"

Justin shrugs. "Dad's got other people to fund his campaign. He can still win without that funding."

Justin's humoring me. The way his dad eagerly answered that guy's questions shows that the cash would certainly help. I lift my eyebrow.

"It doesn't matter. You are worth more than his campaign to me." He brushes a strand of my hair behind my ear.

Would he really put that at risk for me? My heart skips but my stomach drops. No, that's not right. That's too much for him to give me. His dad has worked too hard for this.

"No, I won't let you hurt your dad's campaign." I trace his chiseled jaw, the stubble prickling my fingertips. "Not after all of everyone's hard work. It's only a little more than a month before election. If I have to be a *special friend*, I can deal with it. He needs to win. Deserves it, really. He's got great values. I know that politics is a game. You've got to play to get ahead."

"But I never wanted you to become a pawn."

"Well, you're in it, right?"

"Yeah." His gaze shifts down and, for a moment, I glimpse Justin's only insecurity. He's tied to his parents' political life, and, with how much he clearly loves them, that's non-negotiable.

My fingers grace his chin. I put pressure under it lightly, until his gorgeous green eyes rise to meet my gaze. I lean in, kissing him gently before pulling away. "Like I said before, I'm game."

***

Oops, too much. Water floods my newly potted chrysanthemums. A pool of mud forms, threatening to drown the plants. Mom's green thumb is clearly not genetic. I take off her engagement ring she gave me this summer, carefully placing it in my pocket before I plunge in after the ugly orange flowers. Surprisingly, the coolness of the mud is more soothing than any fancy lotion Marissa used during our manicure nights. I squish the mud between my fingers, enjoying the mini spa-treatment.

"Lucy?" Mom walks over, scratching her cheek and leaving a smudge. "As much as I understand the draw to examine dirt, we need five more pots planted and loaded in the trailer for my fall exhibit this afternoon." She hands me her gardening rag, always tied to the back end of her garden tool-belt. I'm pretty sure it's the only belt she owns.

"Right, got it," I say, rubbing the mud off my hands before draining the extra water from the soil.

She hands me another scoop of potting soil. "To replace what was lost."

"Thanks."

Mom sits down on the steps of the deck. "So, what were Justin's parents like?"

"Nice," I say as I debate how much to share with her. I'm not really in the mood for advice.

She takes out a mini hoe from her belt and uses the end to scrape the dirt from under her nails. "Well, that's pretty boring," she says with a grin that's tilted up in the corner, so much like Eric's when he's playing Batman. With that smile, I know it's safe to share. She's not in over-drive Mom mode. She's just curious.

"No, they aren't boring. Just different than you and Dad."

"Well, I'd certainly hope they are different. I'd hate to be a cookie-cutter mold."

I roll my eyes. She knows she strives to be the non-generic parent. I study her, wondering if she'll expand. I dare not say anything until she does. I'm more careful with my words now, still trying to be more considerate than my instincts guide. Old habits have been hard to break. Just because we have a relationship now, doesn't make it easy. We still fight, but when we're not in the heat of it, I try to remember she's a person too.

"Truthfully," she continues, "dealing with the differences of your significant other's family is part of the process. Your Grandma Jane and I didn't initially see eye-to-eye. You know that."

I laugh; Grandma Jane has always been a well-ironed business woman with a heart of gold. Dad introduced her to Mom during their hippie phase. I can't imagine how horrible that introduction went. At least my introduction was more like a non-introduction. I mean, yeah, we shook hands, but it didn't feel that real at all.

"So, how are they different from us?" Mom pats the step next to her.

"Well," I slide up on the step, knee to knee with her. Smart, Mom. It's much easier to spill when you don't have to look each other in the eye. She hands me the garden hoe, my turn to pick beneath my nails. "I don't really know. We met at this political fundraiser event ... For a moment, everything felt fine. His grandma is really cute, his mom tried to put me at ease, and his sister even gave me a hug.

But the moment I met his dad and some big exec dragged himself into the conversation, the tone shifted. Suddenly, it wasn't about meeting the family. It was some weird political exchange."

"Were you uncomfortable?"

I thought about it. "No, not really. Justin never left my side and included me as much as he could."

"Did his family introduce you to others?"

My stomach dropped. "Kind of. I was introduced as Justin's 'special friend.'"

Mom shifts in her spot and sucks in one of her therapeutic breaths. Uh oh, here comes the Mom advice, whether I want it or not. I find myself taking in a similar breath, just less noisy.

"It's hard for parents to acknowledge their kids' relationships as serious," Mom begins, "but here's the thing. They are. They shape them and whether or not they agree with the relationship, it doesn't mean it doesn't exist. It's important to them. I made that mistake with you and Zach." I cringe, remembering how Zach cheated on me with my best friend Marissa. Mom pats my knee before she continues. "Yeah, he was a jerk. But if I would have acknowledged that you liked him, I may have been able to be there more when everything…"

"Went to hell?" I offer.

"Exactly."

I nod as Mom continues. "But don't interpret that 'special friend' moment as them not acknowledging or liking you. With trying to slide into the governor's seat, they have to be extra careful in everything they say. Who knows what's next for them, maybe a presidential run?"

"Yeah, that's what I told Justin. I can deal with it. It

makes sense, especially when the guy who barged into the conversation is the one giving Mr. Marshall money in hopes he can snag Justin for a reality college bachelor show."

Mom laughs. "Reality TV? Justin!? No, no, no. He's too *real* to do reality TV. His dad isn't forcing him, is he?"

"No. Absolutely not."

Mom nods. "Okay, well, why don't we have Justin's family over for dinner? A way for us all to get to know one another."

I squirm in my seat. Heck, I don't even know them. There's no way I'm ready to introduce his parents to my own.

"Okay, I get it. Take a month. Get to know them before we all meet, all right?"

"Sounds good."

She bends over, readjusting the mums I'd planted so they look right. I bite my tongue as she messes with my work. It's hard not to be insulted when I'm helping her, but really, it's her exhibit. This is not her over-correcting me, or picking me apart to shape perfection. No, it's business. I'll survive the sting.

"So, have you thought about basketball?"

I nod, surprised that the question doesn't bother me. "I'm thinking about it."

"When are tryouts?"

"Next week."

"Well, whatever you decide, I support you. Just make this decision based off of you, no one else." She nods to the lined-up plants and empty pots. "Okay, let's get these done. I'm hoping to snag a shower before I have to leave."

I thrust my hands back in the dirt to plant while Mom arranges some sort of straw hay garland, but it's basketball that's bouncing around in my head. What would playing mean for me this year? I'd have to deal with Coach T, that horrible man who knowingly let the seniors keep bullying me as long as we won. I'd be putting myself out there to scouts and the media again. They didn't ignore my first season, and they definitely wouldn't ignore my return. The pressure would be high.

But, in the evening when I shoot hoops, I have this sense of freedom and invincibility; there's no other feeling like it in my life.

Then there's the Justin factor. Being on the basketball team would mean less time with him. Practices after school, games in the evenings, tournaments on the weekends. It'd basically demolish our time together, which would totally suck.

My stomach nags at me. It's not like that time with Justin will be there anyway. He's captain of the boys' varsity team. He'll be at practice and games just as often as me. If I don't play, at least I'd be around when he's available.

But that reasoning makes me nauseous. I pour the last scoop of soil into the last teal pot. No. I can't base my choice on that. If I chose not to play for that reason, I'd only be gaining an extra hour with Justin a week, sneaking it in before his practice. Saying no to basketball would be a sacrifice that defines me through him. Waiting on him. My heart deflates with the thought. Justin's a part of me. It scares me how much my heart is entwined with his. But I can't be that girl waiting all the time. Especially when Justin isn't waiting for me. It's not like he mentioned quitting ball so we could go on more dates or anything like that.

God, if he did, I'd smack him. That'd be ridiculous.

No, my decision to play basketball or not can't rest on

my time spent with Justin.

It has to be about me and the ball.

My heart thumps against my ribcage and I know. With that feeling, my choice is made. I pull out my phone and call him. Adrenaline floods my system; suddenly I'm ready to run five miles.

"Hey, Lady," he greets me and my stomach flutters. God, I love his smooth, husky voice.

"Hey, what are you up to?"

"Studying. You?"

"Well, I was wondering if you could call Alex and head over?"

"Why?"

"It's time to show Coach T that I don't give up."

CHAPTER FOUR

Justin

"Gawd, why are you so nervous? You know she'll make it." Lucy's friend Laura tosses me the gym towel from my bag. I'm still sweating, despite the fact guys' tryouts ended an hour ago. "What's with the pacing? I've never seen you like this before. Wait, you're not worried about your own spot, are you?"

There's no need to be conceited, so I pretend she didn't ask. She knows I owned tryouts. "It's not that. It's just," I gaze back at the East Gym's door, knowing Lucy's in there with Coach T, a total ass, waiting to find out if he'll give her a second chance. Honestly, he should be the one begging her to return. Lucy told me how he looked the other way her freshman year, but only after I swore not to tell my coach. Every time I see his fat face, it takes all my restraint to not throw a punch.

Thankfully, I know Lucy has the balls to shove her skills in his face. But, does she have the strength? Just talking about the man made her hands shake. And the memories that gym must hold? Crap. She's in there dealing with all that while I'm stuck out here, just waiting.

"She'll be fine, Justin. Really. Sit down." She yanks my arm, dragging me over to the lunch table to rejoin Luke, Alex, and Jake. Laura wraps her arms around Luke, giving him a hug while we wait for the boys' list to be posted. Luke pats her arm. He didn't have the greatest tryout—chickened on the chance for an easy drive—but he made every outside shot. With that in his pocket, plus his attitude and grades, he's golden.

"Don't worry man, you're good."

"Yeah, you're good, Luke," Alex repeats. He's pacing back and forth. The kid cannot keep still when he's nervous. Then again, I'm already to the other end of the table, I guess neither can I. I haven't been this nervous in a long time.

Alex meets me at the end of the table. "How'd I do?" he says under his breath. "I mean, really, Justin. Do I have hope here?"

He beams up at me and I know what he sees. I'm totally his older brother, way more than a cousin. I'm his Jackson. I imagine what Jackson would have said to me and say just that. "You killed it." I clap him on the shoulder, watching the relief flood his face.

Thankfully, it wasn't a lie. Alex is actually better at ball than I was at his age. Way better. Hell, I bet they will start him on junior varsity as a freshman. At that point, I'd only made the sophomore team. But there's no way I'm telling him that. He's got to learn how the process feels.

41

"Thanks." Alex clasps my hand, pulling me in for a quick man-hug. Jake's sitting down, head between his palms. He never does well under pressure and this tryout was no exception. I made sure to show the coaches my belief in Jake's potential. When I fed him, he bit and the ball would swish. But anyone else, even Alex, would leave him throwing up bricks. Too many bricks.

I bite my tongue. Dear God, let him at least make the freshman team. He and Alex are best friends. The wedge that'd create would royally suck. Jake knows Alex is better, that doesn't seem to matter to him. But to not be part of the team? That'd hurt a ton.

A banging on the lockers bordering the cafeteria is the signal our roster is up. Alex's face drains and Jake doesn't move. Luke sighs, pulling himself off the bench and walking toward the South Gym's door, where four pieces of paper hang.

A huddle forms in front of him; he's forced to wait. He's not super patient though, straining on his tiptoes for a view.

I clasp Alex on the shoulder. "Ready to go look?"

"No way, I can't. Can you check for me?"

"Do you really think that's going to work on me?" I yank him up by the back of his t-shirt. "Be a man, go see."

Alex huffs, dragging himself toward the huddled group of guys. Jake still hasn't lifted his head. "You too, Jake. Up you go."

"I sucked. Don't make me look."

"It's part of the deal, dude. Get up. I've got to look too." He reluctantly stands, already looking defeated. I probably should be nice and do it for him. But sitting down and taking the news from me, whether good or bad, is just going to make him feel like a wimp. He's got to own it and do it himself.

I walk next to him though. He doesn't have to do it alone.

Luke pumps his fist in the air. Solid. I've got my forward.

Alex stands a few guys ahead of us in line, not even attempting to peek. Wow. Never knew he had such restraint. A few moments pass and it's finally his turn. He glances up, reading the freshman list and I see his shoulders slump. *Come on, don't be an idiot. Read the other lists too.* Finally, his shoulders straighten and that dorky grin plasters his face. Good.

I push Jake in front of me; together we scan the list. There, smack in the middle, he lands the freshman team. He breathes a huge sigh of relief as I check out who the coach took this year. Alex's name is at the bottom of JV. Sweet! I glance at the varsity list, my name listed on top with a star. Captain again, like last year.

I feign excitement because the freshmen are watching. Really, all I care about is what's going on with Lucy on the other side of that wall. Then I hear it, the high-pitched squeals as the East Gym's door opens. Girls flood out, some smiling and others with swollen, red eyes. I've never NOT made the team. That's seriously got to suck.

I search for Lucy, catching sight of her hanging back in the gym, having a word with the evil coach. He better not be lecturing her or giving her any crap. She nods sternly before exiting.

I meet her at the door. "How'd it go?"

"Eh," she says.

"What? He cut you!"

"Calm down. I'm starting point guard. He just, um, lectured me about how he invested his time into me my freshman year and how he didn't appreciate it when I 'ditched' the team."

"He seriously said that?" Oh my God. I'm telling our coach. That guy needs to be out of here, forever.

"Don't worry. I knew it was coming. It's not like I hadn't practiced what I'd say to him." She winks at me.

"Whoa. Really?" I stand back, amazed at the force that stands before me. Just five months ago, she couldn't stand up for herself. Now? She's stone.

"Yup."

"So you guys are good?"

"Ha, no way. Not good. But we're in agreement. If I ever see him look the other way while a teammate trashes someone, I'm out. If he actually coaches and cares, I'm in. He wasn't pleased that I worded it like that," she shrugs, "but he agreed. He knows he'd be fired if I ever shared the crap he knew about but didn't act on."

"So." I wrap my arms around her waist. "You're doing it? You're in?"

"Yes. Absolutely." She nods to the girls waiting at the table on the other side of the gym. "I've got to go actually. Captain's talk."

"Oh, who's speaking?"

"Jaclyn."

Right. I'd forgotten she was captain. I should've known that. The school's so big, it's hard to keep everyone on my radar.

"And me." Lucy's eyes fill with excitement. "Co-captains. Jaclyn says she's cool with it."

"What!" I say in an Alex-like whoop. I scoop her

near, kissing her forehead. "You are amazing." She laughs, pushing me away.

"I assume you made your team?" She nods to the varsity and JV guys, huddled around another table. Oh, right. My captain's talk. "Go have your chat. We can meet up after, okay?"

"Absolutely." I turn away but my gut turns. My Psych paper's due tomorrow and the strategy meeting with Dad and Paul is tonight. But how Lucy beams back at me is my answer. My heart twists. There's no way I'm missing more of that. We'll hang for dinner then I can buzz back home for the meeting with Dad and Paul. The paper will have to be an all-nighter. No big deal. It's worth it for time with my girl.

***

Paul looks up from his laptop. "Justin, be reasonable."

Dad shifts in his chair, not speaking when he should.

"Dad…" I turn, excluding Paul. "An interview? No way. We both agreed I'm not doing that show. It'd be intentionally leading him on to snag money for your campaign. That's not right. There's no integrity in that."

Dad pulls his hands through his hair, like I do. He rolls his lips in before he speaks. "Justin, the preliminary stats are showing this race is too close. With his funding, we could reach so many more voters."

Paul butts in. "You'll be projected as honest, smart, and responsible. No one will think badly of you. If anything, it'll snag more voters for your father. Plus, fifty grand would make a huge difference this close to the end."

I throw my hands up. It blows my mind why Dad hired

this guy. Paul's always rubbed me the wrong way. Political image adviser? My ass. A reality show is a reality show. It's going to make our whole family look like chumps.

"Please." Dad reaches out and squeezes my arm. "I've got this campaign covered on every side but through social media. The other guy is dominating out there. That's a huge voter percentage that I'm missing. Carl would make sure that interview is posted everywhere online."

I suck in a deep breath. "I'm not single though."

"Actually," Paul looks over his glasses at me, "you are. Single is defined as unmarried. So, even if you are dating, you are technically single. The requirements for the show are a marital status of single." He turns his laptop around, showing me the screen. "Technically, you wouldn't be lying."

"Son, I hate asking you to do something you don't want to do. But this will help us all."

"The media would eat it up, Justin."

"Yes. Eat it up, chew on it for a week, and spit it out to the dogs."

"Justin," Dad's voice drops, "it's TLC. Not MTV."

I want to scream "No!" Moving against this feeling goes against everything I've learned about making life choices.

Dad reaches out and squeezes my arm. "Consider it."

I grit my teeth and stand. "Fine. One interview. But that's it."

"That's all we'll need to get the funding and the social media spin." Paul smiles. "Knew you'd come around."

Dad glances down at the table, pulling out a new file. I wait for him to feel my glare. *Look at me.* But he won't. He's moved his pawn and now it's time to strategize some more. This is not the man I grew up admiring. Politics has a way of turning the greatest people into slime.

He continues to rearrange his folders while Paul packs up and leaves. Finally, alone together, his eyes find mine. "Thank you." He nods to an old family photo on the mantel, the one that includes all of us a few months before Jackson passed away. He's wrapped in our arms, smiling despite the pain. "Family matters. You've done so much for me, son. Thank you for giving a little bit more."

There's the man I know. Where was he five minutes ago? Well, now that he's finally *here*, I'm not wasting the chance to confront him about how he treated Lucy. I pull open the fridge for some turkey and lemonade. I set them on the counter and take a deep breath. If I'm doing this interview, then he's got to fess up to being an ass around Lucy.

"What did you think of Lucy?" I ask before taking a swig of lemonade from the container.

"She's very pretty."

"Yup," I say, waiting for more.

"Polite."

"Uh huh." I eat a slice of turkey as I watch him figure out how he screwed up. His eyebrows furrow, then spread apart as his mouth drops open with his breath.

Aha, got it. There we go.

"Okay. You're right. I honestly don't know how I feel about her. That was my chance to meet her." He rubs his temple. "I really screwed that one up, didn't I?"

"I wouldn't exactly say it went well."

"I'm sorry that Carl threw me off. I kept thinking campaign instead of family. She's important to you, correct?"

"Yes. She's awesome."

"Oh, so I take it you really like her?"

"As I told you last week at dinner, I love her." I set the lemonade down. Why didn't he believe me the first time? Or listen?

"Ah, I see." Dad straightens out his wedding ring. "Well, then I owe her an apology too. I didn't take the time to get to know her, and I definitely want to if she means so much to you."

"Thank you." I hold out the lemonade to Dad. He takes a sip.

"Jeff! How many times have I asked you not to drink from that?" Mom says as she opens the basement door, sweaty from her treadmill run.

"He made me do it," Dad says as he tosses it back to me. Mom laughs and I roll my eyes before I take another long sip.

"Okay, okay." Mom takes the container away while the rim is still in my mouth. "So what'd I miss?"

"Oh, just Dad forcing me to do a reality show."

"Jeffery Marshall." Mom's voice drops low and stern. "You know how I feel about that show."

Dad throws his hands up. "It's only an interview, Christy. Not the show."

"Are you okay with this?"

No. But it's not like I have a choice.

"Justin?"

"Yeah. It's fine. One interview won't hurt. There's no way I'm doing that show next fall though." My eyebrows raise toward Dad.

"I wouldn't want you to either," Dad replies.

"Good. Because you both would be on my bad list if you did that show."

Dad points at me. "Did you know your son is in love?"

I nearly spit lemonade from my mouth. Nice subject change.

"Yes, of course. A mother doesn't miss that." Mom steps away from his side. Usually they are all over each other. I mean, this is better, but… it's weird. There's too much tension. It reminds me of the days leading up to Jackson's death.

"Why didn't you tell me? I messed up meeting her," Dad growls.

"Because Justin told both of us last week, during our only family dinner. Remember?"

He doesn't answer.

"See, this is what I'm talking about when I say you need to pay more attention, Jeff." They stare at one another, silent.

I step back from the counter. Time for a quick exit. "Okay, I've got a paper to write."

"Right now?" Mom calls behind me as I make my way down to the basement. "Didn't you have dinner with Lucy earlier?"

"Yeah."

"Isn't this that twelve-page one? You know the rules. No hanging out with friends until homework is done. You aren't eighteen yet."

"Mom, if I ever miss a deadline or an assignment, feel free to lecture me. Until then," I raise the container of lemonade to her, "cheers."

"Cheers, son!" Dad calls behind her as I close the door. Good. He owes me escape from at least the homework rule. I can't believe she still tries to hold that over me.

"Jeffery, we need to talk." Mom's voice filters through

the door.

I beeline it for the television, turning on football. iPod on and headphones in, I crank Hammock, sure to drown out their arguing tones.

CHAPTER FIVE

Lucy

Coach T tosses his hands up in the air. Face red and blotched, he yells at Chelsey, "Are you kidding!? What was that?"

I tug Chelsey's hand behind the bench, giving it a squeeze as I send her a sideways eye roll. *You're Good. He's crazy.*

"Bottom of the fourth quarter, girls. Two baskets behind. You're killing me!"

I glance out into the bleachers where Eric jumps up and down in his Superman costume, oblivious that Coach T is grilling us. I wave back, loving his enthusiasm for Halloween, even though it's still over a week away. A flash of familiar yellow makes me turn. I hate that Marissa's blond hair captures my attention. After she betrayed me by sleeping with Zach, I go to great lengths to avoid her in school. But right now Marissa's pretty impossible to miss since she's sucking face with Zach in the back corner. Eww.

Why would they even come? Is this their sick idea of a date? Making out in front of me? Whatever. They can do what they want up there. The court is my domain now.

Coach catches my look of disgust, then tosses his clipboard in the air. I reach out and catch it before it slams to the ground, a guaranteed technical foul. Coaches and players can't throw stuff. He knows that.

He glares at the clipboard in my hands. "Is this a joke to you, Zwindler?"

"No, sir. Just waving to my brother."

"And how does that help?" Oh my gosh. For real! I'm so done with his crap.

"It's helping about as much as your incredibly inspiring speech."

Chelsey sucks in a breath as Coach takes a step closer. Rage doesn't even begin to describe that bilious look on his face. He glares at me but I hold his gaze. He can't treat us like that, and he knows it. I've got more on his past behavior than anyone in this gym. Call it blackmail, but whatever. I've got team email threads with his name on it and responses, that include the horrible stuff the seniors said about me.

"Fine." He takes a step back. "Just get Zwindler the f'ing ball."

The ref blows the whistle and we all jump up and dash onto the court, eager to get away from that troll.

"Whoa, Lucy. I can't believe you said that!" Jaclyn squeezes my shoulder. "Thanks. I never would've had the balls to do it." She pats my butt and I laugh. Jaclyn, the queen of the butt pat. I take position at the top of the key, watching Chelsey from the sideline as the ref gives her the ball. The crowd roars, Laura's bouncing around in front of the cheerleaders in a hot witch costume, doing a much better job of rousing the crowd with her dancing than the cheerleaders are doing.

I take a deep breath; the sound deafens in my ears.

Just me, the girls on the court, and the ball. Go.

Chels slaps the ball and I jog backwards a few steps, hands overhead, making as if I'm going to catch a pass. I feign a jump, throwing my defender toward me, but dart the other direction toward the hoop. Mac, Jaclyn, and Grace weave under the basket, creating a brief opening. I dart, catching the ball from Chels. Mac's defender drops away from her to take me on. I toss the ball behind my back to Mac, who throws it up for an easy lay-up.

One basket down.

The defender swears, snatching the ball and returning to the baseline before throwing it back into play. Her throw is lazy, towards the girl Jaclyn defends. Jacyln stretches her freak spider arms, snatching the ball from the air. The lanes open. I sprint for the drive. Jaclyn sends the ball my way.

Defenders collapse in on me. I'd probably make the shot, but it's too risky.

Four seconds left on the clock.

Chelsey blurs past my left peripheral.

Yes. A sharp bounce pass and it's in her hands. She squares up.

Swish.

Bzzzzzzzz.

A deafening roar breaks through the buzzer. "The Eagles Win!" booms from the sound system. I run to Chels, wrapping her in my arms.

"YES, CHELS!"

Jacyln jumps on my back. "We did it!" The rest of the girls rush onto the court, squealing at unbelievable decibels.

Three for three. Not a bad way to launch the season.

I glance back at Coach T, who's clapping and shaking hands with random parents. He looks like a baboon smiling, totally fake. That ugly grin will disappear the moment we step into that locker room. At least we won, but he'll still have a crap load of stuff for us to work on. If the man says one positive word, I'll be shocked. We walk back to the bench to grab our stuff. I glance at the South wall. Empty. Again. Crap.

The South Wall is Justin's spot, where the guy's team stands if they return from their game early to cheer us on. At least, that's where they are supposed to be. Justin still hasn't seen me play and I only had the chance to catch the last half hour of his second game.

I reach into my bag and pull out my phone.

Me: We Won!!!

Justin: Crap!

Me: Crap!? Lol

Justin: No, we're like five minutes away. I was hoping to see you play.

Me: It's okay. There's always next time. It'll be nice to see you! :) How'd you do?

Justin: Nailed it. Luke rolled his ankle though, so Coach pulled Alex up from JV. He did okay.

Immediately, another text alert pops up on screen.

Alex: Don't listen to Justin. I killed it. Five baskets. Walking on frickin' air.

Justin: Whatever. Don't listen to him. He smells.

I laugh, knowing Alex is leaning over Justin's shoulder.

I wish I could watch their actual banter on the court or the bus. Hell, I wish I could see some of them at all. I miss Alex. And Justin? I miss him more than I ever missed basketball. Walking with him from History to Study Hall isn't enough time together. Not even close.

A squeal draws me away from my phone's screen. An arm wraps around my waist, pulling me into a hug. Laura.

"YOU ARE AMAZING!" Victory ice cream when our men return?" I cringe. For Luke and Laura, every game won means ice cream and, as Laura's shared, then some. Ice cream sounds good, but it's a little weird enjoying it with them knowing exactly what happens in the back of Luke's SUV afterwards. Plus, Justin and I need time together.

Alone.

"Rain check?"

"Fine." She leans in and pecks my cheek. "But we're still on for shopping tomorrow night?"

"Absolutely! My schedule's clear." Justin's got that James J. Hill board meeting anyway. He's been nervous about it, constantly pulling out the proposal he submitted for his painting company to be hired to paint the mansion. Pretty sure he's reviewed the thing like twenty times by now.

I glance at the South Gym's doors, still shut and wall still empty. This five minutes is too long. My insides ache to be wrapped up in his strong arms. I force my eyes to wander from the door, so I can appear normal. I catch a glimpse of a blond woman in a maroon and gold hat stepping down the bleachers. Before she leaves, she waves.

Whoa. I know her! Cynthia DeClaire. University of Minnesota girls' basketball coach. Was she here to watch me play? Or was she scouting someone else?

Just then, the South door is thrown in. Alex leads the way,

bouncing and hollering into the gym. Crazy, overconfident freshman. Jen's next with her team of cheerleaders. The crowd cheers when she does a flip. And, like always, Trish cheers the loudest. It's so sweet. They haven't come out yet so I don't get to see much of them together. But when I do see them, they always seem to be supporting one another. I like that. It's the way it should work.

The Junior Varsity team follows the cheerleaders. They look boyishly skinny compared to the seniors behind them who walk in confident and take their spot along the South wall. Justin's the last through the door, his black hair still shiny and extra curled with sweat from the game.

Finally.

My legs carry me to him before I can think.

I jump and he catches me, wrapping my legs around him. Our lips find one another. The ache in my gut ceases. Sweet relief.

"Now, this is the way to celebrate a victory." He laughs gorgeously and I melt.

Then a camera flash blinds us, followed by Dad's signature cough.

Oh, right.

Public.

"Get a room!" Trish taunts with a wink as she walks past with Jen.

I slide down with a laugh but Justin doesn't let me out of his arms. He leans in closer. "Do you mind if I come over? I know it's almost ten."

My heart jumps; time with Justin? Yes! Thank God Mom recently amended my ten o'clock curfew. I can be with Justin until eleven, as long as he's at our house. We haven't had a chance to take advantage of the rule yet.

"Yes."

Justin bends down to my ear as my parents and Eric walk down from the bleachers. The warmth from his breath sends goosebumps running down the back of my legs. Best tingles ever.

He chuckles softly as he feels my reaction, then whispers, "I'm glad you said yes, because, seriously, even if you said no, I planned on being there. You may not know this about me, but I'm amazing at climbing trees. That one outside of your window is seriously tempting." He gives my side a squeeze and steps forward, greeting my dad then giving Mom a hug.

Tree climbing? The thought of Justin climbing in my window makes my heart throttle forward. Maybe I'll have to start leaving it unlocked…

***

Justin rests the bowl of popcorn on his lap as we sit on the back steps. "I've missed this," he says as he strokes a circle on my palm. "Being with you."

"I've missed you too." I reach for a piece of popcorn, but he stops me. He picks it up, placing it in my mouth for me. He waits until I swallow it, before following it with a salty kiss.

"Is it always going to feel like this?" he asks when he pulls away.

"This?"

"The ache of being away from you. The pure bliss of being with you." He shakes his head. "It's like I'm never relaxed unless you're with me."

My heart backflips as his words resonate with me. I

entwine my fingers with his.

"I'm going to make sure we have more time together. More time to just be and not rush around." Justin wraps his arm around me as I shiver, my knit sweater doing little to protect me from the breeze. "Lucy," his tone shifts, "something's come up with the campaign."

"Oh?"

"Involving me and that show…"

"Oh." He isn't doing it, is he? No, he wouldn't. Ever. That's just not him. How would that work for us?

"I have to participate in this promotional interview thing. It'll be online."

"Like, as one of the upcoming college bachelors?"

"Not exactly. It's more a showcase of the potential guys they'd follow." He picks a red leaf off the vine that crawls up the railing of our deck stairs. "I don't want to do it, believe me," he says.

"Then don't. It's your life, Justin."

"It is, but… this really matters to my dad. It could mean the difference in his success, his dream. Twenty minutes of my time is worth that."

"But…" The word slips out before I can restrain myself.

"But, I have a girlfriend." He leans over, kissing my head. "I know. Listen, if you don't want me to do this, if it will hurt you in any way, please let me know and I'll call the whole thing off."

I pluck my own leaf from the vine to pull apart. Will it hurt me? No. Is it embarrassing? Yeah. I'm supposed to be his girlfriend. But, that means I need to stand with him. Only a week ago, I told Justin that I was game. I can handle the political stuff until the election.

He strokes my hair. "I'll call it off."

"No, it's okay. Do what you need to do." My fingers find his and I squeeze. "Just a few more weeks of this nonsense, right?"

"Right."

His phone buzzes on the step above us. He ignores it. It buzzes again. Then again.

"You can look. I won't mind."

Justin sighs, reaching back to grab the phone but not taking his eyes from mine. "I'm only going to look so they'll shut up." He holds the phone in front of me, sharing the screen with me. I love that he doesn't hide anything from me. Not that he's the type of guy who'd cheat. But, I like that he doesn't even give me a chance to doubt who he's responding to.

The phone keeps buzzing in his palm. Fifteen Facebook notifications in, what, twenty-eight seconds? His brow furrows as he opens up the Facebook app. There's a photo of us from after the game. My legs wrapped around Justin, him gazing up into my eyes. We're both tagged. The comments keep rolling in, ranging from *Cutest Couple Ever* to *Get A Room*. Justin laughs until he gets to the comment about my boobs. *Squeezable huge tits* from some guy I've never heard of. Holy crap.

Instantly, I cross my arms in front of myself. Justin motions to turn off the screen, but I stop him, engrossed in what begins to unfold. The tone of the comments shifts. Gone are the sweet or funny ones from people we know. Strangers throw insults and sexual entendres as the photo is shared. Both girls and guys. We stare in disbelief, refreshing the screen. A few of the names I recognize from school tell the strangers to shove it or F off. Good, at least someone else thinks this is cruel.

Then, as some random chick starts estimating the size of Justin's boner, which he clearly doesn't have in the photo, he slams the phone shut.

"What was that?"

"I think we just saw the evil side of Facebook." He shakes his head and asks for my phone. "Do you mind if I untag you?" I hand it over, letting him access my app to undo the tag. Then he takes a moment to do his own.

"That was crazy."

"Yeah," he responds, his brow still furrowed.

"You okay?"

His fists clench. "I hate how they said stuff about you."

I push down the lump in my throat. "Justin, I've dealt with people being asses before. No big deal." Truth is, it really sucked, but Justin will only worry if he knows how much those last comments hurt.

"We'll have to be more careful."

"How? It's the Internet. People will say what they say."

"We can cancel our accounts."

"That's not going to stop the comments or people taking random photos of us at school."

Justin rubs his jaw, clearly still bothered. I lean in, kissing his cheek. "It'll be okay. Once the newness of us blows over, people will get bored. Move on to the next couple, you know?"

"I hope so."

The back screen door opens. "Lucy?" Dad calls out. I bite my tongue. Dad's much more of a curfew enforcer than I expected. Justin clicks his phone on: ten fifty-seven. Yup. Dad's way more on top of the minutes than Mom ever was.

"It's time," Dad says.

60

"I've got three minutes, Dad," I call back.

"All right, three minutes. Then bed."

"Yeah, got it, Dad." I stand up, pulling Justin up behind me.

Justin pulls his fingers through my hair before he touches his forehead to mine. "I'm so sorry I can't see you tomorrow. Campaign lunch, final push to get that vote. We're in crunch time. Then I've got a paper and studying for the Calc II midterm."

"Don't forget the board meeting."

"Right! That too."

That familiar ache returns to my heart, the horrid pull of being apart. I push my lips against his. "I'll miss you."

"Same," he whispers.

The door squeaks open again. "Lucy," Dad calls.

Mom laughs in the background. "Dan, give them a moment. My goodness."

I pull away from Justin. He winks back with a frustrated grin. Seriously, that grin. That jaw. That stubble. "When's the interview?"

"They're coming tomorrow."

CHAPTER SIX

Justin

How do girls wear this stuff? A camera flash blinds me again as I readjust on the curvy red couch. The lights' heat is melting off all of the foundation spackled on my face. I take a quick selfie and Snapchat it to Alex. He mentioned being a bit bummed out Sally missed his game. I really need to call him.

After sitting under the lights for a few minutes, the makeup artist returns taking a pencil to my eye. Makeup was never part of the agreement. Dad owes me big time. I had to cancel my study session with Jen for my Calc II midterm to fit this in. I'm afraid I may have hit my math threshold. I used to aim for A's, but now passing seems damn near unachievable. I hope she's up for rescheduling with me, that is if I can find the time.

"So, Justin." Carl clears his throat with a hack. "Jessie here is going to ask you some questions. Where you live, hobbies, aspirations, the regular stuff." An older woman with a cat sweater and frizzy hair smiles at me from the stool next to the camera. She's interviewing me, off-camera? My heart rate slows. Okay, cool. Maybe my instincts were wrong and this isn't a crude reality show.

"Hello, Justin. So nice to meet you," she says in a smooth voice that no male on earth could define without using the word sexy. "How are you?"

There's a beat in her voice that I recognize. No way. I shift forward toward her. "Were you the voice for the evil female computer in the latest Bond film?"

"That's me," she says with an aunt-like grin.

"Wow. Very nice to meet you."

"Likewise." The way she says it sends goosebumps down my spine. Weird. The computer chick from the film was so hot. Jessie laughs as she pulls out yarn and needles from her purse.

"The industry calls her The Siren," Carl explains. "Her voice draws everyone in. Men identify it as sexy and women find it confident and comforting, like a wise older sister." He clasps Jessie's shoulder and smiles. "As you can see, I've brought in my best to make you look good, Justin."

I nod, still amazed at how that voice comes from such a regular, obsessed-with-knitting type woman. A voice like that shouldn't be legal.

"Shall we get started, Justin?" She shifts her glasses down as she counts the rows she's placed on her needle, then she looks up and smiles at me, like a friendly librarian.

"I'd love to."

"Tell us about yourself. Where do you live? Who's in

your family?"

So I do. I tell her a ton, even about Jackson. Carl's right; she is a siren. I find myself spilling way more information than intended with each new question. She's too easy to talk to. I'm telling everyone it's because of the cat on her sweater, not her voice. Crazy cat ladies are easy to talk to, right?

Jessie clears her throat. "Last question, Justin. How would you describe your perfect girl?"

Lucy's name almost slips off my tongue. I close it, swallowing the urge to explain I already have a girlfriend. "My perfect girl?"

"Yes. What type of girl do you want to spend the rest of your life with?"

Without hesitation, I look into the camera and define Lucy. "She's strong, brave, beautiful and, although she doesn't intend it, she's really funny. She also must be able to survive a tornado."

"Survive a tornado? That's pretty specific."

I nod, remembering my freak encounter with Lucy and a tornado last summer. The camera to my left moves closer, the lens changing for a close-up. "I guess I know what I'm looking for."

"I hope you'll find it."

"I'm pretty sure I will."

***

"Justin, wake up," Jennifer says as she snaps in my face. My eyes fly open and the room's a blur. Clarification comes with a few blinks, however that exit sign in the front of the lecture hall is still fuzzy. Crap, I'll need glasses soon. My first sign of aging and I'm not even eighteen. *Sweet.*

"He's starting the review for midterm. Don't miss this." She hands me her coffee cup.

"I'm not going to take your drink. I'll survive." Truth? I've yet to acquire the taste of that addictive muck.

"Seriously, drink it. Or do you want to miss your only chance to review after you blew me off last week?"

Fine. With a huge swig, I burn a blister to the roof of my mouth. The exit sign instantly clears though… So that's how coffee works.

"Thanks," I say, handing the paper cup back.

"Justin, you've got to give something up. You're killing yourself." She waits for me to answer, so I throw her a shrug. It's not like I have a choice. My calendar's full, I'm dealing with it.

"I'm serious. Be careful."

"Jen," I nod toward the little Calc II professor who just said something about integrals involving trig functions, "the review?"

She purses her lips, refocusing on her own notes.

I focus on mine too, but the example problems just aren't making sense. Calc was never this difficult to understand. Of all years, why does math decide to kick my ass now? Jennifer's notes and numbers flow perfectly down her page. She nods along with the professor, sometimes working ahead. The woman's a saint for agreeing to take post-secondary classes with me. When we get back to school for History, I'm picking her brain about integral functions and whatever that sign means that the professor keeps flashing on the projection up front.

Jen taps my hand, and I find my eyes closed *again*. "It's over. Come on," she holds out her hand, backpack already slung over her shoulders. She pulls me out of my seat. "Justin, your life is killing you."

"Naw. I've got the situation under control. Jack Bauer style. Don't worry, I'm good."

"Doesn't he get near killed and tortured in every episode?"

"*Touché.*"

"What if I decide it's morally wrong for me to help you study?"

"Well," I take her backpack from her as we climb the lecture hall stairs for the back exit, "then I'd be screwed."

"Well, lucky for you, I'm pretty awesome."

"That's true."

"Okay, hand over your schedule. Let's see where you can squeeze some study time in with me." Her voice is full of snark, but I give her my phone anyway as I duck into the car. I need her help and I can cope with attitude. My schedule isn't *that* bad. She's overreacting. If I shifted my Psych project to later Thursday night, we could study after school, before basketball practice. Then after practice, I'll swing on over to the second to last campaign dinner. Absolutely do-able.

"Whoa, Justin." She grows silent, scrolling through my hourly schedule and my list of to do's. "I was joking before, but are you kidding? This is crazy. If your parents knew you were this swamped, they'd never ask you to help with the campaign."

"They don't need to know. I'm keeping up with everything. It's fine." I point to the blue slot on Thursday, after school. "How about then? I'll bump the Psych project later. No big deal."

"Works fine for me." She taps my arm as I pull onto

the highway. "Justin, be honest with yourself. No one can keep this type of schedule up forever. Something will give. Be smart, okay?"

"I'll keep that in mind."

"I'm not kidding."

"I know you're concerned, and I get it. But I'm used to it. I'm doing fine." I turn the radio on. "So, how's everything going with Trish? Still good?"

"Yeah, she's great. It's hard being in different schools. But easier in a way too. We have coffee dates on Tuesdays and Thursdays and make sure to have at least one date night on the weekend."

"You see her that much?" My gut turns and the pain of being away from Lucy rears. God, I miss her.

"How often do you get to see Lucy?"

"I saw her four days ago for thirty-six minutes."

"That's it? Is she cool with that?"

I yank on my hair. "Yeah, I dunno, I hope? It's not like I want it this way. Hell, it's two more days until I can see her again. And that's at her basketball game. But," I shrug, "at least I'll finally get to see her play."

"How come she doesn't go to the fancy campaign luncheons or go door-to-door with you? Is it because of that interview?"

I cringe. Great question for which I have horrid answers. One: I'm too embarrassed about how sleazy everything is now. Risking exposing Lucy to that world again isn't worth it. It's absurd. She could decide she doesn't want to be part of it, and I'm stuck in it. I don't have a choice. Two: That Carl dude won't leave me alone. Everything's gotten so much worse since I did that interview. I've had to attend online Twitter parties, our local paper did two stories on the interview, and some of the guys on the team won't stop talking about all the *action* I'll get if I do the show. And three: I can't be myself at all. Paul's always over my shoulder, watching and directing every move. I don't want Lucy to see me acting like a robotic version of me.

"Protecting her from that stress is important to me," I say instead. My words may as well have been a bumper sticker slapped on my forehead that says "Ballless." Pretty sure I'm the worst boyfriend ever for using "protection" as my excuse. The truth is, I suck.

She rolls her lips in and crosses her arms.

"Jen, don't worry. I'll see her more, you more, everyone more. My priorities aren't backwards. The campaign just needs to end. Only one week more until election day. I can do it."

"I know," Jen finally replies. "But should you?"

I pull into the school lot. Jen hands my phone back as she steps out of the car without another word. Okay, that was a bit dramatic. However, it's clear that post campaign, I'll have a lot of repairing to do.

CHAPTER SEVEN

Lucy

Three steady knocks on the door and a hoot. Our secret code. I close my laptop as Eric peeks his head in. It's amazing how much he's grown in just a few months. Thankfully, he's still my little brother. It's going to suck when my little brother suddenly becomes my big brother. I wonder how our dynamic will switch.

"What's up, bud?" I ask as I open the door all the way.

"Want to play trucks with me?" He nods toward the duffel bag that he started using last week to haul *all* of his vehicles, *all* the time. I don't know if I've ever seen him without it.

"Absolutely. That sounds fun."

A goofy look overtakes his face as he unzips the giant bag, taking out a new fire truck.

"Whoa, where'd you get that one from?"

"The library."

"They let you check out toys?"

"Only if it comes with a book. It's boring though." He crawls up on my bed and moves my pillow to build a ramp.

"I see."

"Zoom," he says and the fire truck flies off the edge of my bed.

"Be careful with that, Eric," Mom says from the other side of the doorway. "If that gets broken…"

Eric holds up his palm. "Okay, Mom. I get it." Whoa. Attitude.

Mom's eyes widen. "I did not teach him that," I say.

"Unfortunately, in the last few weeks he's developed a bit of an attitude. I suspect it has to do with being moved to a new classroom."

Eric ignores her, finding another truck of his own to fling off my bed. Mom taps the doorframe. Her lips roll in then part slightly. If I wasn't looking for it, I would have missed her brief head shake. She plasters a smile on her face for me though. Something's definitely on her mind.

"What's up, Mom?"

"Did you watch Justin's interview yet?"

"Yeah…" My insides squirm. The interview was fine, but I've been dreading Mom's reaction to it.

"Justin did well," she says flatly.

"Okay, Mom. Out with it. What's wrong?"

"He shouldn't be doing that interview at all."

"Yeah, I told you that he didn't want to."

"It's not only that, Lucy. He's dating you."

"He doesn't have a choice at the moment. It's a way to help out his dad."

"I think his dad is taking liberties where he shouldn't. Justin should have refused."

"Well," I bite the inside of my cheek, "that's your opinion. I see Justin as helping his dad. Him doing the interview didn't bother me. I'm sorry that it bothered you, but Justin made the choice and I support that."

Mom nods. "Okay, but be careful, Lucy. I don't want a hidden life for you. After hearing about how his parents blew you off, I worry. Family dynamics are difficult enough. Add politics and now a reality show?"

"He's not doing the show. He did one interview to help promote it as a *potential* candidate."

"Lucy, listen," her voice gets that edge and I clamp down on my tongue... Eight, nine, ten. Deep breath. I will not lose it unless what she says is completely off the wall. And even then, somehow I'll maintain control.

"Yes?" I finally respond.

"I'm entitled to share my feelings."

"Okay."

"Right now, I'm feeling like this is too much for you. It's not fair to you."

I catch another truck that Eric's flung at me from the bed. "Mom, I'm not breaking up with him for this. It's a stressful time. It'll pass."

"He never sees you. This isn't want you want."

"No, it's not what *you* want for me. Right now, it is what it is. We'll get through it and things will get better."

She sucks her cheeks in. "Okay, well at least you know my opinion."

"Why share it though? Just so you can say *I told you so*?" The moment the line leaves my mouth, I know I've gone too far.

"I shared it because I care about you," she says. "If you valued my parenting skills, you'd consider it."

Ooo, sting. Responding to that one has minefield written all over it. So I hold my tongue.

"Consider it," she reemphasizes as she pulls my door closed.

"Zoom!" A black car crashes into my shoulder. Then a red one. I recover the red one, chasing Eric around on the bed, ramming into his socked feet, distracting myself from my anger.

She had no right to say that to me. I was fine with the interview before. Now? I don't know. I want to write her words off, but she pinpointed exactly what I've been trying to ignore— Justin *did* have a choice and he didn't say no.

CHAPTER EIGHT

Justin

That flash of auburn catches my eye the moment I step through the gym doors. Lucy's breaking down the court, driving through two defensive players. Then *swish!* A flawless reverse lay up. Three minutes in and she's already killing it. And that shot? She has no idea how hot she is when she pulls it off. The first time she used it on me, holy crap. I had to harness Batman strength to not grab her and immediately start making out. Of course, she probably would have slapped me.

I force myself to climb up at least three rows before taking a seat. There's no way I'm going to be that boyfriend on the sidelines, acting like a coach. A quick glance through the stands and my heart drops. Her parents and brother aren't here tonight. Bummer. I was looking forward to seeing them. A chance to check off bonding time from my list. Not that it's actually on the list, but I know it's crucial to get to know them for a solid foundation to our relationship.

Lucy's eyes never drift from who she defends. Honestly, I bet I could walk around naked with a megaphone shouting I love her and she wouldn't notice anything but the game. That look of pure intensity... in her own world... doing her thing. I wish I had that power on and off the court to help me escape. It's almost shameful how easily the stands affect my skills. Now when Dad comes to my games, the media shows up. This leads to after-game questions and photo ops. It's to the point where I just want to bolt post-game, but Dad always waves me over and I know I have to do the right thing.

Lucy plants herself on the baseline near me, looks over her shoulder, and winks.

My heart fist pumps. I love that she can so easily do that to me.

She receives a pass from Chelsey. The ball's quickly pushed down, close to the court. She drives a few quick steps before passing it back out to Jaclyn, who pops up a three-pointer. *Swish.*

My phone buzzes in my back pocket. I take it out for a quick glance. A photo of Ian holding a white electric guitar pops up. He's been talking my ear off about buying a new guitar all month. I'm surprised he texted me. He usually calls, a true sign of being homeschooled.

Ian: You get to meet my new baby tonight! Still on for finishing our project after the game?

I reply then turn back to the court as the crowd roars. Jaclyn's slapping Lucy's butt as she books it back down the court for zone defense.

Seriously? I suck! I missed something amazing…Again!

I shut down my phone. Screw this. New rule: around Lucy, I'm completely unreachable.

I reach back, massaging my right shoulder, allowing myself to finally relax. There. My God. I've got to turn off that phone more often.

The game's quick. Lucy and Jaclyn don't even play the last quarter, giving up their positions to some JV players. Classy move. There's no point in running circles when someone else could have court time. It's more fun for everyone if there's actually a game.

I spend the rest of the game flirting with Lucy from across the court. She tosses me her scrunched up nose flirt look, which looks a bit like an awkward bunny and she knows it. This time is gold. Time to just look at one another. She's gorgeous and, as she sticks out her tongue at me, she becomes the cutest thing.

That sassy brunette makes me crazy in a way she'll never understand.

And that scares me more than anything else.

***

"How is it that you still smell like apples even when you're covered in sweat?"

"You think I smell like apples?" She pushes into me.

"Yes. Apples are my favorite fruit."

"Okay, I'll take that." She takes out the elastic in her hair, letting it tumble over her shoulders, drawing my eyes down to her chest. I force myself not to stare, noticing instead how she sticks a sandwich pick at the French fries in front of her.

"You okay?" French fries aren't usually safe in front of this girl.

She picks up three of the crunchiest fries and balances them upright in a teepee. Her crystal blue eyes then find mine and with a sigh, she says, "I miss you."

My hand finds hers, tiny in my palm and always so cold. It's selfish, but I like it that way. As if her hands can only be warm in my own. "I know that this sucks. It's going to get better after the campaign. I swear. Only a few days left."

She nods. "Yeah. I can handle that." She slides her foot up my calf, causing shock waves to travel much higher. Frick. "And then I'll see you more?"

"Yes, trust me. I'm not letting anything take me away from you."

Her smile glows. My heart sinks. It's been a long time since I've seen her look so happy. It shouldn't be like that.

"So, what are you up to after this?" She pops a fry in her mouth.

"Last meeting with Ian to finish our Psych project."

"When do you need to leave?"

I glance at my phone. "Thirty minutes."

A frown briefly shows before she covers it up, using a napkin to wipe her mouth. God, I'm so lucky. Most girls would be lecturing me for neglecting them. Here she is, trying to hold it together for me.

"A few more days?"

"That's it. It'll be post-election, post-midterms."

"Okay."

"Can I call you tonight when we're done?"

"I'd love that."

"It's gonna be late. Like, we're talking past midnight?"

"I'll be up. I'd love more time to hear your voice."

My phone flashes eight twenty-two. Lucy dips her French fry in our malt and winks at me as she eats it. With that wink, my heart becomes heavier, knowing I have to leave soon. It shouldn't hurt like this when she's still so close.

I step out of my side of the booth and slide in next to her. As I wrap her in my arms, I take a whiff. Apples and cinnamon. The perfect apple pie. She rests her head on my shoulder and the ache ceases as the warmth of being with her takes over.

There. Perfect.

***

"Solid. Let's make sure to mention the Pavlovian dogs in the conclusion, and we're set," Ian says as he tosses his pen in the air.

"Right, that woman has conditioned herself to salivate at the mere mention of Pavlov. What's with her?"

"She's devoted her entire career to teaching entry level psychology. How would anyone survive that plight? She's bound to have fallen in love with at least one of those researchers."

"Ha, too true. Here you go. Have at it." I hand over the laptop, letting him finish typing up the final paragraph. Ian's been fun to work with. Thoughtful, funny, and, thankfully, wicked smart. I totally lucked out in the random pairing for this project. We couldn't be more different. A business-minded jock paired with an intellectual musician. But we work well together, complimenting one another's weaknesses.

Ian types the last word and we both let out a breath of relief. "Finally." He shrinks Microsoft Word and dives into iTunes. "Now, onto the important stuff."

I yawn and my fingers itch to bolt and call Lucy.

"Dude, it's like I wrote this playlist." He turns on one of my favorite instrumental tracks from *Lower Case Noises*. "Nice." He rocks forward with the music, continuing to browse. "So, that girl you brought to the September fundraiser? The one with the bacon-wrapped scallops, remember?"

"Yeah? What about her?"

"Just haven't seen her around since you introduced her. Are you guys still a thing?"

My tongue nearly gets bitten off as I try to hold in my real reaction. Instead, I sit up a bit straighter. "Yeah, she's still my girlfriend."

"All right." Ian turns back to the laptop, studying the list again.

"All right?" I laugh. If my blood could change colors, it just became green.

He looks back at me and shrugs. "Just thought it was worth asking. She seems cool." He waves me off. "Don't worry about me. I'm not the hit-on-your-friend's-girl type of guy. I was just curious." He closes my laptop, holding out a hand to haul me off his couch.

Peace.

I clasp it, allowing him to pull me up. I'm too tired for this. "You sure?" I ask. "Man, I've got no time to be friends with someone who's gonna stab me in the back." My blunt words bite, but I don't care. I'm exhausted and, frick, he's talking about Lucy!

He squeezes my shoulder. "I'm not that type of guy.

Bros before hoes, right?" He chuckles. "You can't really blame me for asking, right?"

My gut relaxes; I don't know what's wrong with me. I know he's good. Fishing out the creeps is my specialty. "No, I can't blame you. She's amazing. That's why I'm with her."

"And stunning. You're lucky, man." He walks me to the front door. "Let me know if it doesn't work out, all right?" he says with a wicked smile.

"Tool."

"Whatever." We fist pump. "See you next week? I'll email the project in tonight."

"Sweet."

Once I'm on the road, my finger hovers over Call Lucy. My gut pulls at me and I hesitate longer, as that green, sludge-like feeling creeps back through me. Why didn't it occur to me that other guys might like Lucy? I've been living in a stupid bubble. She's not mine. I don't own her. Just because I'm not seeing her every day doesn't mean other guys aren't scoping her out.

My heart drops when I think of her waiting for my call. I owe her way more than that. A reason to keep being with me.

I nearly push CALL, but the ache from too much separation rips into me. If I hear her voice, the pain will kill me.

No, I need more than that.

A quick U-turn and my heart throttles.

Yes. I need to see Lucy.

Right now.

CHAPTER NINE

Lucy

All right. The Fascinating Life of Whales is only adding to the weight on my eyelids. I click off the National Geographic Channel, glancing again at the clock for what's probably the one thousandth time. Twenty-eight past midnight. I pull up Facebook on my laptop. Anything to distract me from that piece of plastic on the table called a phone.

Eighty-two notifications. Wow, it's only been a week since I logged on. As I scroll through, the notifications are mostly about comments on photos or wall posts about my games. My wall is plastered with pics of Justin and I together that other people have tagged. There are the ones I remember having taken, but there are a lot of quick shots of us holding hands down the hallway or chatting in the parking lot. I scroll through the comments on each photo, gut tense, looking for the vulgar change that we saw before.

The comments are all friendly though. I let out a breath, relaxing. Justin would hate if I found more crude comments.

With a click, I enlarge a photo of Justin and me from the end of the summer. A selfie, white paint on each of our cheeks. That'd make an awesome profile pic.

But…the phone sits idle in front of me. I sigh, rubbing my eyes as they start to tingle. Crap. Only three more days. Right?

I glance back at the photo, allowing Justin's green eyes to penetrate my soul. Then I'm a goner. The dark of the basement overcomes me, exposing everything I've worked so hard to calm.

I miss him so much. There's no way he can miss me this way. It's ripping me apart.

Is Justin so distant because of his schedule? Or, maybe he'd rather just be doing other things than hang out with me?

What if I'm wrong about us?

No, there's that deep glow in me that feels so right with him. When we're together, everything feels perfect. But since we are rarely together, I can't help but wonder if this is meant to be at all.

This love thing is so overwhelming. The strength of it scares me and the risks, terrifying.

What if he doesn't feel as deeply as me? That's totally plausible and would explain how easy it is for him to be away from me. It's not fair that when I'm out with Laura or playing basketball he's always on my mind. I can't escape him. Not that I want to. God, what I wouldn't do to be in his arms. But, thinking of him all the time has become extra painful.

I never imagined that dating Justin Marshall would be so hard.

My eyes catch the clock. Twelve forty-two and still no call.

I take a deep breath, pulling myself together, rubbing the tears off my cheeks. It's time to stop waiting. I can't let myself think he forgot. Being forgotten again… after everything with Zach…

No. I won't go there. Justin's not like that.

In all of his business and exhaustion, he probably accidently fell asleep. Blaming him for that won't help anything.

I shut the laptop and drag myself off the couch. Time to move on and sleep myself. I glance down at my phone, debating whether I have the strength to leave it down here so I won't check it all night long.

My heart aches with the thought of cutting off the possibility of communication and I immediately reach for it. Partially hating myself. But there's no way I want to miss his call in case he does.

The moment I touch the phone it vibrates.

Justin: You still awake?

I take a deep breath as I digest that his first text isn't an apology for not calling. No. Another deep breath. I refuse to be a bitchy girlfriend. This is Justin. He has a reason.

Me: I am. Was about to head to bed.

Justin: Where are you?

Me: Basement. Why?

I wait a few minutes and he doesn't respond.

Me: Where are you?

Justin: For real. You're gorgeous.

I wipe under my eye, black mascara returns on my finger.

Me: Ha, if you could only see me now.
Justin: I do.

What? I spin around, dropping my phone at the site of Justin tapping lightly on my back sliding door. Holy. My heart spins then throws itself, out of control, raging through my chest. Justin's the only person in the world who can do that.

I bound over the couch, softly sliding open the door. Justin reaches out as he steps in from the night air, taking my hand in his. His dark hair holds a slight curl and he looks like he stepped out of a freaking magazine with his dark-washed jeans and a light gray sweater that he wasn't wearing before.

"Hey." Justin says and he steps close, cupping my chin in his palm.

His five o'clock shadow has grown into scruff. I reach out, touching the pricks along his jaw. We lock eyes for a second before he wraps his arms around my waist, pulling me close. His lips find mine, greeting me in a passionate kiss. My knees weaken as I move up against the wall. Warmth spreads through me, my insides again glowing gold. He pulls out of the kiss for a breath, sweeping my bangs out of my face.

"Lucy, I've missed you so much." Carefully, he wipes the area under my eyes. "Were you crying?"

So unarmed from his surprise and kiss, I nod.

"I did this?" he asks.

"No." I wipe away the new tears that have formed. "I'm tired and missing you."

He pulls me into a hug and his fresh scent takes over, relaxing my crazy heart. "What's going on, Lucy?" His voice warms my ear.

"I miss you."

"I miss you too." He pulls out of the hug, cupping my chin again. His beautiful green eyes hold me captive. "I don't think you'll ever know how much I miss you, Lucy. I can't stop thinking about you. Every moment, you're in my heart and the pain is killing me. I'm sorry I didn't call." He leans down, softly kissing my upper lip. "I needed to have you in my arms."

My soul sighs as his words erase all my doubt.

"That's exactly what I was crying about. I need to be near you more. These last two months…"

"They've sucked. I know. Don't worry. It's over now."

"But there's still three more days until the election."

"Yeah, that means three more days of campaign appearances. You like shrimp right?"

"Of course. Who doesn't?"

"Good. Because that's pretty much all I've been eating this month. Please, come to these stupid fundraisers with me?"

"Will your parents mind?"

"I don't care."

"What about studying for your midterms?"

"Lucy," he says as he runs his fingers through my hair. "If I have to chain myself to the wall to study, I will. But I want you to be there, in the same room."

My heart swells. *Yes.* "I want to be there too."

"Okay. This schedule of mine is nonsense. We'll make it work." His head touches mine. "We're together, okay?"

"Right." I smile easily then and I realize it's the first one I haven't forced out in a while.

"Beautiful," he says, running his finger over my lips.

Goosebumps fly over my body, chased by my racing

heart. He leans in, pressing me up against the wall as he takes my hips in his hands. He kisses me softly, until I part my mouth.

I need him. Everything he'll give me.

He responds passionately, understanding this need. His hand travels up my side as he explores my mouth. He pulls my hips, directing us off the wall. I push him towards the couch, crawling on his lap. There's urgency behind each kiss, needing to recover our lost time.

A soft sigh escapes from the back of his throat. I shift, noticing the bulge in his pants. I pull out of his kiss and bite my lip, trying not to grin. He smirks back at me. I blush, never having noticed this sort of reaction before. He pulls me close, kissing me softer now. But with that under me, I know it's too far. It's not what we want. Not now. I slide off to give him a bit of space. I won't tease him. That's just mean.

"No, I need you close," he whispers, pulling me back, repositioning me so I'm across his lap, with my arms wrapped around his neck. I try not to think about the pressure below.

"You're addictive, worse than the rush of sinking a winning shot." Justin sweeps my bangs out of my eyes. "I didn't think anything could feel more powerful than that."

"It's scary, isn't it?"

"You don't have to be scared with me. I'm not letting *this* go."

I snuggle closer toward his rock solid chest and relax in the calm of his scent. "Being in your arms is like the perfect burrito."

"Steak, barbecoa, rice, black beans, hot salsa, sour cream, corn, and cheese," he says while kissing me between each ingredient. "Delicious." His lips find mine again, and we lose one another to our lips, tongues, and necks. Eventually, his kisses slow and he slides over, arms wrapped around me while lying next to me on the couch.

"Lucy," he whispers as he tries to stifle a yawn that only triggers my own. He puts his finger in my mouth, a running joke that he knows I hate.

I pinch him with a growl. "Seems like it's time for you to go," I tease. Which sucks, because it's true. It's almost two.

"I'll pick you up in the morning? I want you to meet my family. For real, at my home."

"What time?"

"Is nine thirty too early?"

"Nope."

"Awesome. We're having Sunday brunch."

He lifts me with him without any strain as he rises from the couch. His lips are on mine as he walks back to the sliding door. "I don't know if I can make it seven more hours."

"Me either."

"Okay. New plan. I'm picking you up at eight o'clock." He kisses me softly before setting my feet to the floor. "I love you."

"I love you too," I say as he slides out quietly through the back door.

***

Whoa. Talk about a pendulum shift. Mr. Marshall waves at me as he flips pancakes wearing flannel pants, a T-shirt, and a blue dress robe. Mrs. Marshall's pouring orange juice in yoga pants and a workout tank, glowing after her morning run.

The last time I saw them they were all suit and ball gown.

"Lucy, we're so pleased Justin invited you for brunch."

"Me too. Thanks for having me." I keep my hands folded as Justin leads me to sit on the bar stool across from his mom. My kitchen island usually has some soil experiment on it. Here? I can see my reflection in the countertop.

I clasp my hands tight. Do not smudge the granite countertop.

"You want to fry up the bacon, Justin?"

"Sure," he says, sliding from beside me with a confident nod.

"Lucy, I hope you don't think it's rude if I ask you to help?" Mrs. Marshall asks with a look that's so much like Justin's. That smile wasn't at the fundraiser dinner. Seeing it now helps.

"Please do! What can I do?" Yes, helping is way easier. Better than just sitting and staring.

"There's a spiral ham in the fridge. Do you mind cutting it up?"

"Absolutely, no problem."

I scoot off the stool and open the stainless steel vault they call a fridge. On the bottom shelf, I find the ham in a netted bag. Nine pounds. Whoa. This is a family-only brunch, right?

"There's a cutting board in the lower left drawer. You'll find the serving platter and knife over on the back counter."

"Thanks." I slide my fingers through the netting, lifting the ham up on the countertop.

Okay, cutting a pre-sliced spiral ham? No problem. I easily pull open the netting, thankful for the rebuilt muscles from my summer of painting. I'll slice up and arrange the most impressive spiral ham Justin's folks have ever seen.

I dig the knife in, slicing quick to release the plastic wrap. Water squirts back at me, spraying my sweater and pooling over the cutting board. Towel-less, I try scooping the water into the middle of the board. Without any edges to the board, the battle turns on me. I bite my tongue as it oozes out, spilling over the countertop and onto the floor. Crap. Crap. Crap.

I clear my throat and force my voice to be steady. "Justin, where can I get a towel?"

"Use the one hanging on the oven, dear," his mom replies instead. Thankfully, she doesn't look over.

Oven door. Okay, that's five steps away, max. I abandon the ham to walk across the kitchen, super-calm-like. Three steps away, then suddenly, *SPLAT!*

My gut tightens as I turn around. No, please no.

Like a top, the ham spins on the floor.

"Oh my gosh." I lunge for the ham. Five-second rule!

My foot doesn't land though. Instead it slides on the puddle of ham juice. I gasp as my back hits Justin's kitchen floor. A cool wetness slides under my head and neck. Ham juice. Nasty.

"I'm so sorry," I gasp as I roll, grabbing the ham from the ground. I hold it over my chest and squeeze my eyes shut. Is this really happening?

A moment passes before Justin leans over me and I peek upward. "You okay down there?" he asks, biting back a gorgeous smirk.

"Oh, give her room." Mrs. Marshall pushes him aside and helps me up.

"I'm so sorry, Mrs. Marshall. I didn't mean to ruin your ham." I ring out juice from the back of my sweater, debating how I can save face. As the juice drips out of my hair, the smell of ham overcomes me. Screw it. There's no way I can make this okay.

I take a deep breath. "Okay, I'm sorry. Listen, that girl you met at the fundraiser in that pretty lace dress? That's not me. This," I twist my hair, squeezing the rest of the water from it, "is me."

Then Mr. Marshall begins to laugh. "Well, that guy in the suit who's politically correct, also not me."

"Same with that woman in the red dress." Mrs. Marshall smiles and nudges me.

Justin steps closer then, pulling me into his arms. "Mmm, you smell like pig. Delicious."

"Aww, see, Christy? This explains Justin's forever obsession with bacon. They're perfect for one another."

I clasp a hand over my mouth, trying not to laugh. Justin reaches my love handle, tickling me until I crack.

"Welcome to our home," Mrs. Marshall says as she gives me a sideways hug. "You fit in well here."

"Hey," a new voice adds to the mix. Tonya walks into the kitchen towards the ham juice.

"Be careful!" I say as she steps into the wetness. Her foot slides up, landing her butt-down in the puddle.

I rush to her side, sliding again, this time on my thigh, and ending up sloshing more ham juice toward her.

Tonya starts laughing, thank God.

"What is this stuff?" she says.

"Ham juice. Totally my fault." I squirm to get up before helping her off the floor.

"Yuck."

"I'm sorry. It's nasty."

"Yup," Mr. Marshall says, throwing us towels. "You fit in well here. Nice choice, son."

CHAPTER TEN

Justin

Jeff Marshall, 28%. Tim Montgomery, 36%. Not all precincts reporting.

My chest rattles as I glance at Dad. He nods at the screen before turning around to the crowd, offering a confident clap. "It's okay, folks. The numbers are only beginning to roll in. We're doing fine." He clasps hands with a volunteer, still building relationships and caring about others' views. He's got to win. He'd be such a caring governor.

Mom sighs at me from across the room. In the next hour or two, our life will change completely. It doesn't matter which way the vote falls. The bile in my stomach turns over. The thought of "living" at the governor's mansion doesn't seem fun. Dad reassured me I wasn't expected to move in and that they'll be splitting time between the houses. That relief was awesome. I love my basement bedroom. Plus, not living there will make it a bit easier to deal with all the watchers. People assume I'm used to it with all the attention from school. But here? On the political side? The closer Dad gets to his dream, the closer I'm being watched. It's a bit too creepy for me.

I try to concentrate on my Psych textbook. I still have three chapters to read before tomorrow's test, but all I can make out are blurry blocks which I imagine must be paragraphs. The more I concentrate, the worse it gets. I rub my eyes as someone pats my back while passing. "Just you wait, Justin," they say. "Soon it'll be your campaign!" Nausea takes over as I freeze, the room still moves in circles around me. The walls swell and beat with each humid breath I suck in. No. I'm never going to become a politician. I smile at the guy, which is enough for him so he moves on. Thank goodness. That's not a conversation I'm ever planning to have with anyone. I try to refocus on the text but the room starts spinning again. Did I eat today? Pretty sure I grabbed a banana on the way out the door. But rarely do I go a few hours without a small bite of protein or super-carb to charge me until my next big meal. The room pulsates again. Dad sips a dark liquid from his tumbler while I rub my damp palms against my dress pants. How does he stay so calm? I'm a mess.

My phone vibrates. A text from Lucy. Finally!

Lucy: Game's finished. You still want me to come?

Me: Heck yes. I'm going crazy without you here.

Lucy: I'll be there as soon as I can. Got to shower first.

An image of Lucy bare in the shower flashes before me. I take a deep breath, pushing it aside. I've got to control those. I don't know how I'm ever going to survive dating this girl.

"There you go." Tonya pats my shoulder. "That's the first smile I've seen in a while."

My face heats so she peeks at my phone.

"No way. Private," I say as I pull it from her view.

"Oh my gosh, are you sexting?" She snatches the phone, reading the text.

"Are you kidding me? I'm not an idiot. Just texting, *normally*, with Lucy."

"Na-ha," she laughs as she reads. "You were totally picturing her in the shower." She hip-checks me lightly. "Don't be such a guy."

"Do you really think I'm like that?"

"I'd hope not."

"I was just trying to figure out what to write back."

"Sure," Tonya says as she hands back the phone. "Well, go ahead."

Me: You always look nice. Just come.

I hand it back to her. "See?"

"Yup…you ended your text with come."

"And I'm the immature one?"

She tosses her hair over her shoulder as she walks away. It's been a while since Tonya has played the annoying big sister. With her living in downtown Minneapolis, we usually get along fine. But tonight? The stress seems to be dominating, rubbing us both into a tween-like rawness.

Paul waves me over then. *Fine.* I owe him common decency as he's brought Dad this far. But after he slipped me a letter he drafted this morning expressing my *earnest interest* in that reality show this morning, he'll forever be a weasel to me. It's insane that he thought I'd sign that thing.

Paul slicks his hair back. Correction. He's a snake.

"Justin, it's a good night. I can feel it," he says, too upbeat, sloshing the drink in his hand. "Is Lucy here?"

I shake my head as I'm about to say "not yet," but he holds up his hand, interrupting.

"Good, because Carl's arriving in five. He told us to count on that fifty grand for advertising, but he hasn't delivered on the promise yet. He says it's coming tonight."

"Wait, he hasn't given it to you? I did that interview weeks ago. And you already spent it?" Is he kidding me?

"Yup. On that family ad series we ran a few weeks ago."

My chest boils. "Paul, Dad has a policy that we don't spend money unless it's in the bank."

"It was a signed pledge. Don't worry so much. He's on his way now with the check. It's how things are usually done."

I glance at Dad, who catches my look of disdain with a cocked eye.

"Don't go running off to tell him." Paul's words slither. "It'll just make him worry. It's no matter. As long as Lucy's not here, we're good."

"Why would Lucy being here matter?"

"You know you need to appear single and available. You've got to play the part."

The doors of the ballroom swing open and, on cue, Carl struts through. Too tall, too round, and too bald.

"It'll be fine, leave it to me. It's not like you're going to end up on that show."

"Well, you better grab that check soon."

"Oh, why is that, son?" Paul steps near me. Is he trying to be intimidating? I look down, towering over his five-seven frame.

"Because Lucy's on her way. And I plan to kiss her the moment she walks through those doors."

Paul's face pales. "No. Tell her not to come."

"I don't live my life fakely, Paul. I did the interview. That was it."

"Justin, come on. It's only a bit more time."

"Your time is up." My gosh, I sound like such an entitled jerk, but I don't care. "Go fix this mess. Right now."

My phone vibrates.

Lucy: I'll be there in twenty minutes.

"Is that Lucy?"

"Yup, she's in the parking lot."

"Justin, don't screw everything up for Jeff. Starting his term as governor with a campaign in debt won't look good. Think about it." Paul steps away from me then, quickly maneuvering his way through the masses to greet Carl.

A tray of bruschetta appears before me. "Take it. You've got to eat, man." Ian reaches out, clasping my hand in greeting.

"I appreciate it. I'm starved." The coolness of the tomatoes pop against the cheese and salty bread. My stomach aches, pleading for more.

"You missed three tray passes that included bacon. What's wrong with you? I know you're nervous, but you need sustenance to get through tonight."

I nod. "Right, right."

Paul shakes Carl's hand, leading him away from the main doors into the depths of the crowd. A bead of sweat drips down his sideburns. Good, let him suffer.

"What's so entertaining?" Ian follows my glare. "The bald creep?"

"Pretty much, yup."

"He's weird. He once took every olive from a tray I was passing. Put them in his pockets and winked at me like people do it all the time. The guy is slime."

I clasp Ian's shoulder. "Exactly." Ian's got character judging down. "We should really hang out outside of Psych sometime."

"Absolutely. I play at a coffee shop every Saturday morning. I'll text you the address. Pop in to listen, then afterward we can do whatever."

"Perfect."

"Okay, I've got to keep passing." He nods for me to take another bruschetta. "Eat."

I do, then watch him pass through the crowd without even bumping an elbow, skillfully making his way toward the volunteers that are already too sloshed from the open bar.

Paul catches my eye as Carl hands him a credit card. He swipes the card through a small attachment on his iPad.

Good. He got it.

Paul grins back at me, a little too smug. He's crazy if he thinks I'm not telling Dad the type of person he employs. I pull my hands through my hair. Paul's got to go. But I'll wait to tell Dad until morning. He doesn't need to deal with that now.

Someone turns up the mega TV behind the bar. Another precinct report. My gut tightens.

Jeff Marshall 41%. Tim Montgomery 40%. Not all precincts yet reporting.

The room cheers and I swear the ceiling moves three feet higher. Dad responds minimally with that nod he does when one of my games is way too close. With the games, I have more control, the power to do something about it.

But this? Nothing can be done in the final countdown.

Just then, the back French doors open, revealing Lucy in the white dress I bought her, her hair all wrapped up tight on top of her head. I grin, weaving my way through the crowd, loving that she didn't waste our time together with a blow dryer or finding a new outfit. Smart girl.

"Hi, how's everything going?" Lucy asks on tiptoes, trying to see the TV report over the crowd.

I step in front of her, blocking her view. "Great now that you're here." I scoop my hand around her waist, pulling her close.

A classic Paul throat-clear ensues. Sorry, Paul. I'm not playing your games anymore.

I lift Lucy up, bringing her to my lips for an intense kiss, before slowly lowering her to the ground. Someone whistles and Lucy blushes.

Okay, so I put on a bit of a show.

"That good, huh?" She laughs at my overreaction, slipping her hand in mine so I can lead her through the crowd. I don't hesitate, leading her straight past Carl. His eyes bulge like an octopus about to devour itself.

Mom pulls Lucy into a hug. "Happy you could make it."

"I barely did. The game went long."

"I can't believe they had a game on election night." She shakes her head. "What type of values are they teaching you kids?"

"Don't worry, everyone on the team who's eighteen got a free pass from school to vote. Though," she shrugs, "I can't guarantee they didn't use that time to go grab a coffee and browse Facebook."

"Hmm, maybe if…no, *when* your father is in office, I'll

find a way to make sure schools can provide chaperones."

I laugh. "To a bunch of eighteen-year-olds?"

"A woman can dream," she says before taking a sip of her white wine. "Where's Alex tonight?"

"A game." The one against our ultimate rivals. The guys hated me when I said I'd have to bow out. Especially Alex. He wouldn't let up. Coach understood. But, still. I hate letting people down. Mom nods while aimlessly looking through the crowd. Her ability to listen tonight is less than stellar. I won't hold that against her though. Heck, I can barely keep a thought straight tonight.

The commercials finally end and the anchor chats about the end of duck migration while he waits for more precinct updates. The chatter in the banquet has turned into a low hum, as if the electricity in the air is snuffing the noise out. I let my hand find that lower place on Lucy's back, rubbing it as I wait for the anchor to speak. I glance down at the hot way her back curves, allowing myself to momentarily blank out from this hell.

"And now," the anchor bellows. My eyes snap back to the screen. "CNN, MSNBC, and FOX are reporting their predictions for Minnesota's next Governor."

My heart stops.

"Jeff Marshall with 49.5% of precinct report! Tim Montgomery, 43%."

The room roars. Millions of pounds lift from my shoulder and for a moment, I'm free.

My heart flies as Lucy jumps up and down with cheers. Mom grabs my hand, gasping, before springing forward onto Dad's arm. Dad gives his signature nod, then slowly his straight face cracks, hinting at a smile. He leans in towards Mom, giving her cheek a quick kiss.

"SPEECH, SPEECH!"

Dad holds up his hand. "Let's wait until it's official folks."

The anchor bellows again, "This just in. All precincts reporting. Can't wait to meet you on Capitol Hill, Mr. Marshall." Below his statement, the scrolling bar highlights Dad's name. 53% of the precinct vote. Then that millions of pounds missing from my shoulders detours, slamming me in the gut.

Change is coming.

"Okay," Dad hollers, "*now* we can celebrate! Where's my family?"

Lucy pushes me forward to join my parents and Tonya. Dad pulls us together. We hug in a huddle. Yeah, it's lame, but I don't care. Not tonight. Dad deserves this. A mess of words pour from us as we embrace. This new ache gets pushed aside. It'll go away. Change is always hard. Right now, I'm focused on him. Finally, Dad takes a moment to make sure his eyes meet with each of ours individually. "I love you guys. I'd never be here without you." With that said, he loosens his grasp of Tonya and me. We step back as he scoops in to give Mom a huge kiss. I bounce backward the moment I hear Mom calling Dad "Mr. Governor" under her breath. Okay, that's enough.

But the crowd loves it and everyone catcalls and cheers. Only Carl and Paul stand stoic.

Lucy wraps her arm around my waist. "Congratulations! All your hard work was worth it. I'm so excited for your family!"

"Thanks," I say as I take a deep breath. I smile back at her, even though my gut aches.

"What's wrong?" she asks low so no one can hear. With

everyone celebrating around us and patting my back, her eyes are the only ones that are sincere. She's totally in-tune. "Justin?"

I pull her in close for a hug. "For some reason, I feel like we lost," I whisper.

CHAPTER ELEVEN

Lucy

I slide my fingers into my woven, fingerless gloves, wrapping them around my water bottle. Forty-seven degrees is heavenly in Minnesota in mid-November. I know it's horrible, but in this moment, I'm thankful for global warming. For once the sting of Minnesota's winter isn't infringing upon its fall.

"We went for caramel. Hope that's cool," Laura says as she slides a fresh pie in front of me. "Fork or spoon?" Laura digs in with her own spoon while Jennifer joins us at the table.

"Fork's great."

She hands me a wimpy plastic fork and shrugs. "It's all they had."

"No matter, it'll do." I dig in through the flaky crust,

scooping up an apple slice covered in the caramel goo. The crusts melt the moment it touches my tongue. The apple's tartness slices through the sugary caramel. Oh, man. Heavenly, hot, melty goo. "You two taking Family Consumer Science may be the best thing that's ever happened to me. I hope this got an A."

Jennifer sighs after her bite, angling her face up towards the sun. "A+. I'm like, the best cook."

Laura clears her throat, biting her lip and holding back a grin.

"Umm," I say, remembering how Jennifer managed to burn mac and cheese during our last girls' night.

Jennifer rolls her eyes. "Okay, so Laura had *some* pointers to offer. But I measured the ingredients and stuff."

"Right. That counts as cooking."

The moment Jennifer closes her eyes and angles her face toward the sun, Laura mouths, "I re-measured."

"I heard that," Jennifer says.

"You hear everything," Laura pouts.

"It's my superpower."

"I want a superpower."

"Oh hush up, you can cook." Jennifer loops her hair up into a high messy bun. The football and lacrosse players sitting across the quad all ogle her. I purposely make my eyes skip over Zach. The sight of him still makes my skin crawl.

"Seriously, Jennifer. You've got to stop doing that." Laura throws a piece of crust at her. "It's not fair to all the chicks that actually want to get with dicks, ya know?"

I nearly choke on an apple slice. Crap, Laura. She loves to run away with words. Thankfully, Jennifer laughs. I'm still surprised that Jennifer dared to tell Laura about Trish, especially with Laura being from the south. I have no idea how that conversation went but, clearly, Laura's embraced it.

Jennifer nods back towards the table. "If you want a piece of them, I'm not stopping you."

"No need," Laura sits up straighter, emphasizing her southern accent. "I'm a lady, thank you." Now I'm laughing. Laura is the opposite of ladylike. She's already downed over half the pie.

"Well, then do you mind sharing more than a quarter of the pie with Jen and me?" I ask, scooping up a huge bite. She shoos my hand away.

"Excuse me? Did you make this pie?"

Jennifer opens her mouth to fight for me.

"Oh, don't even try to make a case for you cooking this, Jen."

Jen falls silent. I reach across with my fork, trying to slide past Laura's guard. Fail.

"Yeah, that's what I thought," Laura says teasingly. She scoops up the pie tin as she stands. "My pie."

I lift my eyebrow. "Point proven. *Not* a lady."

"Oh, hush up," Laura says with a wink as she weaves her way through the courtyard over to Luke. She passes a table of guys with Marissa perched on the end. Marissa plays with her hair and occasionally moves the sweater off her shoulder so she can massage her neck. Her eyes catch mine. My gut drops and I chicken out, breaking her glare. Seriously. Why does she keep doing that? All week she's been trying to catch my attention. It's driving me crazy.

I pretend to stretch, really checking out to see what the heck Zach's up to. He's on his phone again. Did they break up? I guess I haven't seen them smashed up against the lockers for a while.

Marissa's flirting squeal rings through the courtyard. Jennifer covers her ears.

"Does she have any idea what she sounds like?"

"Yup." I cover my ears as she does it again. "She knows it's super high-pitched but," I pause as some guy wraps his arm around Marissa's waist for a side hug, briefly brushing her ass. "It's never failed her."

"Uh. And *that* is why I don't like guys."

"They're not all bad."

"Justin's a freak of nature, you know that."

"Yeah, I lucked out." I know I have my stupid goofy grin across my face. I really did luck out with Justin. Like, pigs flew. Stars aligned. I have no idea what I did right to get such a perfect boyfriend. I don't deserve him, but, God, I'm so happy to be with him. I dare not doubt the laws of the universe. Jen's lucky too. She has Trish. They're always so sweet together. I love that Jen and I can gush about our loves to one another. No one else wants to hear that stuff.

"How's Trish? Is she coming out with everyone tomorrow night?" It's crazy awesome to have my own "everyone." Laura, Luke, Jake, Justin, me, Jen, Trish, and sometimes the guy from Justin's Psych class, Ian. When I was friends with Marissa, I was fooled into thinking I had a group. But really, we just hopped from table to table annoying people. I'm surprised Marissa runs the act solo now.

"Nah, she can't make it." Jen sighs, finally looking at me and not up at the sky. She picks at her fingernail polish, just like the night she told me she was a lesbian. I've learned since that rarely will Jen ruin a manicure.

"What's up?"

"She's pulling away. Taking longer to return texts, phone calls." She shakes her head. "Ever since I mentioned coming out together at the winter formal. She's just… changed."

"Has she come out at her school yet?"

"I thought so? I mean, her friends know. Just like my friends know. Her parents know… I don't get it. It's really confusing."

"Have you tried talking to her about it?"

"A few times. But she kind of shuts down."

Jen scrapes all the purple off her thumb nail. "I'm afraid she's going to dump me."

"Really? Are you sure you're reading this right?"

"Yeah. I dunno? I'm trying to keep things consistent but special too. Little surprises here and there. Honestly, do you think I'm coming on too strong? Or not strong enough?" She nods over to Marissa. "I don't do things like that. Maybe I'm doing it wrong?"

"Do *not* use Marissa as an example, trust me."

"How do you balance the act with Justin?"

"I don't know. It sort of just unfolds." It's natural. How do I explain this? "I let things just happen with Justin. I acted so long in my friendship with Marissa. There isn't enough energy left for me to act with him."

"Yeah," Jen says as she gazes over at the empty brick wall.

I reach over and squeeze her arm. "It'll work out, Jen. It will."

When she looks back at me, her eyes are red. "I love her. I mean, I think I love her. How do I even know what real love is? Crap." She wipes a tear away, making sure her mascara is still set. "I have no idea what I'm doing."

"That's okay. I don't think any of us do." Watching the doubt on Jennifer's face rattles me. What am I saying? Don't I know if I love Justin?

I search my heart and everything feels solid. Yes, I love him. I do.

But Jen's right. How is love defined? What if we have no idea what we're doing?

The bell rings then and Jen forces out a smile, grabbing her books. "Thank you."

"No problem." I yank myself out of my own black hole of thoughts. There's nothing pretty down there.

"Have fun at English. I'll tell Justin you say hi in Calc II. Oh, crap! Justin! His birthday is in a few weeks. What are we going to do?"

I smash my hand against my face as my gut drops. I've never dated a guy on his birthday before. Let alone a guy I loved. And his eighteenth birthday? It'd be easy to say I'll just throw a huge drunk party. That'd be the cliché way. But Justin's not like that. Plus, I know his family will want to help celebrate too.

"Aw, don't stress about it too much, Luce. Ask him what he wants to do. If it's Justin, it'll be pretty easy. Trust me."

"Right. I'll see you tomorrow night?"

"Yup."

"Call me if you need to, okay?"

"I will," she says as she walks away. I want to throw my backpack at the guy who just looked at her butt. Seriously?

***

Saturday morning is starred on my planner from now through the end of the year. Justin's evenings are still crammed full. Post-secondary sounds like a nightmare. Paul also insists that Justin show up at all of his dad's public appearances, and Justin's been helping organize a huge fundraiser for the Twin Cities branch of the Leukemia Society. That's sucked away two Friday evenings, but he needed to be there. He lights up when he talks about the kids he meets when he volunteers. It helps him connect with Jackson again.

I miss Justin a lot. When accidently bumping into to one another at Subway on Tuesday brought us more time together than we'd had in weeks, he swore that from now on early Saturday mornings are for us. Crawling into Justin's car this morning brought back all the memories of carpooling to work together last summer. Tensions were always high during our morning drive, and this morning the tension during the ride was so insanely high it was ridiculous. Of course, now the tensions there because I want to kiss him rather than slap his ego silly.

I hold my coat closed as I walk with Justin into the coffee shop. The chill nips at me. In less than a week, the freezing cold trampled the perfect fall weather.

Justin opens the door to the coffee shop. The roasted bean smell immediately infiltrates my clothes. Crap, shouldn't have worn wool. I'm going to have to air this thing out before re-wearing it at school.

I wave at Ian who's setting up his guitar in the back corner. He's been fun to get to know. He's an endless surprise. A broad shouldered, football-esque looking guy, who'd rather read or play music than discuss sports. Maybe he doesn't feel compelled to care about sports because he's homeschooled? Either way, it's nice to meet a guy who doesn't raise sports up on a pedestal.

Not that Justin only talks about sports. He may talk about a game, but he doesn't seem compelled to throw out professional athletes' names. People always expect us to have a lot to say about basketball, but really, we rarely talk about it. Especially professionally. It's nice that Justin is just the "there's sports on TV" type guy while he does something else. I don't think I could dedicate every Sunday morning to football. Thankfully, even if Justin was like that, he's not the type of guy who'd expect me to sacrifice three hours a day. Heck, he's so busy, I doubt *he'd* sacrifice three hours a day to watching a game if he could.

Justin squeezes my hand while he orders our drinks. No, Justin would rather spend that three hours with me. And that's why he's amazing.

"What?" Justin nudges me with his elbow.

"Just thinking."

"Do you want a scone too?"

"No," I beam back at him as we walk toward our regular booth. "I'm just happy."

"Oh?"

"Mmm, hmm. I love spending time with you."

"I know. I can't wait for winter break. I may have to be careful that you don't get sick of me."

"Why's that?"

"Because I'll see you every day." He holds my gaze. His dimples deep from the crease in his smile.

My chest warms with the thought of spending every evening in Justin's arms. We rummage through our bags, pulling out our laptops to tackle essays. English for me. Psych for him. We've discovered that as long as we're in public, we're pretty good at studying together.

But his basement?

No productivity there. We've tried sitting on opposite couches or using headphones. But, inevitably, one of us just gives into the hormonal rush. Let's just say we'd get A's in making out.

"Why are you blushing?" Justin taps on my notebook.

"Me? Blushing? Never."

"Seriously…" His foot rubs up against my leg. "What's going on in that head of yours today?"

"I have no idea what you mean," I say with a sly grin.

The angle of Justin's chin sharpens as he tries to figure me out. He didn't shave this morning, so he looks even older than near eighteen. He's just so… *smokin' hot*… without even trying.

"That." Justin nudges me again and leans in. "That look. It's driving me crazy."

"Oh?" Driving Justin crazy is one of my favorite things to do. Well, crazy in the good way. And, as he slides out of his side of the booth and into mine, I'm pretty sure I've taken this the good way.

He leans in, his breath warm on my ear and his hand on my leg. "Do you want me to ask them to change the order to go? Study somewhere else?"

I answer by touching his jaw, feeling the prick of his stubble. How is it possible he's this sexy at nine in the morning on a Saturday?

"Well, that answers that." He slides out of the booth, crossing quickly to the counter to change our order.

"Why aren't you packed up?" he teases as he returns with our drinks.

"I like watching you."

He pulls my laptop and notebook toward him, sliding them into my bag for me. "Well, I'm holding you personally responsible if I bomb this essay."

I drop my little game, knowing how important grades are to him. "Okay, okay. Come on." I tap the seat next to me. "We can study. For real. I'll stop looking at you like that."

He weaves his fingers through mine, pulling me up and out of the booth.

"Never stop looking at me like that. You promise?" he whispers with his hand on my lower back, leading me toward the door.

"I promise."

"You know grades mean nothing to me compared to you." He waves goodbye to Ian in the corner as he opens the door. "The cleaning crew is at our house this morning, so…"

"Oh? Does that matter? I mean, we'll just be writing papers." I wink at him.

"Those looks are going to end me." He opens the passenger door, reaching across my body to help buckle me in.

"Is that a bad thing?"

"No."

He gets in the driver's seat and starts the car.

"Where are we going?"

"You'll see."

I reach out and turn over his hand to draw circles on his palm. His Adam's apple goes up and down with a groan. He pulls off the highway, onto a frontage road, and into a deserted park. These parks are never deserted in the summer. Hmm. Okay, winter, maybe you do have something to offer?

"So, what's your essay about?"

Justin takes my palm to his mouth, and starts kissing it.

"Theory?" I ask, trying not to sigh as he leans closer, his kiss traveling up my arm. "Psych statistics?"

He tugs me closer to him, his hand on my thigh. I give in when his kisses reach my lips. There's an intensity there I've never felt before. Whoa. He lowers my seat, angling on top of me. The warmth spreading through me makes me suddenly aware that this is our first make out session without parents roaming on the floor above.

Oh God. He's driving me wild. The way his lips explore mine, the way his chest is so solid beneath his shirt.

I open my eyes, somehow finding myself maneuvered into the back seat. My heart flips, while butterflies crash and play bumper cars in my gut.

He kisses my throat, down to my collarbone.

The blood whooshes in my head. How far does he want to go? Am I ready for this?

His lips return to mine and everything in me burns. Those hands find their way under my shirt, resting on my stomach. The touch is heavenly and warm.

Yes. I want more. I'm ready.

But for what?

I don't know… I don't know. What is he comfortable with?

What am I comfortable with?

Everything?…No?

"I don't know," I answer out loud, gasping the moment his hand cups my bra.

Crap. No. I didn't mean stop. Did I?

But he does. Justin, like a gentleman, pulls back.

"Sorry…" He sits up, running his hands through his hair. "I… You're just…" He shakes his head. "You're my kryptonite. I'm not strong enough to keep control."

I sit up, pulling my hair back into a bun. "No, I didn't mean that exactly. My mind was going a million miles an hour. I loved every moment of it, honestly." I reach out, touching his hand.

He squeezes back. "We should probably talk about this stuff."

"Yeah."

"Will talking about this be weird for you? We've only been together a little over three months."

My stomach flips. It's only been three months? Wow. Zach and I were together for two. Time passes so quickly when you're with someone you love. It's a cruel joke, as I want all the time in the world with him.

"No, we can talk about it." I pull my sweater closed as I remember his hand briefly touching my chest. "Is there much to talk about though? You told me this summer you want to wait to have sex until you're married."

He pauses for a long time, keeping my hand warm in his. "What do you want?"

"You…but," the butterflies in my stomach crash violently together and I know I have to tell the truth, "not this soon."

He nods. "Right."

"So what do you want?"

"Lucy, I had no idea how hard it'd be around you. You just…kryptonite." He brushes the bangs from my face.

"Wasn't kryptonite bad for Superman?"

He smiles back. "You know what I mean."

"I don't want to be bad for you."

"Lucy, you will never be bad for me. Ever."

One of our phones buzzes in the front seat.

"So...what are you saying?" My chest vibrates, wondering if sex is back on the option list. It'd change every kiss and every intention we have when we're alone together.

"You do crazy things to me, but we need to be smart about it." He touches my cheek. "I love how confident you feel with me."

I nod, ignoring another buzzing cell.

"Did you feel that way with Zach?"

The mere mention of his name makes the hairs on my arms stand up. Definitely not. "Zach was a creep. My body knew it."

"I know, but wasn't it scary wondering all the time how far he'd go?"

"Yeah," I admit. There's no use hiding anything from Justin.

"Okay. Well, I don't want you to ever feel like that with me."

"It's different with you, Justin. I do feel safe."

"I know. But I love you. And I don't want to cause you any stress." He sighs. "We'll figure this out. But in the meantime, maybe I won't be taking you to empty parking lots."

"Justin, this was awesome. I loved it."

"I know. But it's me. I just...I don't trust myself."

A phone rings again.

"Who is that?"

Justin reaches forwards and grabs his phone. "It's Jen." He dials her number. Jen's sobs pour out the phone. "We'll be right over. Hang in there. We'll see you soon." Justin hangs up.

"What happened?"

"Trish dumped Jen this morning."

My heart drops through the floor. How could it happen to them? They were perfect for each other. Trish seemed fine last night. If they can break up...

No. I won't even go there. Today is about Jen.

Justin turns on the ignition.

Time to go be a real friend.

CHAPTER TWELVE

Justin

Lucy taps my arm. "Uh, Justin?" she says, nodding toward my speedometer.

Whoa, twenty miles over the speed limit. "Right, thanks." I squeeze her hand back as I press the brake. Most guys would be pissed if their girlfriend pointed that out but I can't handle a ticket on my conscience right now. Plus, she's right. I'm going way too fast. How can I be upset about that?

"It's okay. I know you want to get to Jen's quickly."

"Yeah, this sucks for her," I say as I push away the real reason for my heavy foot. It's not that I don't want to get to Jen's, I *do*. It's that I can't process what I just did. I wiggle, attempting to hide what's left of the most amazing make out session ever. The evidence proves that even with

114

a conviction to respect Lucy, I'm weak. Why can't I keep my shit together? I almost made her say "No." I pushed her into doubt. What type of guy does that to the girl he loves?

But she does something to me; my brain turns off with the way she pulls her hands through my hair, her tongue on my teeth, the curve of her hips under my palms.

Shit.

I readjust again. *Calm down.* We pass twenty-two trees. *Okay, there.* It's down. I move one more time, feeling pretty awesome she didn't notice what was going on.

"You okay? Worried about Jen?"

"Yeah." She's so sweet. Thinking I'm that good of a person. This makes my gut drop though. I should be worried about Jen. And I am. How could Trish do this to her? It totally sucks.

"Wedgie?" she asks with a cocked eyebrow.

Her words bust my train of thought off rail. I burst out laughing. "Who says wedgie anymore?"

With her hair now up in a bun, her neck is exposed. A quarter-sized red mark grabs my eye. Holy hell. That's a hickey. I don't even remember doing that.

"Is that it, then?" she teases.

"No," I cough.

"Uh-huh."

I flip down her mirror, trying to suppress my smile. I should feel horrible about this too. But, in truth, it's the first hickey I've given a girl. I'm kinda proud.

"Take a look at your neck."

Lucy's gasp is followed by a swat to my arm. "Justin!"

"Sorry." I start pulling my hands through my hair, but stop midway. It's such an odd nervous tick. It needs to stop. She's examining the mark in the mirror. Crap, it's huge.

And it's just going to get redder, right? Purple too?

I reach over, touching her arm. "Does it hurt?"

"Nah." She shuts the mirror. "I didn't notice it until you pointed it out. Don't worry about it."

"You have a game on Monday. How are you going to hide that?"

She smiles. "I was friends with Marissa for a long time. I've gotten many How-To-Hide-Hickey makeup tutorials. No biggie."

Many tutorials? How many hickeys has she had?

She gets a cockeyed expression on her face, then bursts out in laughter again. "Zach and I kissed, but no hickeys. Don't worry. This is my first," she says with a wink.

Her first? I frickin' rock!

"I stopped Zach before we got that far," Lucy clarifies. "With you, I was lost in it all."

I rub my jaw. "Ditto."

She doesn't say anything, just reaches over so we can hold hands again.

"Do you think Jen will be okay?"

I pause, thinking about how strong I know Jen is. Plus, back when we "dated" we spent tons of time alone at the picnic table during her lifeguard breaks, pretending to have "couple time" when really we were just checking out girls. Trish was her first girlfriend. There would be more.

"Long term, Jen will be fine. But right now? I don't know." I've never seen the fresh side of a breakup before.

"I can't believe Trish dumped her," Lucy says through a light breath.

"It's so out of the blue. They always seemed so cool together."

Lucy shakes her head. "Jen told me last week she

116

thought Trish may break up with her. That she was pulling away."

I bite my tongue. Jen should have told me this on the way to class. She used to tell me everything. What's changed with her?… Or is it me? Maybe when Jen bolted from the car a few weeks ago all pissed off about how little time I was spending with Lucy, she was really talking about herself.

Shit. I did tell Jen I'd see her more after the campaign, but that ended a few weeks ago. I shouldn't have made her wait. I should have made time for her. No matter how hard I try lately, something slips through the cracks. There never used to be cracks before Dad's run for governor. No matter what I do, I can't seem to hold everything together. Jackson could've pulled it off. I wish he was here to tell me how. Dad used to be a good example, but he's taken on too much slime on the political front. He's missing family dinners and mingling with people he used to have no respect for. I guess their open pocketbooks helped gain his respect again. He better calm down a bit and find himself. If he's around Paul, he's a man I don't know.

I pull up Jen's driveway and take a deep breath. "You ready?"

"Absolutely."

***

Jen chokes back another wad of crud. Lucy hands her a Kleenex and whispers, "It's going to be okay," while stroking her hair.

"Not ready for a commitment? But we were together… dating! Isn't that a commitment already?" Jen blows into the tissue as I shift in the chair across from her. I hold my tongue, thankful I'm wiser than Alex would be if he was here and not commenting on the superfluous amount of snot involved in a girl breakdown.

"I know," Lucy says like a mother.

I reach out and squeeze Jen's hand. Seriously, I suck at this. I take a deep breath before I throw myself out there. "There will be other girls, Jen," I offer. More fish. More ice-cream flavors. That sort of thing. Lucy's eyes pop wide. Uh oh, wrong thing to say. Jen's chest heaves, followed with a sob of such depth that her ribs rattle.

Crap.

"Trish is it. I don't want someone else," she says through her snot-filled sob.

"I know," Lucy says over and over again, patting her arm. "This sucks. I'm sorry this hurts so much." Her words are like a blanket. I lean back, letting Lucy be the leader here. I'm out of my element. She nods to the place next to me, where Jen's legs rest.

Right. I can do that.

I slide onto the couch, lifting Jen's legs on my lap. I put my hands on her calves and Jen's full-body sobs seem to lessen with my touch. Okay, this I'm used to. My hands know Jen. Not like sexually, but in a "hold me, protect me" way. I can do that.

Jen's voice cracks. "She didn't want to go with me to the winter formal. I told her we didn't have to go. We didn't have to come out together in that way. But finally she confessed it wasn't that." She takes a deep breath. "She loves me, but I'm just not her type."

"Not her type? What the hell is wrong with her? Jen, you're a total babe. Funny, smart, and killer hot." The words fly out of my mouth. My hand flies over it, realizing that

that confession may not be totally cool with Lucy.

But Lucy smiles at me and mouths, "Keep going."

Okay. I take a deep breath. "Everything about you is awesome, Jen. Trish is crazy."

Jen wipes the tears from her eyes. "You're just saying that."

"No," I cough, remembering the first time I saw her from across the cafeteria. "I'm telling the truth." I squeeze her calf lightly. "You know that. Come on, I followed you around like a puppy our freshman year, remember? Begging you to date me."

She cracks a smile and my gut relaxes. "It took me a full year to say yes."

Okay. This is working. I look to Lucy. How much does she want me to share?

Lucy nods for me to continue.

Okay then...

"You were gorgeous, kind, and composed. Still are. You're one of the smartest girls I know, but you never shove it in anyone's face."

"I am?" She cocks her head to look at me.

"You know you are."

"But you're a guy."

As if that totally discredits my ability to tell if she's beautiful?

"I look at girls all the time. I know what I'm talking about." Lucy tosses me a look. Okay, that might've been too far.

She turns Jen's head up towards her, taking over. "Don't worry. You're totally hot to girls too. The most beautiful girl in school, no doubt. I'd be lining up to date you if, well..."

"You didn't like dicks so much." Jen forces out a laugh.

119

Lucy tosses her hand over her mouth as she chortles. "Right. That's it."

"Sorry, I'm all vag," Jen says back with a slight shrug.

"Whoa!" I say. "You guys talk like *that*?"

Jen ignores me, instead swinging her legs off my lap and sitting up. "Okay. I can handle this."

That's all it took? A funny joke? I was expecting this to take hours. That wasn't so bad.

"I can do this," Jen says with that intense look of concentration she has before an exam. Her eyebrows are slightly turned in as she bites the corner of her lip. "Right. First thing on the list. Return the winter formal dress." Jen storms from the room, getting right to her agenda.

How did she just swing from heartbreak to moving on so quickly?

"That was easier than I thought," I whispered to Lucy.

"*This* is only beginning. Hold up."

"No, really. I know Jen, I think she's fine. Once she's concentrated on a to-do list, she's set."

She shakes her head, tracing a circle on my palm. "I know heartbreak. We've only hit the surface here. Trust me."

"You know heartbreak?" Did she love Zach?

"It was a different type of heartbreak. Leaving basketball destroyed me."

I squeeze her hand. We don't talk about what happens on the court much. I've rarely seen her play. And when I do? My brain launches into must-make-out mode the moment she steps off the court.

And here I thought I was an in-tune boyfriend. I'm failing in every aspect.

"Are you glad you're playing again?"

"Yup. Every time I'm back on the court, I feel like I'm flying. I'm very happy there."

"How's everything with Coach T?"

"He's still a total jerk." Of course. Why would that suddenly change?

Jen walks in then, dragging a big purple bag. "Here we go. Ready for the mall?"

Lucy folds her hands in her lap, just waiting. This is girl code for something. I hold my breath, not daring to move.

"Do you want to see it?" Jen offers. "I picked it out sophomore year. Perfect for the big senior winter formal, you know. I knew I had to have it when I saw it on the rack." She laughs as she unzips the bag. "I didn't even acknowledge I was gay back then. And," she twirls with the dress against her body, "it still fits."

Okay. What the hell is going on? Why is she so giddy?

She giggles as she opens up the bag, yanking out a pink shiny dress. "Isn't it gorgeous?"

Lucy stands up to look. "The beading is beautiful. Love the silk. Great choice."

"Yeah," Jen says quietly and I stand up too. I'm supposed to, right? "No matter," she says after a deep breath. "We'll return it."

Is she crazy? "Can you still return it? You bought it sophomore year, right? Craigslist will probably work best."

Jen's face pales.

Okay, clearly that was the wrong thing to say. Practicality is obviously not the correct route.

"Right," Jen's voice shakes. "I, umm..." She turns to Lucy. "Do you have your dress yet?" Lucy shakes her head. "Perfect." She nods back toward me. "This dress will look great with Justin's dark features."

I want to point out that there's no way Jen's size two dress will fit Lucy's curves. But I'm smarter than that. One girl will feel too skinny and the other fat. I'm not going there.

Jen sniffs again and her chest rattles. Oh crap. I reach for the Kleenex box. Here comes more snot.

"When I bought this dress, I picked it out because it compliments your features so well." She tries to laugh. "Isn't that funny? We'd only been dating a few months and I'd already planned the dress for our senior winter formal." She shakes her head. "Ridiculous."

Then the sob erupts.

Lucy steps forward, taking the dress from her hands. She holds it up next to me. "Jen, you're right. This dress does look great with Justin."

Is she serious? I eye Lucy. That thing will look like lingerie on her. My stomach warms. I take a slow breath to cool it off. Not the time to be picturing Lucy in something like that.

Lucy winks at me. "Yeah. This dress definitely belongs next to Justin. Since you can't return it and this dress is way too nice to be Craigslisted, I think this dress needs to go to the dance with him."

Jen's lips twitch. "Good. I'm glad you'll wear it. Glad it'll…" tears stream down her face as she spits out the last words, "…be used."

Lucy pulls her into a hug as she hands the dress back.

"Go to the dance with Justin, Jen. Wear your dress."

"I couldn't do that to you." She sucks back more snot.

Lucy holds Jen's shoulders, looking her in the eye. "How long have you been head of the counsel planning this dance?"

"Since sophomore year."

"Right. And you're the president of student council now, correct?"

"Yeah…"

"Jen, I refuse to let you miss this dance."

I stand in awe, watching Lucy do what many girls wouldn't dare: Give away their date to the biggest dance of the year. Prom's an afterthought compared to this formal. To girls, winter formal means everything. They pretend it's a freakin' mini-wedding. Insanity.

I step forward, taking Jen's hand. "Will you please go to winter formal with me?"

She sniffs, looking at Lucy. "Are you sure?"

Lucy smiles. "You've seen me try to dance. Really, you'll be saving me, big time."

"Are you sure, Justin?"

I smile, remembering how much fun we had at last year's dance. And remembering that freshman fantasy of bringing Jen as my date for our senior year. The night was going to be epic. Now, I get that chance. But, it means I won't get that epic night with Lucy. I was going to treat her like a queen, or let her have her Cinderella moment, or whatever girls look forward to at this stuff. This isn't what I wanted. Lucy deserves that.

Lucy's lip lifts, her eyebrows rise, waiting for me to say yes. Clearly, she wants Jen to come first with this. How did I land such an amazing girl? Sacrificing so much to make her friend happy. To make everything okay.

"I'd love to walk you down that grand aisle, Jen. Will you come with me?"

"Yeah." She sniffs. "Okay." She reaches out, pulling me into a hug, whispering into my neck. "You've always been my protector. I couldn't go with anyone else."

"I'll always be there," I offer.

Lucy hangs the dress back up in the bag. Hands down, she's the most amazing girl I've ever met.

CHAPTER THIRTEEN

Lucy

I stand on my tiptoes, camera held above the crowd with the viewfinder on. Sweet, a straight shot down the aisle. This should do. At least, I hope Jen will think so. I had no idea parking would be so hard in St. Paul. There's a snowstorm coming so I figured it'd be deserted, but it seemed as though everyone and their mom decided to come out to watch the grand march anyway.

Crackled audio of Clair De Lune blasts through the DJ's speakers as the first junior class couple takes their position under the archway at the top of the aisle. Someone must be spacing the couples every five steps because the timing is awesome. With the strobe-light effect of all the flashing cameras, this really does feel like a wedding or a Hollywood event.

Finally, the juniors blend into the seniors. I wait for a glimpse of Jen's pink dress.

Yellow, blue, bold pink, black…there. Pink and flowing. Her shoulders are relaxed, her smile bright. Good. She deserves this. My heart thumps as I allow my eyes to drift from Jen to Justin. But not just Justin. It's Justin in a tux. He blows me away, the way the tux hugs his broad shoulders, just to nip in at the waist that I love to drape my arm around. My knees start to wobble, and suddenly I want to jump the rope and pull him close. Somehow, Justin in a tux makes him more intimate and exposed than I've ever seen him before.

My fingers remember to click as I ogle him, making sure to keep the camera angle just right. Who knew that all of Marissa's camera instructions would actually come in handy and allow me to function on autopilot?

They take their time walking down the aisle, then make the turn in front of the crowd toward the dance floor. The crowd sighs with pleasure as they pass, her arm wrapped through his. So elegant.

"I knew they'd end up back together," someone says.

"They're the most perfect couple in the world. Look! Happy endings do happen. Glad Justin threw that Lucy chick out. I wonder if he'll still do the reality show next fall if he's dating Jennifer again?"

I bite the inside of my cheek. None of that's true, but man it stings. What's so bad about me? I move a few steps away from them, snapping a few more photos as Justin and Jen disappear together onto the dance floor.

I force myself to stay firmly planted in my new spot so I can snag shots of Luke and Laura as well. I'm not running out of here until my friend duty is complete. But it's hard to pay attention with that dark head of hair dancing in the crowd. Justin twirls Jen around and she laughs. He pulls her back in, wrapping her in a hug. He moves easily into another move and my jaw drops. He really can dance. Wow. I'm a stumbling fool on the dance floor. Maybe it's a good thing I didn't come with him.

Finally, Laura appears wearing the coral gown we picked out together in October. It's stunning. The golden one I have hanging in my closet has a similar flow. We planned it that way, so we could do a stupid twirl dance that we made up in the dressing room together. I bite my lip, remembering I'd removed the tags. No big deal. I'll wear it next year.

The crowd of observers has thinned a bit now. I step up closer to the red velvet rope that separates us common folk from the dancers. Soon the band will announce it's time for the parents and friends to leave so the dinner can start. Laura winks at me as she crosses in front of the rope. I wave back and mouth, "Gorgeous!"

There. Friend duty complete.

I'm about to leave when Marissa steps up the aisle with one of the football players. Everyone else wore long ball gowns, but Marissa took the short mini-dress route with a keyhole exposing her cleavage. Nearly a clubbing outfit.

I cringe as I watch her walk with this new guy who's cute and buff, but as he swerves it's obvious he's a bit tipsy. Surprised he got past the wall of chaperones. He pulls her too close to his hip, hand brushing her butt. A remaining parent gasps. My heart drops.

What is Marissa doing with him?

She directs him through the turn of the aisle, taking a place on the dance floor. Immediately, he's all up on her, grinding like crazy to the classical music. What the heck? Isn't that for later, when the room darkens, and the music is just right? Not now. Nasty choice.

Marissa doesn't seem to care though. Nope, in fact, she grinds back.

I hear her mom squeal from behind me, "Look, George. Doesn't she look hot in that dress?"

Her dad nods, never looking up from his phone. I don't think I've ever seen him without that thing glued to his palm. I've never liked him with his long hair greased back. It's creepy. Thankfully, he wasn't around much when we used to hang out.

Oh, awesome. Marissa's turned around and her date moved in, wrapping himself around her so he's way too close to her butt. Her body moves with the music in pleasure. Wow. She's putting on a good show. But that's just it—it's a show. I know that smile. It's the same one she'd use when we'd leave her house whenever both parents were home. This isn't fun for her at all.

Free from staring at her date's face, she scans the dance floor for someone. Then I feel it, the pressure of her eyes landing on my own. She stops dancing, straightening up for a second, and then nods to me. Her smile disappears as she holds her gaze.

What's happening to you? I ask with my eyes.

Hers are blank.

My insides squirm. I want to pull her away from that creep, take her home, and talk. But about what?

How she cheated with my boyfriend?

Used me?

Bullied me through the disguise of a friend? This doesn't make sense. I should never want to speak with her again.

Marissa pushes her butt back into that guy with a grin as the DJ announces it's time for dinner to start. Translation: observers, get out.

I scan the dancers, looking for Jen and Justin. A soft flash of pink catches my eye. She's speaking with some of her cheerleading friends. Justin's not there though. Maybe he's getting their table?

A black head of hair near the escalator makes my heart jolt. But it's not Justin, just the same head of hair. His dad stands with his back turned to Christy and Tonya. He's tapping away on his iPad, oblivious to Justin's mom asking him a question. He's in his own world. Well, not totally, it seems he now lives in the same tech-realm as Marissa's dad.

A security guard comes up to the rope. "I know it looks fun, but it's time to go home," she says, ushering me away like I'm part of all the underclassmen here who came to dream. I glance back one last time for Justin's black hair. Nothing. I sigh, moving out the door with the younger students and parents.

As I'm stepping into the skyway to avoid the frigid December weather below, I hear my name called. I whip around to the most gorgeous sight—Justin running toward me. He pulls me close, kissing my forehead. "I know I'm here with Jen tonight," he brushes the bangs out of my eyes, "but I want you to know how much I wish I was with you."

As his words hit me, my eyes sting. It's not like I hadn't imagined going to the winter formal since I first heard of it freshman year. Or having a romantic date with Justin where I could wow him with what I wore.

I hug him, holding everything back.

This is for Jennifer. I can be strong for her.

"You look more gorgeous right now in your black pants, snow boots, and sweater, than any girl on that dance floor." He pulls me up, his lips finding mine. "Can I see you tonight? I'll sneak away from the hotel for a bit."

I nod, knowing if I speak that I'm going to lose it. How does he always know the right thing to say?

"All right. I'll text you." He leans in again, kissing my head. "I love you."

"I love you too."

"Later?"

"Yup."

He waves as he weaves his way back toward the formal. I take a deep breath, reviewing basketball plays as I make it back to Dad's car. As I turn on the ignition, the tears begin to fall. *Get a grip.* This is not a big deal. Jennifer needed Justin tonight. This is the right thing to do. I'm Jen's friend. Would Marissa have ever done something like that for me?

No.

I smile, wiping away the tears from my cheek. No, she wouldn't have. Which means I escaped becoming Marissa. I know how to be a good friend.

At least there's that.

***

I white-knuckle the steering wheel as I strain to see through the blowing snow. I'm not a bad driver, but driving in a snowstorm freaks me out. It doesn't matter that I'm only crawling along at twenty miles an hour with all the other cars. With the sun gone, it feels like eighty when driving in near white out. The intensity of this storm came out of nowhere.

I'm a fool for not taking Dad up on his offer to drive me downtown. There's no way they would've let me drive if they knew the storm was going to be this bad. The weatherman said a few inches. My ass.

The car in the far left lane swerves a bit. My heart leaps in my throat, choking me for a moment. Thankfully, the middle lane between us is empty as its rear floats over where the line should be. The car takes a moment to regain its traction, pushing forward back into its lane. I let out a breath of relief, keeping the car rolling along. If I stop on this unplowed highway, I'll never get moving again.

Suddenly, a red SUV flies by on my left side. Are you kidding me? Just because you have four-wheel drive doesn't mean you have superpowers. The SUV blows past a compact car way out in front of me. I'm smart enough to not follow too close in this weather. But the speed of the SUV clearly freaks the compact driver out so it slows, then it spins out, accelerating as it whips around between lanes.

I pump my brakes to the thrumming beat in my head as I close in. Too close. There's no way I'm not going to slam him, so I swerve right and let go. Suddenly, I'm turning slowly. I glance at the man in the compact whose face is pale. Slow crashing is torture. *Please ice, take me away from him and keep me on the road.*

I miss the compact's side mirror by a few inches. I let my breath out and brace before plunging into the shallow ditch. My head bangs against the seat, but that's it. Okay, I grasp the steering wheel, waiting for the next hit. I give it a full minute before I'm brave enough to glance back. Nothing. No one's angling my direction. I'm out of the crash zone. Thank God. The blue car that stayed a good distance behind me rolls past. My heart relaxes. No accident. No injuries.

My wheels spin the moment I throw the car in reverse. The ditch is shallow, but it's at enough of an angle where there's no way I can get out of here without someone else's help. The cat litter and shovel in the trunk won't even help. I grab the emergency blanket before climbing out, wrapping it around my shoulders. Why didn't I wear a coat? Stupid skyways and their no-weather promises. I trudge deeper into the snow, away from the road and toward the sound wall. There's no point in waiting for a tow truck. They're probably already backed up. The coolness of the snow stings my legs as I trudge up the exit ramp.

I take a left and walk a few blocks before I spot our study date coffee shop. The bell rings as I open the door. A Christmas carol CD plays. Tom, the barista, knocks on the counter. "The usual? Black tea?"

"That'd be great. Thanks."

I pull out my phone and speak to Dad while I wait. The storm has been upgraded to blizzard status. As long as I'm safe, he can't risk driving Mom's car with the way it slides over regular winter roads. He'll look for another ride or, worst-case scenario, he'll find a place for me to stay. Not the best situation, but I'll survive.

I force a smile as I take the tea from Tom and my heart sinks. Looks like I probably won't be seeing Justin after the dance tonight.

"What's going on, Lucy?" Tom asks.

"I was downtown to take photos of friends for a school dance, but ended up in the ditch on my route home."

"You okay?" His brow folds in.

"Yeah, it happened slowly. No big deal. Car should be fine too. I know you close soon, but is it okay if I hang out?

My dad's trying to figure out a way to get me home."

"No problem. Grab a book. Your booth is available."

Of course it is. Everyone else is smart enough to be home. The place is empty. I pull some dystopian novel off the shelf and curl up in the booth. Tom slides a muffin and scone in front of me. "On the house," he says.

"Thank you." Both blueberry. My favorite. He didn't have to do this, but I really appreciate it. I could be here forever.

"Hey," a familiar voice says. I glance up and Ian's staring down at me. "What's up?"

"I ended up in a ditch. So I thought I'd come hang out."

I pat the table for him to join me. He pulls a chair up to the end of the booth. Leaving Justin's side open. Nice.

"Why are you still here in this storm?" I glance at the white curtain of snow beating the windows. "Did you drive in to play guitar this evening?"

"Nah, I played this morning but then Tom's second barista called in sick. I fill in for him time to time, so I offered to help. Not much to do this weekend."

"No homework?"

"Just turned in my post-secondary final essays yesterday. And I've got no high school homework. My mom always blocks off December from schoolwork."

"Wow. A whole month?" What I wouldn't do for a month break in the middle of the school year. That's amazing!

"Yup. The holidays are really crazy around our house, so we do coursework in the summer. My dad grew up Jewish and my mom's Christian. They never settled on what religion they wanted for me, so we celebrate all of it."

"Nice." I bet he scores major gifts.

He laughs. "If you're thinking presents, you can stop. We only get one gift each year."

"One?"

"Yup." He shrugs. "Not a big deal. I buy myself everything I need anyway. With four brothers and three sisters, one gift is plenty."

"Seven siblings?" I'm suddenly picturing the old lady who lived in a shoe.

"Yup."

"Wow. Do you know all of their names?"

Ian laughs again. "Of course I do. Do you know your brother's name?"

"Yeah, but that's one brother."

"If you had more, you'd remember them. Trust me."

"Are you the oldest?"

"Second oldest."

"How come I didn't know this about you before? All the time we've hung out in the group, you've failed to mention your huge family. Do you not like them?"

"We get along great. I love my family." He readjusts his glasses. "But I prefer to not be defined by them. We only moved here a year ago. It's been nice having a group of friends who don't think I'm a freak for having seven siblings."

I drop my voice. "Is that why you homeschool?"

"Because of my freaky family fertility?" He laughs again and I like it. It's relaxed and honest, like him. "I've always been homeschooled. Mom was an English teacher and Dad was a biologist when they started homeschooling my older sister. Now they both have PhD's in research. Their hours can be wonky so traditional school schedules stand in the way of our family functioning. Plus," he sighs, "they have a lot to offer education-wise that I couldn't get from traditional school. The fieldwork assignments Dad has us do are amazing. And Mom has *ins* where we can research ancient texts that the public can't see, rather than seeing a photo of them in a textbook."

"Sounds surreal."

"It is, but I do miss people. We were part of a homeschool co-op before we moved. Haven't been able to connect with one here yet that holds a similar teaching philosophy. That's why I was so thrilled when I met you guys."

"So what do you do for fun?"

"Music. Read. Study politics."

I laugh. "Well it's perfect you are friends with Justin then."

Now Ian chuckles. "I'm friends with Justin because he's cool. I've worked enough of his dad's events to know Justin isn't there because he loves politics."

"Yeah. He's there because he loves his dad."

"Exactly."

I lean back in the booth. This isn't that bad. Ian is easy to talk to, and I like how he interprets Justin. I have a sneaky suspicion most guys are more jealous of him than they let on. But with Ian? Not a trace.

"You want to play a game while we wait out the storm?" he asks.

"Sure."

"Cards?"

"Sure, but I warn you I don't come from a card-playing family. You'll have to teach me."

"No problem," he says as he gets up to grab a deck of cards off the game shelf.

I study him as he walks away. He's got broad shoulders. Not athletic broad, but still the type of shoulders that are hot. And he's a good guy. I'll have to set him up with someone. But, as he slides a board with holes in front of me and casually leans back to shuffle the cards, I don't know if I should. He seems like the type to just ask a girl out if he wants to date them. I won't push it.

"Okay, so cribbage is really a math game, but if you prefer something like solitaire we can play that."

I groan. I've always hated solitaire. It's mind-numbing and frustrating for me while everyone else loves it. But math? It's ridiculous how soothing numbers are to my brain.

"Oh? No cribbage?" He pulls the board back.

"No, definitely cribbage. I can't handle solitaire. Bores me to death."

"Really? I thought most girls liked solitaire."

"I'm not most girls."

"So math, huh?"

"Yep."

"All right then. I warn you though, I'm really good at cribbage."

"Is that so? Well," I lean in, "I'm really good at math. I bet I can keep up."

We play cribbage for an hour before the snowfall starts to slow. We come out pretty even on wins/losses. Joe leaves, only having to walk down the road to his apartment, giving Ian the key. We stay another hour, playing every game on the shelf. Finally, the snowfall stops.

Then I receive the hundredth frustrated text from Dad.

Dad: Okay. I give up. No one can get you and this is only a brief lull in this blizzard. There's a hotel six

blocks down the road. Can you walk there? I'll book you a room.

My heart tanks. Definitely no Justin tonight. I'm tempted to text him but he's at the dance. I'm not going to take him away from Jen right now. This can wait.

"Did your dad find you a ride?"

"Nope."

"How far out do you live?"

"Twenty-five minutes down the highway, but in this? A few days?"

"Hmm." Ian takes out his phone. "One sec," he says before moving away from the table. He shakes his head as he returns. "No luck with my family either. I'm going to sleep here since I have to open in the morning anyway."

"Here? Where?"

"The floor. Or a booth?"

I sigh, grabbing my purse. "There's a hotel up the street. My dad booked me a room. I'm sure they have others open, too."

Ian hesitates a second and blushes. "I'll walk you there, but I can't stay." He bends down to pick some muffin up off the floor. There's a hole in the tip of his well-worn shoes. Oh my gosh. I'm such an entitled jerk. Why'd I assume he could afford a hotel? Heck, I couldn't afford a room out of my own pocket right now.

"Ian, you're staying at the hotel."

"No, it's okay."

"You can share my room. No big deal. We'll get two beds. I refuse to leave if you plan on sleeping on this floor."

"I don't know…"

I put my purse back down and spread the emergency blanket out on the tiled floor. "Fine. I'll sleep here tonight."

I go to lie down, but Ian takes my arm, keeping me upright.

"All right, all right. I'll stay with you." He picks up the blanket and hands it to me, before holding open the door. The below zero air stings my cheeks. It's going to be a long six blocks. "Wait, is Justin going to kill me?"

"Don't worry about Justin. He's staying in a suite with our group of friends at the dance tonight. He'll be fine with it. Same situation. *Friends*." Okay, so I had to clarify. This definitely makes me a bit nervous. I've never stayed in a hotel with anyone but my family. Ian isn't exactly who I pictured when I imagined my first night alone with a guy.

"Absolutely. I understand." He pulls the door closed, sliding in the key. "Thanks, Lucy. This is kind of awesome of you."

"Don't worry about it. I'm glad I won't be alone. I'd be bored to death. Did you bring the cards?"

"Got 'em."

"Then we'll be good."

"They better have TV," he says as we bend forward to keep warm while we walk. "Ghosthunters is having a marathon tonight."

"Seriously? Are you a bit of a nerd?"

"Totally." Okay, a Ghosthunters marathon with Ian in a hotel room. Not how I pictured tonight when I was a freshman, but it definitely holds the promise of fun.

"How about I'll watch some Ghosthunters, but only if you are willing to rotate it with the Blue Planet episodes on Discovery."

"Blue Planet, huh?" He nudges me. "You're a total nerd too."

"Everyone's got their thing. Whatever."

CHAPTER FOURTEEN

Justin

"Ooh," Laura says as she flips through her phone with an eyebrow raised. She pounces, landing on the couch in front of me, next to Luke. "Did you get a text from Lucy tonight?"

"Not yet." I reach in my back pocket. Did I miss one? I'm sure I would have felt the buzz. No missed texts. Weird.

Laura rolls her lips in, holding in a smirk. "You may want to text her."

"Is she okay?"

"Don't worry about her. She's in good hands." Laura giggles, taking a Twizzler from our poker pile.

Good hands?

Me: Hey, Lady. I've been missing you. What's up?

It doesn't take long for the phone to vibrate in return.

Lucy: Oddly enough, I'm watching Ghosthunters with Ian in St. Paul.

Me: What? How'd that come up?

Lucy: Got stuck in a ditch near the coffee shop. Ian was there. We couldn't get a ride home. My dad got us a motel room.

Lucy's in a motel room with Ian?

"And, there it is." Laura giggles.

"Is what?"

"That delicious jealous look."

Me: Your dad got you both a hotel room, together?

Lucy: He doesn't know Ian's here. Couldn't leave him sleeping on the coffee shop floor though.

I toss a Twizzler at Laura as I step out of the suite. It's way too loud in here with Luke, Laura, Jen, and Tiffany, and Allison, and their boyfriends.

My phone rings twice before Lucy picks up.

"Hey, Justin," she says. "Hold on a sec." She continues, speaking to someone else in the room. "I'm just gonna step outside, Ian? Okay?"

Ian's voice drifts through the phone from the background. "No problem. Tell Justin I say hello. Don't forget your blanket."

Blanket? I shake my head, throwing the image of them snuggled in a blanket together in a bed out of my mind. That's ridiculous.

"It's so nice to hear your voice," Lucy says to me now. The wind whooshes past. She's outside?

"Are you okay?"

"Yep. Totally fine. A little cold," she says with a laugh.

"You should have called me."

"And made you worry all night?" The way she says it

bothers me. I want to worry about her. She's my girlfriend. "No way. I'm safe and having a good time. Did you have fun tonight?"

"Sure. It was great. Jen didn't even mention Trish. She loved it. So that was good."

"Good." A gust of wind drowns out her next words.

"What did you say?"

"Nothing."

"No, really."

She sighs as the wind dies down again. "Ian's great. We're having fun, but I wish you were here with me."

My gut relaxes. Take that, jealous green monster. I win.

"I'd keep you warmer than Ian, for sure."

She laughs and I can totally picture her smile with a slight blush. "So, when can I see you again?"

"As soon as possible, I promise."

"Sounds good," she says and her voice shakes. She's shivering.

"Cold?"

"A bit."

"Okay, go inside and get warm? So…Ghosthunters, huh?"

"Don't judge. It's actually really cool. There's another marathon on your birthday in a week. Maybe I'll throw you a Ghosthunters party."

Shoot. It never occurred to me that she'd plan something. I knew I should've told her yesterday about my parents' gift.

"It's okay, Justin. Don't worry. I won't throw you a Ghosthunters party. I've got different plans. Way better, promise."

"Lucy." Crap. This isn't supposed to happen this way. I

take a deep breath. "I wanted to tell you this in person, but there can't be a party."

"That's okay. We don't need to do a party. Maybe you and I can just grab dinner with your family?"

My gut twists. "Actually, I won't be home on my birthday."

"That's okay. We can do it the day before or after. We can work around your schedule. No worries."

"No…"

"I'm confused."

I take a deep breath, hating what I'm about to say. "My parents are taking me on a two-week birthday vacation to Hawaii over the holidays."

"Oh." Another gush of wind rips through the phone. There's a horrible long pause before she finally continues. "Well, that's awesome. A great eighteenth birthday gift. You'll have fun." She may fool most with that confidence, but I can totally tell the forced enthusiasm behind her voice.

My voice drops as some cheerleaders in the suite next to ours spill out of their room in bikinis for the hotel pool. I turn away from them as they squeal hello. "I don't want to go. Being away from you on my birthday will suck."

"And Christmas." Her voice is soft and more distant.

"I'm sorry."

"It's okay." She breathes in quick through her nose and I can tell she's fighting off tears. "You have the vacation of a lifetime. You all deserve to escape this winter wasteland. Especially before the inauguration. When do you leave?"

"In two days."

"When do you return?"

"New Year's Eve."

"All right. Will you be around for a New Year's kiss?"

"I won't miss it. I promise."

"So, what are you doing tomorrow?" The chattering of her teeth can't be ignored. This conversation is going to give her pneumonia.

"Everything in my power to get to you. Listen, you should probably go back inside. I don't want you to get sick."

Her teeth click away. "It's the weather, not you. But yeah, I need to go. I love you," she offers.

"I love you too. Call me when you wake up."

"I don't want to wake you."

"Trust me, I'll be awake. There's no way I'll be sleeping knowing you are in a hotel room with another guy."

"It's Ian." I swear I can hear her eyes roll.

"Well, he is a guy. Just sayin'."

***

"So what are the chances that our flight will be canceled?" I try not to sound too optimistic as I pull out of Jen's driveway, chatting with Mom on the phone.

"They've cleared the runway. Flights are on schedule now. Honey," Mom says, "I know you want to see Lucy, but I don't think it's going to happen before we go. I'm sorry."

I smack the steering wheel. After two nights and a day cooped up in a hotel suite with six people, I'm at the end of my rope and have a stiff neck from sleeping on the floor. All I want to do is be with Lucy and she's still stuck in St. Paul. Screw you, Super Blizzard. You ruined everything.

"Are the roads near the coffee shop available yet?"

"No, I checked. The plows won't be able to tackle those streets until tomorrow morning. They're starting major highways in that area right now."

"Our streets are fine."

"Different town and plow availability. Give her a call, Justin. She'll understand."

"She doesn't have a cell phone charger."

"Well, does she have a room number?"

"Yeah."

"We'll pay whatever it costs her per minute. Just come home and call her while you pack. We need to be out of the house in an hour to get to the airport."

Jen lives down the block from me, so it doesn't take long before I'm home. I nod to Dad as I walk through the kitchen towards the basement. "Welcome home."

"Thanks."

"I put my suitcase downstairs for you."

"Great," I say, a little too short.

Dad taps my arm. "Justin. I know this isn't ideal. But drop the attitude. Your mom has been planning this for a long time. Way before Lucy came into the picture. After all the stuff you've been juggling, she wanted this escape for you. Don't disappoint her."

I let out a slow breath as I step into the basement, wishing that for once I was allowed to be a teenager and just be pissed off, but Dad's right. Mom doesn't deserve this. *He* might, but Mom doesn't. Hell, they're bringing me to Hawaii. That's one amazing birthday gift.

I turn around, looking as at ease as possible. "Yeah, you're right. Good reality check."

"I'm proud of you, son. Jackson would be too." He pats me on the back and I return a smile, holding in my inner cringe as I pull the basement door closed. His pride for me is always doubled with a reflection on Jackson. Maybe he thinks it makes me feel better, but it doesn't. I'm always missing Jackson, and trying to live up to the life he never had and could never give my parents. It's hard trying to be both of us.

Slam. My fist flies into the punching bag hanging in our back room. I punch the crap out of it for every reason possible. Losing a brother. Not being enough on my own. Trying to always keep my shit together for everyone else. Who cares about what I want? Lucy, I want her and I won't even get a birthday or Christmas kiss! Finally, my brain buzzes. Endorphins. There, better. Sweat drips down my back.

Packing doesn't take too long. I toss all the summer stuff in my bottom drawer in the suitcase and add a few pairs of boxers. A three-minute shower later and I toss my toothbrush and electric razor in the suitcase too. Laptop's in its case. Ready to roll.

I Google Lucy's hotel and call the front desk. A woman transfers me to the room, but there's no answer.

I swear and yank on my hair. I've seriously got to stop doing that or I'm going to go bald like Uncle Alex. I fling myself back into the leather couch, dialing the front desk for another transfer. Maybe she's just in the shower?

But still, no answer.

I stretch out my neck, hating how anxious this makes me. I'm normally able to keep things balanced but not being able to talk to her is driving me crazy. What if this is the end? Our plane crashes and her last memory of me is how I complained about Luke snoring. Of all moments, *that's* when her phone had to bite it.

Or what if something else is going on in that hotel room? It's not that I don't trust her, but the situation is iffy. Who wouldn't make a move on a girl like Lucy after three days? She's incredible, even I'd flirt! Flirt? Seriously? What am I thinking? It could be so much worse than that. I know Ian, but guys are insane. There's so many horrible things he could do to her…

My gut yanks at me, knowing I just crossed a major line. Okay, I'm taking the easy route in hating Ian. He's a good guy. Plus, if he touched her, Lucy would easily kick his soft musician ass. The pluses of dating a strong girl.

I grab a water from the fridge. *Okay, chill out, you're totally unhinged.*

The truth is that I want to be the one stuck in that hotel with her. Why can't that be my birthday gift?

"Justin, we leave in ten minutes," Mom calls from above.

I try the number one last time. No answer. It's dinnertime so she's probably trudging through the snow to get food. I leave a voicemail message, but it's totally awkward because I mention Ian way too much. I don't want her to think I'm not trusting her. I'm not the possessive boyfriend type of guy.

I pull my laptop out and try my last form of communication. Email. At least it's some sort of goodbye that she can read when electronics aren't trying to screw us over.

Okay. I crack my knuckles.

Dear Lucy…

CHAPTER FIFTEEN

Lucy

The anchor gives a cocky look to the camera that matches his grin. "St. Paul roads will be cleared of the four and a half feet of snow by tomorrow morning. Talk about a surprise storm." He brushes his fake tuft of hair and laughs with the female co-anchor. "I'm still shoveling off our back deck."

"Really? Your back deck? You have the audacity to say that? And *you're* shoveling? Doubtful." Ian says to the television from the edge of his bed.

"Good to know you're getting your household up and running again, Charles." She looks at the camera. "Like Charles, many Minnesotans are already moving on from the storm."

Yes, if by many you mean few. We're still stuck here!

The screen switches to a shot of the airport and I hold

in a groan. Justin's supposed to fly out this evening. *Please be closed, please be closed.*

"The runways were cleared this morning. Commercial flights resumed on time this afternoon." They zoom in on a plane taxing on the runway. The anchorman fake chuckles, then says, "Here's a flight heading off to Hawaii. Soon-to-be Governor Marshall and family are reported to be on board." They cut back to the newsroom. Both anchors raise their mugs. "Happy holiday vacation to you."

Then I'm watching the plane take off into the gray winter sky.

Justin.

He didn't even say goodbye. I grip the comforter at the end of my bed. There's a phone here. "Why didn't he call?" I accidently say out loud.

Ian turns off the television. "Lucy, he must have tried. I mean, it's Justin. He calls if he's going to be five minutes late."

I shake my head. "No, he didn't. Ian, you know I haven't left the room for over a day."

"Right, because it's too cold?"

"Yeah, too cold." My eyes sting.

"He must've called." Ian reaches over and puts the phone to his ear.

"See, no messages."

He nods in agreement as he dials out. Dad's going to freak when he gets this ridiculous eighty-cents-per-minute phone bill for local calls. Robbery.

"Hello. Yes, thank you, we have enough towels for the day. I'm checking to see if any calls have come in for Lucy Zwindler? We've been waiting for some." He nods, looking at me. "Five calls? And you transferred them up here? We didn't get them." He checks the back of the phone. "Yes, our ringer's on. You transferred them to room 108?"

Ian throws up his hands. "Yes, 108. We are room 108. Not 107."

I slink off the corner of the bed and hit the floor. She transferred them to the wrong room. I take a deep breath, struggling to hold back the tears. Because she's an idiot, I missed his calls. I had been calling Justin on the room's line but then his phone ran out of battery. Also, Dad called to tell me to stop since the motel was charging eighty cents a minute.

Ian paces back and forth. "What did the callers sound like? Okay, we'll call them back. Thank you."

He rocks the phone back into the receiver. I jump as he kicks the heater. Whoa.

"This is a joke! Room 107? We better get this bill free since no one is staying in that room." He rubs his forehead. "Okay, so one more night?"

"Yeah, one more." But really, it's like fifteen. Fifteen nights of being away from Justin. It's going to kill me. Not being in his arms, not smelling that fresh scent or feeling his scruff against my cheek.

The cracking starts from my chest. I swallow, trying to keep everything under control. But they come. The tears show up, spilling down my cheeks.

Ian moves off of his bed, inching toward me across the carpet. "Come here," he says and I do, crawling over into an awkward hug. For three days, we haven't touched. Ian's been nothing but a gentleman, even stepping outside when I shower. Most guys wouldn't be that aware of privacy needs. I've decided he's genuinely more respectful because he has so many siblings.

He pulls me to his chest. His clothing still smells like

the coffee house, but more mocha-like. He pats my back. "I know it sucks. You'll talk to him tomorrow. It'll work out."

"Thanks. I'm sorry. I know I'm overreacting."

"No. Don't apologize. Trust me, if I had to be away from my girlfriend for that long without saying goodbye, I'd be pissed."

I pull out of his embrace, leaning back against my bed. He does the same to his. "So you have a girlfriend?" I ask.

He smiles crookedly. "I guess I should have emphasized the *if* a bit more." He shakes his head. "No girlfriend."

"Did you leave one back in St. Louis?"

"I had some girls I went out on dates with, but nothing serious."

"Have you asked anyone out here yet?"

"Still working on meeting the right one to ask."

"You'll meet her. I'll keep my eyes open at school. Introduce you to someone cool."

"That's okay. I'll bump into her myself. I operate better that way."

"I get that," I say, zoning in on the weird floral pattern on the carpeted floor.

"He's lucky," Ian says softly, almost to himself.

"Justin?" I ask.

"Yeah." He smiles at me, his blond hair still disheveled from his earlier trek to grab us lunch.

"Why?"

"He has you."

I suppress my blush. I know he's not talking about *me*, me. He's talking about the type of relationship that Justin and I have. We are lucky. It's true.

"You'll find your girl someday, Ian. I've spent three days with you. You're nothing short of awesome."

Ian stands, then helps me off the floor. "Want to escape this place to find some dinner? No reason to stay in now that you don't have to wait for his call anymore."

My face heats. He knew I was waiting in here only for Justin's call, and he indulged it with going on all the errands and food runs in the record snow and cold. All so I wouldn't have to miss Justin's call. Wow.

"You're an awesome friend, you know that? Right?"

Ian laughs, pulling me close to wrap the emergency blanket around my shoulders. I'll never leave home in the winter without a coat again.

"Whatever. That Chinese place opened up again. Sound good?"

"Yeah, that'll be great."

***

I scroll through my email, opening Justin's goodbye one more time.

Dear Lucy,

I hate that I'm leaving you without saying goodbye. I wish I could hold you, whisper in your ear that I love you and you're beautiful.

Please know that you are everything to me. For the first time in my life, I'm insanely jealous. I wish I was the one stuck in that motel room with you.

I can't wait for New Years when I can hold you in my arms again. Warning, I'll probably never let you go.

Skype me / text me / call me the moment you can.

I love you,

Justin.

One day until he's back. I can make it.

I've forced the weeks to pass quickly, keeping every moment busy. Shopping with Jen and Laura. Snow-tubing with the group. Hanging out with Ian at the coffee house. Pretty sure not a day has passed where I haven't had something planned as I wait for my bedtime Skype date. Staring at Justin's gorgeous, tan face is the way to fall asleep. For sure.

On today's distraction agenda? Picking up my Christmas gift.

I close the laptop and throw on some lip gloss, waiting at the door near the garage. It was a weird Christmas, having no gifts under the tree. They promised something was coming, but I'd have to wait until today.

"I'm ready!" I call out.

"We're coming," Mom says as she walks through the swinging kitchen door, a bulky old video camera in hand.

"Is this really a video-worthy gift?"

"Yes, definitely."

I sidestep, making a mental note to freak out no matter what the gift is. Even if it's an elephant ride. Though, that'd be pretty cool. Especially in winter. But really, whether it's an elephant ride or a family field trip to learn about recycling, I'm going to pretend it's awesome.

After the year I've given them, they deserve at least that much from me.

Mom climbs into the car, but I stop to trace the dent and small scrape in the bumper before I open my door. Amazing that's all that happened. Score one for me. Okay, really for the soft snow, but still.

Dad and Eric join us. "You ready, Lucy?"

"I'm excited. Where are we going?"

"You'll see." He opens the garage door and pulls the car out a few feet before stopping. "And, we're here."

"Here?"

Dad snorts. "Yup."

I climb out of the car, hesitantly.

"Go look beside the house, on the basketball court," Mom explains.

Basketball court? Did they get me a new hoop in the middle of winter?

I peek around the side of the house. A red car with a small gold bow stuck on the hood is brilliant against the white snow.

"Are you kidding me?" A car? They got me a car! I run my hands over the perfect cherry paint job.

I peek in the windows. Leather interior. Spacious. CD player and iPhone nesting dock.

"Whoa," I say, looking back in disbelief. Dad's standing there with his arms crossed while Mom videos. "Is this really for me?"

"Yep," Dad says, stepping up and opening the driver door for me. "It's a Volvo S60. A little big, but you can fit all the stuff you want when you move away to college. And," he points to the shifting thing. "All-wheel drive for the weather. Super safe."

"Wow. I can't even…I mean. Are you sure?"

Mom rests her hand on my shoulder. "Lucy, we're very proud of you. You've worked hard on many things. You deserve this."

"Climb in," Dad instructs.

The leather seats are easy to slide into. My thumb looks for a button on the side. Score, they heat. I rest my hands on the wheel and my feet reach the pedals easily too. Dad must've adjusted this to Mom's settings. Smart.

The passenger door opens and Dad joins me. He points to all the knobs and features and I appropriately ooo and ahhh.

"Dad, this thing is amazing! Thank you so much," I lean over, giving him a hug.

"You're welcome."

"You know you didn't have to do this. I know it's a lot. And with college coming up..."

"Don't worry; I bought it used. And Lucy, it was time for you to have your own car."

"Sorry about landing yours in a ditch."

"No, that's not what this is about." He takes a deep breath. "You're in a more serious relationship now, right?"

I don't move. Not acknowledging is safer than doing so.

"Well," Dad taps the shifter. "If anything was to happen within that relationship that you're not comfortable with, I don't want you to be stuck there. You should have a way to drive home."

I roll my lips in. Not comfortable with? Is this his version of the sex talk?

"Dad, Justin's not like that."

Dad coughs. "It doesn't have to be *that*. It could just be a fight or being sick of a political conversation at one of his dad's events." He reaches inside and opens the glove compartment, clearly feeling a bit awkward about this too. "You deserve to have control over your transportation."

"Does this mean Justin isn't allowed to drive me anymore?"

"No, he can. The car gives you a bit more freedom though."

I nod. "Thanks, Dad."

He taps my knee. "Okay, now go thank your mom."

I squeeze his arm before climbing out of the car. "I can't believe you got me a freakin' car," I say as I hug Mom.

"You deserve it, Lucy. Merry Christmas."

"Thank you."

"Should we go for a drive?"

"Yes!" I squeal. "Climb in."

"Pop the trunk."

I do and Dad pulls out a new booster seat for Eric. He shrugs. "Figure you may as well have this to help us out from time to time."

"Sure. I'd love to drive Eric around." At this point, they could make me commit to biweekly Boy Scout meeting transportation and I'd be fine with it. They bought me a car!

Once the booster is installed, I push the ignition button. So weird. My key's in the cup holder. "Where to?"

"Everywhere," Dad says.

I pull out of the driveway and that's exactly where we go. I've got a whole day to waste before I can see Justin. We have lunch in Stillwater, ride roller coasters at the Mall of America, and end the night ice skating at The Depot in Minneapolis.

Finally, it's eleven o'clock and I throw on a cute t-shirt and pj pants. I crawl under my covers with my laptop. Three minutes later, Skype does its signature ding.

"Hey, Lady." Justin's face pops up on the screen. His golden tan reminds me of his shirtless summer painting and my stomach heats. It's not fair how easily he makes me melt.

"Hi, you're all dressed up."

He shrugs. "Yeah."

"You look nice. Can I see?"

He rolls his eyes, standing up and backing away from his screen. His white linen pants and light blue dress shirt make my palms sweat. He tugs on the pants. "I didn't know I was supposed to bring business wear, so Tonya dragged me out a few hours ago and we snagged these."

"I like them," I say, trying to suppress my blush. Seriously, he's so hot.

"You do?" He turns around, pretending to model them. "Well, maybe I'll keep them then."

"Yum. Please do."

That makes him laugh as he returns to the computer, pulling his hand through his hair. I smile, remembering how I used to think he did that because he thought he was hot, when actually it's a nervous tick.

"Something bothering you?"

"I can't talk long. We're leaving for dinner soon. It's *amazing* that a random political dinner is happening tonight, here in Hawaii, where Dad can meet and greet."

"So, this wasn't a birthday trip?"

"It was. I mean, we've done tons of awesome stuff. Climbing that volcano was incredible and surfing, I think I'm addicted. Mom made an itinerary that didn't include any dinners… until Paul showed up. Now Dad's dragging us to this thing tonight."

"Paul? He showed up on your birthday trip? Isn't that a bit weird?"

"Yup." Justin rolls in his lips, obviously pissed.

"What did he want?"

"He wants me to do the reality show next fall."

"What? Why?" My eyes pop. I thought Justin was far past that.

"Tonya thinks he's probably invested in the show, but I'm not about to ask him."

"Well, what did you say when he asked again?"

"Hell no, of course."

I tap the keyboard, trying to piece everything together. "Why would your Dad need to meet people in Hawaii anyway? That's about as far away from Minnesota as you can get."

"I dunno." He squeezes the bridge of his nose.

"Justin?" He's totally holding something back. "What is it?"

"Pretty sure he's gearing up for a presidential race, even though he always promised our family he never wanted to be president."

"Are you kidding me?"

"Paul says it's standard practice, just in case he wants to make the leap in the future. Create and maintain connections, you know?"

"How do you feel about that?"

"I wouldn't put anything past Paul."

Justin looks up from the laptop, answering someone in the other room with a wave. He rolls his lips in as he turns back to the screen. "I'm sorry. I've got to go."

"I'll definitely see you tomorrow night at Watson's, right?"

"Yes. My flight gets in around ten-ish. I'll meet you at the party. There's nothing in this world that will steal away our New Year's kiss."

"I can't wait."

"Me too." He looks over the screen. "Coming," he says to them. "Okay, I've really got to go. Our car's here. I'll see you tomorrow, Lady." He adds a wink and my heart kerplunks. I love it when he calls me that.

"Sounds good. I love you."

"Love you too. And, by the way," he leans into the screen and drops his voice to a whisper, "you look beautiful." He waves goodbye quickly as he ends the Skype call and the box on my screen fades to black.

I get up and fling my pillow across the room. My heart aches as the photo of Justin teases me from my desk. Twenty hours until he can hold me and this terrible ache in my gut goes away. I take a deep breath, pulling my hands through my hair and yanking it the way Justin does with his own.

Is it bad that I hate this?

My computer dings—an iMessage from Ian.

Ian: Up for another virtual battle to the death?

Me: Sure.

Ian: Pick your poison.

Me: Let's mix it up tonight. How about Scrabble?

Ian: Are you sure you want to go there? Think of all the tournaments I've won.

Me: Hell yes. I'm going to kick your home-schooled ass.

He sends me the link and I toss up my first word— Alone.

Ding

Ian: Lonely?

I bite my lip, not knowing how to respond. Before I can come up with something clever his word pops up on the Scrabble board—Present.

My heart sinks. Here's this guy posting the word that I wish my own boyfriend could claim.

That he's present.

One more day.

CHAPTER SIXTEEN

Justin

Hell must be filled with baggage claims. Where are our frickin' bags? Give me a break. We've waited thirty minutes! Dad steps up from the bench and places his hand on my shoulder.

"Someplace to be?"

"Dad, it's New Year's. I promised Lucy I wouldn't miss it." The gears of the conveyor belt start moving. Finally! Nothing drops out of the chute, but at least it's moving.

He checks his watch. "It's almost eleven-fifteen. You should be able to make it in time."

"Yeah, in time to say goodbye."

Dad laughs in a way that's too similar to my own. I used to like it, but now it pisses me off. It's getting harder to be his son after being around his fakeness this year.

"You're eighteen now," he says. "I'm not holding a curfew over you."

"Lucy's sixteen. Her parents will be expecting her home shortly after midnight."

He nods. "Good parents."

"Yeah." *Clunk.* Something bounces on the metal above. There's an ear piercing creak while the door opens. A purple bag tumbles down the ramp and bangs into the baggage carousel, just below the sign that states *Handles With Care.* Yeah, *right.* I step up to the carrousel, away from Dad. He's been on his Bluetooth since we got off the plane. It's like he was replaced with a clone that's just a little off. I can't stand it. I eye Dad, wondering if he is backing Paul's recent approach about the reality show.

A chunky gray duffle gets stuck up the ramp, clogging the bags behind it.

Are you kidding me?

The other passengers from the flight start mumbling. Someone steps away to call security.

Nope. No time for that. I jump up on the belt and reach up the ramp. "Justin!" Mom calls sharply in the background.

I yank, and the bag drags free.

There.

I jump down to a short applause. I swear, if this ends up in the paper tomorrow, I'm going to freak. We were in the paper three times in Hawaii. Why? Umm, we climbed a volcano. That's the opposite of newsworthy in Hawaii. Heck, it's highly possible we were in the paper here and Lucy didn't tell me.

I whip out my phone as more unrecognizable baggage falls.

Me: Dude, were we in the paper here?

Alex replies immediately.

Alex: Heck yes. Did you forget to work out while you were there? Getting a bit of a belly.

He attaches a photo from The Trib of our family with surfboards on the beach.

Me: Whatever, I look totally ripped.

Alex: One person's opinion. ;-) Happy new years.

Me: You too. Don't be an idiot.

I worry about Alex. He's always been a lot of fun but the past few months on JV have gone to his head. It didn't even faze him when Suzie dumped him a few months ago. Since, I've counted a rotation of four different girls clinging to his arm after our games.

I'm going to have to have a talk with him.

Finally, a purple piece of luggage falls from the chute onto the ramp. Mom's bag. All right, here we go. I haul each of our bags over to my lazy family on the bench. "Okay, let's go." I kick Tonya lightly in the shin. "Come on."

She stretches and feigns a yawn. "Just five more minutes of sleep?"

I reach out, yanking her off the bench. "Now."

"Ouch!"

Dad steps between us. "Justin, a word. *Now*."

He puts his hand on my shoulder and leads me a few steps away from the bench where Mom continues to gather our things.

"Your attitude needs to stop. Listen, I know you miss Lucy. We'll get you to the party in time. Relax."

"It's not that." But it is. I mean, it is but it isn't. God, it's everything.

"What's going on?"

161

"Why did you invite Paul?" I say between my teeth, hating that this is coming out here.

"Justin, we went through this a few days ago. I didn't invite him. He flew in when the opportunity for the meet and greet arrived. It was a prime chance to make connections. I didn't realize it bothered you so much."

I suppress an urge to throw my hands up. My insides roar.

"Why are you so angry?" he says.

"Did Paul tell you the other reason he came?"

His brow furrows. "No, what's up?"

"He asked me to be on that reality show again."

Dad shakes his head, stepping away from me. "I made it clear you'd do the interview, but no show. Paul knows that."

I puff out my cheeks, thrilled I stopped myself from ripping up the proof. I pull out a folder from my carry on and hand it over. "He showed up with the contract, Dad."

Dad reviews the pages and his face pales. "Justin, I didn't know. I thought this was taken care of."

"Yeah, you messed up."

"This should be a non-issue now. I'm sorry, son."

He waits for me to apologize, but I can't. For the first time, forgiveness isn't quick on my tongue. The whole puzzle hasn't come together yet. It's too slimy and invasive.

"I promise I'll deal with this," he says with a thick slap to the contract.

Right. That's his "I promise" phrase he uses on the campaign trail.

Mom and Tonya are waiting near the skyway to the parking lot. We all wheel our bags across, waiting while Dad grabs the car. I'm glad we drove ourselves. It's way too pretentious to ask Dad's driver to pick us up on New Year's.

"Where's the party, Justin?"

"Watson's." He always throws the New Year's Bash. Parents think it's clean, because for the most part it is, but someone always sneaks in booze. When we pull onto the highway, he pushes the speed limit. He gets it. At least there's that.

Finally, at a quarter to twelve, we pull in front of Watson's mansion. Music blares from the windows. I climb out, thanking them, and run to the front door. I don't even care what they think. Tonya yells something from the window. The longer we were stuck in that condo together, the more we fought. It's annoying, but I'm okay with it. At least I'll always know she's my sister. Amazing how Jackson's death still makes me appreciate her more.

I yank open the huge oak doors. Immediately, I'm stuck in the clog of the entrance, people way too close. I push through elbows and a couple grinding to find a clearing. Then the recognition begins. People cheering my name, like I'm some sort of Frat King. It's easier to wave back, pretending to give a rip about them when the only thing I care about is finding her.

I glance through the living room, looking for that dark flash of auburn hair, as people pull me into photos. Someone gives me the lowdown on drinks. Red cups have the booze. Yellow is free. All right, avoid all red cups, not even holding it for someone. There's no way I'm going to be implicated in underage drinking tonight. With Dad's inauguration only a few days away, I'm not that stupid.

Pretty sure I've said, "The volcano was awesome!" about one hundred times by the time I get out of the living room. In the game room, I finally spot her leaning on a bar stool, looking unbelievably squeezable in tight jeans and a pink sweater. She laughs and Ian claps her back. She's back here with Ian? Well, okay, Laura, Luke, and Jen are there too.

But still.

Ian.

I take a deep breath, pushing away my desire to slug him in the face. Not reasonable. From the way it sounds, he did everything right. I redirect, focusing on Lucy's bare skin where her sweater drops away from her shoulder.

"Hey, Lady," I say as I touch it.

She whips around and screams, smashing her face into me as she wraps me in a hug.

A band of barbed wire removes itself from my chest. I take a deep breath with her in my arms. She still smells like apples. My muscles loosen. *Finally.*

"I thought you weren't going to make it," she whispers.

"I'm here."

"Good." She smiles, pulling away, letting others say hello. I never let her out of my reach though. I hug Jen and Laura and fist pump Luke and Ian.

"Nice to see you again, man. Trip good?" Ian says after he pulls back.

"Yeah, it was awesome. Hey, thanks for helping Lucy out in the storm."

"Nah. She helped me. If it wasn't for her, I'd have been sleeping on a tiled floor." He claps her shoulder making the hairs on the back of my neck stand on end.

"Yeah, she's pretty awesome." I say, pulling her a little closer. Jen lifts an eyebrow.

Okay, yeah. I'm being possessive. Kill me.

"So, how was your flight?" Jen asks, breaking the tension I'd just made.

"Good." I step back from Lucy a bit. I'm cool. Relaxed. "Long though. Happy to be back. What'd I miss over break?"

"Lucy got a new ride," Laura chirps.

"What? A car?"

"My parents gave it to me yesterday. I was planning on telling you but thought it'd be more fun to show you in person."

"Sweet. Can't wait!" This is awesome. I don't have a ride home. More time with Lucy! "Did you drive?" I look around for a red cup, just in case. She puts a yellow one to her lips and takes a sip of something clear. Sweet.

"I did. Need a ride?" Her smile lifts to the left and her eyes bore into me. With that one look, I'm ready to leave with her. This party is lame in comparison.

"That'd be great," I say when I come out of the when-can-we-make-out trance.

Suddenly, someone cuts the track of Justin Timberlake and announces through the intercom, "Two minutes until New Years."

"I'm *not* missing the ball drop this year," Laura pulls Luke off the chair. "Come on, we're going downstairs to watch in the theater. Want to come?"

"Why not?" Lucy answers.

Ian rubs his palms against his pants. "I've actually got to cut to pick up my sister from her party."

"But it's almost midnight!" Laura pretends to pout.

"It's a half an hour drive. Got to get us both home before one. Curfew." He gives Jen, Laura, and, of course, Lucy a quick hug. "Great to see y'all." I wave to him as he disappears into the living room crowd. I know his game plan; leave before the pressure to kiss. It's balls-less, but

I get it. If it wasn't for my fake relationship with Jen, I would've done the same thing the last few years.

We all weave our way through the party as the music starts to blare again. Lucy pauses for a second, watching Marissa twisting high to low on a table with a skirt that hides nothing. All she needs is a stripper pole. I put my hand on Lucy's shoulder, giving her a reassuring squeeze. I lean in. "I'm so happy you're not friends with her anymore."

"Me too," she says, but there's an odd tone in her voice. Huh.

On the way to the basement theater, a few more people stop and snap quick photos with us. Our faces will be all over Instagram and Facebook tonight. Thankfully, Lucy doesn't seem as attached to her phone as most girls. She probably has no idea how often we are tagged on those apps.

The theater's packed. Alex is standing up front, shouting something obscene at the screen with a red cup sloshing in his hand.

Seriously? He's a freshman. Who the hell invited him here?

I wrap my arms around Lucy, keeping myself from running across the room and dragging him down. I'll do that later.

Finally, the ball starts to drop and the lights lower. Lucy steps backward towards me, and I snuggle my nose to her hair. Once the apple smell gets me, my lips are lost. I start kissing behind her ear, then down her neck. She pushes back into me and I turn her, finding her lips long before everyone shouts Happy New Year.

Those lips are so soft, fitting perfectly to mine. I need more of this, but not in front of everyone. This kiss will not end up on Instagram.

I pull away for a second. "Want to find someplace else?"

She doesn't answer with words. Her lips find mine, pushing me out of the room.

I beeline for the second stairway that no one really knows about. Watson gave Jen and me a tour long ago, in case we ever needed a room. Lucy and I fumble up the stairs as we kiss, coming out briefly in the kitchen where I open another door for the backstairs up to the bedrooms. Lucy stumbles on the stairs behind me with a laugh.

Finally, we get to the top together and I throw open a guest room door.

Empty.

Thank God.

I wrap my arms around her waist. I can't get close enough though and it's not until she lands on her back on the bed that I realize I pushed her there. I roll next to her, bringing my fingers through her hair as my tongue explores her mouth. We kiss like that forever as I summon superpowers to keep my hands from wandering.

"Screw it," she whispers as she reaches under my shirt, resting her palm against my abs. Her skin is like fire as her touch explores. Holy hot.

"I've missed you," she says.

The room becomes a humid inferno. My hands fly under her sweater then, resting against her undershirt. I slip my fingers under that too. Her skin is so smooth over the curve of her hip. She takes a moment's break from kissing my neck, yanking her sweater over her head, leaving on a tank top that shows more boobs off than ever before. Holy hell, she's gorgeous.

"It's too hot in here. Sorry," she says, wiping her brow.

"Do not apologize for that." I pull her near, kissing her neck. "You're the hot one."

Her palms find my bare skin again and then she moves to take my hoodie off. It gets caught over my head and she giggles as I yank it off for her. Before I have a chance to joke, her lips find my collarbone and her hands are electric on my chest.

This. Is. Amazing.

I press into her hip, no use trying to hide the evidence that she's driving me wild. But I can't let this go further. I will not let her feel uncomfortable.

This is it.

I will not be a douchebag boyfriend, not when we haven't talked about this yet.

When her lips meet my stomach, I start to shutter. Insanity.

"You okay?" she whispers.

"Yeah, I…" I take a breath. "I'm…" but I can't find a word. There are no words for this.

She smiles before wrapping her arm around my chest and curling into my side. We don't say anything as I calm down. I stroke her back until my shuddering stops.

There.

Control.

"I love you," I say, kissing her hair.

"I love you too."

"So, what'd I miss while I was gone?"

"Me missing you."

"No really, tell me everything. I want to pretend like we were never apart."

So she does. I hold her while she tells me about how Jen's doing better, shopping with Laura, and how she's worried about Alex. I stroke her hair as I say, "Yeah, I'm worried about him too. What's going on there?"

"I don't know." She sighs, sitting up and pulling away from me. "But we should probably make sure he's got a safe way home."

"No, we can't bring him home. We'll take him to my place."

"Oh?"

"If his dad sees him like that, he's ruined."

"Maybe that would be best? I hated my parents for everything they did when I was friends with Marissa, but they were right to do it."

"You don't know my Uncle Alex." He's harsh. Not worth Alex's first mistake. "I'd rather take a shot at Alex before I send him to the lions, you know?"

"Okay, well, I've got to be home by one. So," she checks her phone, "we've got to get going. I'm sorry. I wish I could stay with you here forever, but with the new car there's no way I can afford missing this special curfew."

"Right," I say as she climbs off the bed and I sit up on the side.

"I can't wait for summer," she says as she bends over to tie her shoe.

"Why?"

"Because you're always shirtless when you're painting."

CHAPTER SEVENTEEN

Lucy

Justin wraps his arms around me as we step out of the bedroom. No one's in the hallway, thank God. My face is beet-red, like a guilty tomato. Not that we did anything bad, but I definitely pushed things in there more than I've done before.

A heaving noise jolts me as we pass the room next door. A coughing fit follows. Gross. Justin and I both stop in place and glance at one another. Should we look? When the coughing abruptly stops, we hear a gurgle. I step into the room. There's no way I can leave someone knowing they are choking. A very familiar pair of yellow pumps sprawl across the floor.

Oh, God. Please no.

Another heave.

Another choke.

"Can you wait for me out here?" I ask Justin.

"Marissa?"

"Yeah."

I step into the room. The rancid smell of puke makes me heave. I peer around the corner. Marissa lies on the carpet, topless, her hair disheveled. Her cheek's deep in a pool of her own puke. I pull her hair up out of the goo, and rub her bare back as she heaves again. Another choke, so this time I slap.

She groans and flips over, her eyes struggling for focus. She smiles as barf trails down her chin. "Lucy?"

"Do you need help in there?" Justin asks from behind the door.

"No, I'm good." I take my sweater off, throwing it over her bare chest and cover her butt in this black thong with a blanket from the bed. "Don't come in. Go grab Alex and I'll be down soon. I'll meet you outside."

I grab the binder off my wrist, quickly throwing Marissa's hair up in a bun.

"Why are you naked?"

"The guys, they just…" But she doesn't finish her sentence.

"What did they do?"

She retches again and I turn her over, her spew splattering on the cuff of my jeans. *Eww.*

"Sorry," she says hoarsely.

"Marissa, what did they do to you?"

"I don't know."

I take a deep breath, asking the question I fear most. "Were you raped?"

"No. Nothing went in," she says. "Panties stayed on.

My rules."

"Where are your clothes?"

She rolls over, groaning and closing her eyes. I crawl around the room, collecting her bra and skirt. I have no idea where her shirt is.

"Come on, sit up, babe," I say softly. My stomach cringes. Why am I helping her?

She reaches up, allowing me to lift her. "Thanks," she mutters.

That's why. I'm helping her because she needs me. I don't care if she's a total bitch. No one deserves to be treated like this. I clasp her bra around her chest and slip her skirt on like she's a toddler. I throw my sweater over her head too.

There, at least now I can get her out. There's no way I'm leaving her here. There's always a chance that whoever those guys were may come back for more.

I throw open my phone, texting Justin.

Me: Is there a back door to this place?

Justin: Go out the kitchen, back door is just past the fridge.

Me: I'll meet you there. Can you grab my jacket from the game room closet? My keys are in my black coat. I parked down the hill. A red Volvo S60. I'll meet you with Marissa out back.

I throw my arm under hers, letting her lean against me. "Lucy," she says over and over.

"I've got you. Let's get you home."

She wraps her arms around my waist, giving me a hug. "I always knew you were my best friend."

I bite my tongue as I guide her from the room. This isn't the time to remind her how she used me and stabbed me in the back with my ex. The stairs are tricky with her deadweight, causing us to stumble down the last two. Our bodies hit the door at the bottom, flying into the kitchen. A few people look at us for a second, but then continue their conversation. I guess seeing a trashed girl helped from the house is normal here.

The cold winter air bites as we step outside. My car's waiting down the sidewalk. Marissa's heel catches on an ice slab the first step out the door. I lunge to catch her, but slide. My face stings in the snow.

Four hands reach out, helping both of us up.

"Thanks," I say to Alex.

"Yeah," is all he says as he immediately drops my arm, returning to the car like a scolded dog.

Wow. Where's the Alex I used to love?

"It's really icy here. Do you mind if I just carry her?" Justin asks, nodding down towards her ridiculous skirt.

"No, it's freezing. Let's get her inside."

With one swoop, Justin lifts Marissa into his arms. Her butt cheeks are totally hanging out, but Justin makes sure to keep his hands clear as he slides her into the car.

Alex sits in front, eyeing the back seat in the mirror.

I cross her legs and glare back at him. His eyes shift away and he closes the mirror fast. For real, Justin better smack sense into him tonight. Or else I will.

"I'll be out in one second," Justin says before he closes the door and runs back into Watson's.

I gaze at the dashboard. Two minutes to one. Mom is going to kill me.

I dial our home number. Mom picks up not even through the first ring. "Lucy, are you all right?" her voice has a stressed-out edge.

"Yeah, I'm fine. I'm on my way home. Listen, I'm so sorry. I'm going to be late."

She pauses for a moment before continuing, her voice too steady. "Your curfew is one o'clock, Lucinda."

"I know, I know. But I have a reason."

I gaze at Marissa. Crap. Should I cover for her? No, that's not worth pissing my parents off.

"I'm waiting," Mom says.

"It's Marissa, Mom. I found her in trouble."

Mom sucks in one of her therapeutic breaths. "Lucinda. You can't expect me to believe you are with Marissa tonight, do you? It's Justin, isn't it? Lost track of time? Just tell me the truth."

"I am telling the truth. Why don't you believe me?"

"Would you?"

I take a deep breath. No, but still. Marissa slumps against my shoulder. "I'll prove it, one sec. Do you have your phone?"

"It's right next to me."

"Okay, look for my text."

I swipe my screen to the camera, taking a reverse shot of Marissa conked out and drooling on my shoulder and text it to Mom.

"There, did you get it?"

I hear her phone vibrate.

"Oh, dear. Is she okay?"

"I think so. I'm taking her to her place and then I'll come home."

"Yeah. Let me know if you need anything; I'll stay up."

"Thanks," I say, turning off the call as Justin opens up the door again. He passes me a bowl he took from Watson's kitchen.

"For, well…you know. New car and all."

"Smart."

He climbs in, tossing another plastic bowl at Alex's head.

"I won't need that shit," Alex spits back.

"Right," Justin says shortly as he starts my car, throwing us into reverse.

By the time we reach the end of the driveway, Alex's head is between his legs, retching into the bowl. I roll down the window, the air too revolting. Alex better de-stink my car after this.

After a few minutes, Justin pulls up his driveway. Alex looks back to me, paled. "Lucy, I'm sorry."

Justin shakes his head "Alex, out. You'll have much more to say tomorrow. I promise."

I climb out of the car, meeting Justin in the cold.

"This isn't the way I imagined our night ending," he says, touching his forehead to mine.

"Me either."

"Happy New Year." His warm lips brush the skin between my eyes before he steps away. Alex is half bent up the walkway, hands on his knees, vomiting in the snow.

That's going to be nasty in the morning.

Ten minutes later, I'm helping Marissa to her front door. The lights are still on inside so I knock. No answer. Marissa's limp now. I drag her to the side of the garage door and plug in the code, thankful the number's still engraved in my memory.

We pass through her kitchen. Her mom's leg hangs over the end of the couch, peeking out from the other room. Thankfully, I don't have to be worried about Marissa's parents being super pissed. They've known she's been drinking for a while now.

"I'm putting you down, okay?" I lower Marissa to the hardwood floor as she groans. "I'll let your mom know you're home."

"No." She shakes her head slowly. "Don't wake her. She's wasted." Marissa starts crawling away toward the stairway. I ignore her. Her mom needs to know in case Marissa gets sicker. I touch her mom's leg lightly and call her name, but she won't stir.

Seriously? No wonder Marissa does this stuff. I always thought her parents were cool, but this is weird. I wonder how hard Marissa worked to keep this secret from me.

Marissa groans as she pulls herself up the steps. *Shit.* I can't leave her like this. I follow her up and help her into bed. With a washcloth from her bathroom, I wipe the barf smell from her neck. She pulls her gray, ragged bunny close. Her lips part as her breaths deepen into snores. As I leave, I turn out her bedroom light, leaving the one on in the hallway in case she needs it.

Will she even remember it was me?

Do I want her to?

***

I sift through my closet. *Ugh.* Nothing that screams I'm dating the governor's son. Inauguration Day officially sucks. Not that I'm going to the event, but still. People know who I'm dating and what's going on. I've been trying to go but Coach T keeps blocking me, claiming athletic department rules: a player must be present in school the day of an event in order to participate in said event.

And, of course, tonight of all nights is the game that

determines the district champions and who gets to go to State. The inauguration is at noon, so it's total crap that they won't let me leave, even for an hour. Amazing how they stick to some rules but totally turn their heads away from others. They're champions at that.

I button up this "smart vest" that Marissa once made me buy, pairing it with a white button-down shirt.

Intellectual?

No. It's tight across the chest and lands way too high above my hips, making my love handles look way larger than I ever thought possible.

Totally foolish. Why would I even try to put something on that Marissa suggested? She's ridiculous. I've bumped into her in the hall nearly every day this past week. Not once has she acknowledged how I helped her. How can you be responsive to someone but not remember anything? It's gonna take me a long time to wrap my mind around "blacking out" and the excuses surrounding it.

The frustrating thing is that I want to speak to her. I need to. The first week back from break has been nothing but horrendous to her. When she thinks no one is watching, her face falls, pale and blank. Around the guys? She keeps playing her game. Maybe she doesn't know how to stop? But after the topless photos of her hit Tumblr, it's definitely a dangerous one to play.

Why in the world would she let them take pictures of her?

Yeah, she was drunk. But she was obviously posing. Marissa is far from perfect. Hell, she's a conniving she-witch. She still had a bit of integrity though… until Zach.

Okay, I've got to just choose something to wear before I'm late. With all of these clothes, there's got to be something special, but no. Fine, I'll go with what I love. I yank my favorite gray v-neck T-shirt out of my laundry bin and pair it with my favorite pair of jeans. At least I'll feel like myself.

Fifteen minutes later, I slide through the classroom door at the last chime of the bell. Everyone glares at me. I straighten out my top. Why didn't I go shopping for today? Mr. Tate clears his throat, calling attention to the analysis for chapter fifteen of *Crime and Punishment*. I pull out my notebook, focusing on the mother's reaction to Raskolnikov. My neck prickles and, yup, they're still studying me. Did I miss something?

Suddenly, there's a tug on my sleeve and a note is slipped into my hand from this drama club guy who's never spoken to me before.

So when are you available? ~ Ryder

Available? What?

Buzz. Crap, I forgot to leave my phone in my locker. I reach in my bag, moving it under my sweater so hopefully Mr. Tate doesn't hear it and take it. I keep my eyes on the board as I move, knowing there's no way I can check the text until the two-hour block is done. My leg rests against the bag, so I can feel each text come in. They never seem to stop. What if something's wrong? If Mom or Dad were in an accident, surely the school nurse would come get me, right? When class is nearly done, I can't take it anymore, opting to use the one bathroom pass we get a quarter. As I walk in, a girl from the sophomore basketball team leaves. "Hey, excited for your game tonight?" I ask.

"It should be fine." She steps away from me.

"Well, if you want to practice before the game, we could. I like to keep busy with a ball before our games. I'd

178

love to help."

"No thanks." She scowls at me then.

"Um, okay? Another time?"

She walks past me and I swear she whispers "Doubtful." Okay, that was rude. I was only offering to help. I step into the bathroom, thankful it's empty as I pull out my phone to figure out what's behind this Bermuda Triangle affect.

Fourteen missed texts from Justin. Reading each text is like someone reaching down my windpipe and squeezing my lungs. It's then I glance up, experiencing everything he just warned about, pasted to the mirror—a photo of Justin and I together at the party, in the bedroom. Me kneeling on the floor in front of him. My back completely bare. Justin, shirtless, stretching backwards.

Oh my God.

The position makes me look like I'm giving him a bl…

Weight presses in on my chest. My breath struggles to maintain support.

Who did this? And why the hell am I topless? I was wearing a tank top and tying my shoe! This Photoshopping is insanely good. There's no way people are going to believe this is fake.

Marissa's the only person I know who understands that program, but she couldn't have taken this shot. She was down the hall having her own photo shoot. Heck, there's no way anyone could have taken this picture unless they were tucked in a tree on the other side of the lake with some sort of telephoto lens.

I scroll through Justin's texts again. He lists websites where I should *not* go. So of course, I switch over to my browser as I close myself into a stall and pull up each trashy gossip site.

The photo is everyone's newest post: *The Governor's Son Who Knows How to Get Some.* On one blog, there's even a photo that includes curved side boob. My fingers tremble as I stare at this fake piece of flesh edited into my body. This can't be happening. My fingers hover over the respond button, but what do I say?

The bell rings then and I suck in a deep breath, not letting go. Girls wander in, laughing at the photo on the wall. Some gasp and others just call me a slut. Frozen, each moment of torture from my freshman year flies back at me. My stomach turns over as fear overrules reason. Sweat drips down my back as I brace myself. That stall door will fly open and I'll be dragged out by my hair… No! I close my eyes, fighting it. No, no, no. I cannot do this again. I *will* not be this girl again. These girls have no idea I'm here. The photos are not real. I'm stronger than this now. Going back to that place is not an option for me. I take a deep breath, opening the stall door. I vowed this summer to never spend my life acting afraid anymore.

A few girls gasp as I walk out and wash my hands. I take the photo from the wall, crumpling it and throwing it in the trash. Then I step out into the hall and move towards Math class. Each step is work, but I move forward.

Laura catches my arm. "Lucy, are you okay? Who took that photo? Holy crap. I'd feel so violated!"

I clench my teeth. "Laura, the photos aren't real."

"You don't have to pretend with me, Lucy, I swear. I mean, everyone knows Justin took you up to the room at the party."

"It's not real. Someone Photoshopped it."

She pulls a handful of photos out of her bag. "I've been taking them down in the girls' bathrooms," she explains.

She gazes into my eyes and I stare back.

"I'm telling the truth."

Her eyebrows fold in, then after a moment, fall back in place. "All right, girl, I believe you. But these look freakishly real. What are you going to do?"

"I'm going to keep going."

"Dude, go home. Your parents will understand."

"What? Am I supposed to show them this?"

"Lucy, these photos are everywhere. They're going to find out anyway."

"I can't go home. I have the game tonight."

"So you're going to stay here? That's like serving yourself up on a platter for ridicule." A girl walks past, whispering "whore" as she bumps my shoulder. "See." Laura flips her off.

"I'll endure it." The scars left on my hip and butt ache now. They're the only evidence left of the horrid year of being beat up and thrown against the gym lockers. "Laura, trust me. I've handled worse."

Before Statistics starts, I slip out my phone under my desk and try to figure out how to respond to Justin. This must be a disaster for him on his dad's big day.

Me: Are you okay?

My phone vibrates in response. Suddenly, Mrs. Peterson, the old bat, is standing at my desk, hand extended.

"You know the rules, Lucy. I'll need to confiscate this for the day."

"No, please. I'll go put it in my locker right now." My eyes meet hers. "Please, not today."

"Since this is your first offense, I'll tolerate it. Be back before the bell rings though, otherwise you are tardy." She nods toward the door. *Thank God.* I read Justin's response on the way to my locker.

Justin: Don't worry about me. Is everything okay for you?

No. But how can I tell him that?

I put my phone into my locker. I can't lie to him, but I don't think he can handle the truth right now. I'll respond later once I figure out how.

After Math, I opt to risk losing the phone again, slipping it into my backpack again. The rest of the day passes with a heated face as I shuffle from class to class. Teachers glare at me. I pray none of them approach me, totally avoiding the health teacher who tried to catch up with me after class. There's no way I can handle an STD talk right now. *No thanks.* Justin keeps texting, asking if I'm okay. I still don't know how to respond. If I tell him the truth, I'm afraid he'll leave the inauguration. Plus, somehow I think having him here will make it worse.

My strength cracks with each whispered insult. Only my experience of surviving a history of brutal bullying gives me the superglue to keep moving on. But when a guy catches my eye then looks at his junk, that I'm-going-to-lose-it sting returns to my eyes. *Screw this.* I'm out of here. The teacher calls my name as I stand from my desk, seven minutes early. As I bolt to my locker, I pass Alex walking out of the bathroom. His eyes skip right over me.

"Um, Alex? Excuse me?" I say sharply. The last time I saw him he was throwing up in Justin's driveway and now he's ignoring me? *Um, no.*

"Whatever, Lucy. You and Justin are such hypocrites." He walks away from me then. Actually walks away!

I grab his sleeve. "The photos aren't real, Alex."

He shrugs me off, not saying anything as he crosses in

front of me. "Alex, what has happened to you?" I say under my breath. He hesitates for a second, so I know he hears me, but then moves on.

Somehow, him blowing me off is what finally breaks me. Tears fall. I gasp as the final bell rings, ducking my head as kids pour out into the halls. I pull open the only door where I know it's safe and shut myself in the janitor's closet. Hugged by its total darkness. There's safety in being alone.

I wave my hand above my head, yanking the cord that's always hung above.

The light flickers on and that's when I realize this isn't my closet anymore. Marissa stares back at me, face swollen and mascara-streaked, sitting on the bucket that used to be my loser throne.

"Hey," she says, her voice cracking. "Welcome back."

CHAPTER EIGHTEEN

Justin

I duck out of the main ballroom, phoning Lucy for the thousandth time. She hasn't called back, and it's killing me. I slam my phone shut as it once again goes to her voicemail. Maybe she's ignoring my calls because she thinks I failed her.

Did I?

Dad's support staff follows me into the side conference room, pulling the curtain as Dad joins. His fingers pull on his tie, loosening it, as his eyes find mine then drop away. I've never seen him more disappointed in my life.

He doesn't believe me. *They're fake*, I scream back with my eyes, the same words I've told him all day. I've never given Dad a reason to not trust me and now he's tossing me to the wind. He has no right to treat me that way.

Paul hovers behind Dad's left shoulder, helping him take off his sport coat. A bead of sweat drips down his brow. He's such a creep. They exchange some words before Paul finally leaves his side. That should be one of *us* standing there. Probably Mom, but she's on the couch, listening to an education proposal from a volunteer. When Paul finally leaves Dad alone, I step forward. I've had enough of this guy and Dad's tolerance for his crap. I cut to the chase. "Why is Paul still here?"

"To help deal with incidents like yours," Dad explained.

Right. Everything in me wants to explode. I've never felt this way before. I don't answer him, he doesn't deserve it. He doesn't deserve any of this. Heck, maybe it's a good thing these photos ruined his day.

A few staff members shoot me scornful looks as I walk away. Uncle Alex won't even look at me. And Alex? He's monopolizing the cheese tray. Nice of him to finally show up. I can't believe he bailed on the actual event. He chose a Math test over this? Yeah, right. He's still pissed about what I said to him on New Year's.

I eye my phone; two minutes until Dad said I can leave. That's just enough time to catch the last half of Lucy's game. I gather my laptop bag and move towards the exit, only to run into Paul.

"Where do you think you're going?"

It takes every ounce of control for me to not shove him away. Dad must have sensed it, because soon his hand rests on my shoulder. For the first time in my life, I feel that electric impulse to shrug it off, but I don't. I can't do that here. Here, I can't do anything I feel.

"I'm heading out to Lucy's game," I look at Dad, "like we discussed yesterday."

Dad rubs the bridge of his nose before pulling his hands through his hair. He's about to say something, but then Paul jumps in.

"After your viral debut with that girl this morning, it's best for you not to see her in public today. Let it blow over a little bit, just a few days, so it doesn't damage your father's reputation before he gets a chance to begin."

That girl? My fists ball up and my brain goes warp speed into trying to control the maniac that wants to break Paul's nose.

Dad clears his throat. "I have to agree, son. I'm sorry. You can see her after the game. But showing up there? The gossip blogs are probably waiting to pounce on you. We can't take the hit from more photos right now."

"Dad, they're fake."

He holds up his hand. "We'll discuss this later. Please give me the time I need to handle it correctly. The number of emails I've received today about my inability to raise my own son outweighs everything else. I'm temporarily at a loss for what to do with you. I never dreamed you would be the issue on a day like today. My own son…"

Whoa.

"Dad," I lower my voice and take a step with Dad away from Paul, "I never meant to disappoint you. And…" I struggle to find words when everything in me wants to blow him off. I deserve way better than this, but I am better than he is. I will maintain control. "I'm sorry you feel that way but I'm a good son."

He's quiet for a moment, then swears under his breath. "Just give me the time I need to figure this out. Okay?"

Paul glances at me like I'm an immature fourteen-year-old who was just caught humping a statue.

"Fine," I spit out as I distance myself from them both. Dad rubs his forehead as I leave. He better be questioning who he is right now. How could he imply I wasn't a good son? I'm nearly killing myself trying to support his dream. Not to mention giving up another night with Lucy.

Tonya tugs on my sleeve. "Want to grab some fresh air?"

"Hell, yes." We step out into the back hallway. Empty. My back finds the wall, sinking down to the floor. She slides down next to me.

"Bad day, huh?"

One of the worst. But is it? No. Jackson's diagnosis, his failed remission, his death…. Those will always be the worst. This simply blows.

"Justin, it'll pass. You're only eighteen. No one can expect you to be perfect all the time."

"Tonya, the photos are altered."

She picks at her bracelet. "Listen, I know you don't want to talk about your sex life with me. But let's not lie to one another," she says softly. "I'm not going to stop loving you, you know that."

My eyes burn. "I know you love me. Thank you. But, I'm telling the truth. That didn't happen. Those photos are doctored."

"Okay."

"Okay? So you believe me?"

"I'd be a fool not to. You're my brother and you've never given me reason to doubt you before." Like an injection of drugs, her words give me a bit of peace and confidence.

"Thanks." I give her a little nudge. "Now if only Mom and Dad can realize that too."

"So if they aren't real. What did happen?"

My face heats as I tell her everything. It's uncomfortable to share how Lucy and I made out on the stairs, on the bed, and how my shirt did come off but her tank top stayed on. About how she bent down to tie her shoe, and how I stretched backward, just as someone must have been waiting with their camera to catch an incriminating shot.

That was it.

She doesn't move much as she takes it in.

"Lucy'd tell you the same story."

"How's Lucy handling everything?"

"I have no idea. She won't tell me."

"Maybe the school doesn't know about it?" she offers.

"No, trust me. I've gotten tons of texts. Everyone knows."

She takes a deep breath. "Right. Well, let's figure this out. First, you've got to tend to the more immediate needs of Lucy and our parents. Then there's the big stuff. Dad's political image. Your image with your business and school." Her words send cracks in the foundation beneath me. The painting business. Crap, The Hill House. They could pull my bid over this!

"And then there's the whole fact that Lucy's sixteen and you're eighteen."

"We didn't even…They're fake!"

"I know, I know. But the photographer could be charged with child pornography or something. I'm just saying we've got angles to work with. We need to find the photographer. Who would have a vendetta against you and Lucy?"

"Lucy's ex-boyfriend isn't smart enough to pull this off. Her ex-best friend was wasted in the other room."

"Any enemies?"

At that exact moment, Paul steps out far down the hallway, opening up his phone, and it clicks.

"The entertainment guy. He could do this!" He'd have amazing access to photographers and Photoshop professionals.

"The reality-show guy?"

"Yes." I fill her in on the donation, Paul's insistence on my cooperation with the interview and showing up in Hawaii with the contract.

"Well," she brushes off her skirt and stands up, "it's a place to start. I'll do some research with my lawyer before we present it to Mom and Dad."

"Your *lawyer*? Marc showed up for your fashion show, and then came out for BBQ with us. You went *home* with him. Call him what he is, your boyfriend."

Tonya rolls her eyes. "It's nothing serious… In the meantime, let's focus on the stuff closest to you first. Lucy, her parents, and Mom and Dad." She looks down at me. "You coming?"

"No, I need a little more time from that place. I'll be back inside soon."

"Okay. Don't worry, I've got your back."

"Thanks."

She steps back into the room as Alex slides out. He only notices me after he shuts the door, before trying to yank it open again. I reach up, grabbing him by the waist of his pants, and pull him down next to me.

"We need to talk."

"Fine," he sulks.

"Did you see Lucy at school?"

"Yeah."

"Was she okay?"

"Would you be?" he snaps back. He reaches into his back pocket, taking out a wad of paper and handing it to me. "I collected these from the guys' locker room." He slaps the printed photos into my hand and my gut turns. Wow, Luke wasn't kidding when he said they were everywhere. He glares at me, searching for something.

"The photos are fake, Alex."

"You really expect me to believe that? I'm sorry, but you're such a hypocrite. After that lecture you give me New Year's morning, and you did this that exact night?" He scratches his nose. "How am I supposed to…"

"What, dude?"

His eyes meet mine again. "Nothing. I can't believe you gave me *growing up* advice about self-image, drinking, and sex when you've been doing this stuff with Lucy."

"Okay, first of all, Lucy is it for me. I'm not with a new girl every other week like you've been doing. Second of all, I respect Lucy. Third, the photos are fake." I take him by the shoulder. "I'd own up to you if they were real, Alex. I promise you that. And fourth, I'm eighteen. You're fifteen. Comparing the two is not the same."

"They're really fake?"

"Yes. Fake. Some creep Photoshopped these. I swear."

"Looks like you."

"Argh. It is me. They edited her back to look bare." I take a deep breath, then explain the entire scenario to him. How many times will I have to tell people about one of the most private but best moments with Lucy ever? It sucked that it isn't ours anymore.

"Okay, well, if they really are fake, then you should know Lucy spent the afternoon hiding in the janitor's closet with Marissa."

"What? Why didn't you tell me?"

"I saw them both sneak in at different times of the day." He shrugs. "Ever since Lucy told me about that closet at the end of the summer, I've watched it."

"Why?"

"Something to do. It gives me a chance to play hero and encourage other kids when everything else I did felt wrong." He stares at the plain wall in front of us. I wait for more, but he doesn't offer anything up.

"Why would she be with Marissa?" I ask out of curiosity, but also to help him through his thoughts. Lucy never told me much of what happened the night with Marissa after the party, but I can't imagine they bonded. Not with what Marissa did to her this summer.

"Dude, I saw Lucy's face today. You didn't. She's pretending to be strong, but she's a mess. Marissa's a total mess. Misery in company."

"I can't believe she's with Marissa when she won't even answer my calls."

"Maybe she's trying to hide how bad it hurts?"

"Why would she hide that from me?"

"Because you're perfect?"

"I'm not perfect."

"Shut up." He rolls his eyes. "You know you are."

If only he knew how much stuff I'm trying to juggle at the same time to keep everyone happy. Or if he knew how I resist my natural impulse when asked a question to snap and tell people to go away. Well, everyone but Lucy. The only thing that stresses me out with her is how much I suck with finding time to be near her.

"I'm far from perfect. I could and should be much better."

"Nah," he sucks in a deep breath. "That's your flaw, man." I cock an eyebrow, waiting for him to continue. "You're trying your best for everyone else. You want to meet everyone's expectations but your own. Where are your priorities?"

"Where they've always been," I say, frustrated. "Family—Lucy included—school, and work."

Alex's eyes drop to study the carpet. "You never asked me about when Sally and I broke up."

My gut sinks and my heart smacks to the floor.

Family. My priority.

His eyes meet mine, moist. "You haven't called me in ages, man." He shakes his head. "The only time we've spent together this year is when you dragged me to your house last week when I was drunk." He holds up his hands. "I'm not blaming you for my stupid decisions. I knew what I was doing when I made them. It was easier than trying to live up to your life. It sucked when you stopped caring about me. I know Jackson's gone, but you're a brother to me and it sucks that it's not the other way around."

The impact of his words hits me like a freight train. I failed him. We sit together silent for a while. Finally, I find my voice. "Alex, I'm sorry. You've always been my younger brother. I've never dragged anyone drunk home from a party before and stayed up all night cleaning up their puke."

"Really?"

"Yeah," I elbow him, "and you're probably the only guy I'd ever care enough about to do it for again. Don't try to live a life like mine. Be yourself. That's all I want for you."

He smiles back at me, and I know we're good.

"So, Sally? What happened there?"

"She broke up with me because I got a big head."

"So, you just continued to let it inflate?"

He stretches his arms across his chest. "It was a lot easier than trying to correct my mistakes. But easier isn't better, we both know that, right?" Alex says and for the first time all day my heart feels hope. The weight that's been between us the past few months lifts a bit.

"Yes. Definitely."

"So," he nods towards the front door on the other end of the hall. "Are you going to stick with Uncle Jeff's agenda tonight? Or ditch it for Lucy?"

Now, that's Alex. When he's himself, he's simply awesome. He's right. It's wrong that I'm still here. Why respect my dad when he doesn't respect me? No wonder Lucy hasn't responded to my texts or calls.

He kicks my shoe. "You're eighteen, man. You don't have to be here." He nods back to the door. "Hell, no one in that room wants you around anyway. Just go." He stands up and extends a hand, pulling me off the ground. "Be the guy you want to be. Not the guy everyone else wants, okay?"

"Thanks, Alex," I say as I take off down the hall. "I owe you a future reality check."

"Consider it even, man. Now run!"

CHAPTER NINETEEN

Lucy

He's not here. Marissa rolls her eyes at me as she catches me looking for him at the South door. We didn't say much in the closet after I turned the light back off. There was mostly silence and a lot of tears. She followed me to the game though, making sure I made it. Nice, I guess? I still don't know what to make of it.

McKenzie passes me the ball. The gym door opens as I release it from my hands. Is it him?

No.

Brick shot, off the backboard.

Someone boos from the crowd. Jaclyn wraps her arm around my waist, pulling me close. "Lucy, you've got to get over today. Please, get your head in the game. We need you. We're dying here."

"Right, sorry." I rub my eyes, hating myself for being so weak. I used to be able to play basketball with my entire team hating me. Now, I can't even sink an easy jump shot. Being called a slut isn't new. I've played with those names sneered down my back before. Without Justin here, it's like I can't function.

And that scares me. It's not right.

A ball flies toward my head and I duck. Crap. That was supposed to be a pass.

"TIME OUT." Coach T's voice booms from the sideline. "Zwindler, outside, now." He steps through the gym door that leads to the locker room. I follow, though I'd rather drink shards of glass.

"What's wrong out there?" he says with a brash tone.

"Bad day."

"Well, your bad day is ruining us. I'm well aware that you've had bad days before, but that's never stopped you."

"I know." The cracks in the steps below my feet look like spiderwebs.

He yanks at the whistle around his neck. "Don't lose this for us, Zwindler. It's the division championship game. Don't you want to go to State?"

"Of course I do."

He steps toward me and the stench of his BO is overwhelming. "Then don't let the fact you're a slut ruin everything." His words sting my cheek as he steps out the door.

Everything in my writhes. I hate him. He's the worst coach and human being I've ever met. Why the heck am I even playing for him again?

Because Justin made me.

No, he didn't make me. He just helped me see how

much I missed basketball. I was delusional to think playing with Coach T again would be worth it. He called me a slut! I'm such an idiot. With Justin and Alex, sure, basketball was fun. Why did I think this year could be different? Over the summer, Justin and Alex always made basketball a blast. It's not like they are ever around when I play now.

Wait, who am I doing this for?

Screw Coach T.

I'm done.

I fly down the stairs to the locker room. I plow through the door, tearing my jersey off.

"Hey, watch it."

I jump, turning towards the voice. Marissa pulls my sweaty jersey off her head.

"Nice," she says, tossing it back at me.

I turn my back to her. I know we had a moment in the closet, but I can't deal with her right now. Not with everything she's done to me. My fingers struggle to remember my locker combo with Marissa's eyes on my back.

"Lucy." Marissa taps her toe on the concrete floor.

"WHAT?" The word flies harshly out of my mouth. That toe tap ruled my life last year. I'm so over being treated like that.

Marissa holds her hands up. "Sorry," she says, which receives a huge eye roll from me. *Yeah, right.*

"Where are you going?"

"Home. Where I belong. I'm done with this."

She leans against the locker next to mine as my fingers finally remember the combo. "Lucy, I think you're making the wrong decision. You belong up there."

An absurd laugh flies from my mouth. "I belong up

there? Marissa, you were the one who convinced me to give up basketball."

"I was wrong," she says quietly, which makes me stop and actually look at her. "Come on. Obviously, I was wrong. Look at my life right now. It's horrid."

I nod; no use arguing that.

"If I could do what you do up there, I'd never give it up."

"Marissa, I don't play basketball for the attention."

"I know. It's not that. You love it. You're passionate about it. I'm not passionate about anything but myself and that landed me topless, posing for stupid guys, and plastered all over Tumblr. Somewhere between June and now, I lost myself. I claim to be a photographer? I quit yearbook class. I don't even know how it happened…"

Is she trying to relate to me? "The photos of me were fake, Marissa."

She laughs lightly. "Lucy, you wouldn't even change your bra in front of me. There's no way the photos of you and Justin are real. I'm not saying you're a skank. I'm saying I am."

"Okay?" What is she getting at here? I pull on sweats over my shorts.

"Don't give up what you love for anyone. You've made it through an entire season before with a team who hated you. You can make it through one more game with a few people in the stands who don't respect you. Who cares what people think? Your friends know they are fake, right?"

"Yeah."

"Then go play. Don't let crap stand in your way."

"I can't." I slam my locker shut. "I just can't."

"Why? You're stronger than that. Why do you think

I worked so hard to keep you less than me? Keeping you hidden was impossible… Obviously, it didn't work. Justin saw you for you."

Justin. Hearing his name is like having a brick thrown against my chest. Why isn't he here? Sure, I never texted him back. But what was I supposed to say? *I'm fine.* I'm not fine. I can't even grasp how this happened to us. Just because I didn't return his text doesn't mean he shouldn't be here. He promised he wouldn't miss the game.

I can't believe he's not following through. Do I matter to him? Heat drains from my face. That's just it—he can't care about me the way I do for him. Wouldn't I be higher on the priority list? He should be here, especially after today.

"You're not playing because Justin's not here, huh?" Marissa sits down on the bench, crossing her legs.

I gaze up at the ceiling, refusing to meet her eyes.

"Lucy, don't define yourself by a guy. Trust me, you'll become less than nothing." The whistle blows above us, signaling the end of the third quarter. "Go do your thing up there. If Justin doesn't show, who cares? It's your thing, not his. Go do it."

She stands then and leaves, without even a goodbye. I turn back toward my locker, the squeak of the door letting me know I'm finally alone. The back of my knees find the bench and I sit, contemplating the person I'd just met. The real Marissa. Weird. I don't know if I think she's mean or honest or… I dunno? The important thing is something extra is tugging at my gut. The truth. Whoa, she's right. How is it possible the only person making sense to me today is Marissa? I've let Justin define me, just like I let Marissa do last year.

I've got to get back up there and play. Coach T probably

won't let me back on the court, but I've got to try. He owes me. I yank off my sweats down to my shorts and pull my jersey back over my head. If he doesn't let me on, so be it.

And Justin? Maybe he's up there now and maybe he isn't. It doesn't matter. I'm throwing all of the weight of this lie and Justin's messed up priorities back onto the court.

The light from the gym blinds me for a second as I yank open the door. I gulp, literally swallowing my pride. Coach T meets me at the end of the bench, hands on his fat hips.

"I want to play."

"I knew you'd come around."

"No, I'm not playing because of you. I'm playing for me. Got that?"

"Whatever. Just win." He calls Kiley off the court right before the ref blows the whistle. "You're in."

I step on the court and dart between the opponent's pass, swiping the ball from the air. I drive toward our basket. Easy lay up. Two points. The other team grabs the ball to toss in from the baseline. There's no way I'm running all the way back to the other side to wait to defend.

Jaclyn nods to me, understanding my game plan. "PRESS," she yells. Coach T slams his clipboard on the chair. He only likes to press for the last three minutes of a game but I totally don't care. We're doing this our way.

Jaclyn steals the ball after two passes then tosses it to me. Their redhead center is on me so I bounce it back, finding my sweet spot on the three-point line. Hands up and, *smack,* the ball's back in my hands. Lines aligned in my palm before I let go.

Swish.

Three more.

As I fly down the court, nothing matters anymore but my teammates and the game. The bleachers disappear and the doors don't exist. Coach T's shouts fade. Good, glad to get rid of his toxic boom. The only thing taunting me is the scoreboard. But, no matter how hard I fight against it, there's just not enough time.

Not enough time to repair all of my mistakes from earlier in the game.

The final buzzer rings, solidifying the score. Eighty-seven to seventy-nine. My feet halt at center court. I lost the game. We're not going to State and the season's over, all because I momentarily forgot how to be myself. My teammates join me. Jacyln wraps her arm around me.

"I'm sorry, guys." My head hangs as the noise and the bleachers come back into view. It all crushes in on me. "I'm so sorry. I suck."

"No," Jaclyn taps me, "this isn't your fault. We've all had bad days. What do you always say when we attribute a win to you?"

"We win as a team, we lose as a team," Chelsey says for me. "There's always next year."

"But not for some of you," I say, fully aware of the seniors in the group.

Jacyln and McKenna look at one another. "Honestly, I'm glad it's over. Coach T's a nightmare."

"As evidenced by the fact he just left the gym. The only good thing about the season being over!" Chelsey chimes.

"All right, girls, let's go congratulate the other team." Jaclyn puts her hand in the circle and we yell "Eagles!" before breaking away. The gym fills with applause. No one's yelling slut or booing anymore. They are all cheering for us, louder than the fans of the team who won. Is it possible

I imagined that many people cared about the photos? To think I believed I was above caring what people think. I'm just as shallow as before.

We clasp the hands of the new division champs. A blond woman in a blazer hangs out near the baseline, waving me over. My heart skips a beat as I recognize her again, the coach from the University of Minnesota Golden Gophers.

"Quite a game," she says.

"Yeah," I sigh, "I…"

"Bad day?"

"You have no idea." …Oh God. Wait. What if she has an idea?

"We all have bad days. But in the two seasons I've followed your playing, I've only seen you have one. That's forgivable."

"Thanks."

"Your last quarter was amazing. The stats…Wow."

"I don't even remember what happened, honestly."

"Good, then I won't throw numbers at you. I don't like my players having big heads." She winks. Her players? "Here's my card. You're a junior, correct? Give me a call this spring. I'd love to talk to you about a future as a Golden Gopher."

I gaze at the card in my palm, hesitating like an idiot. "Thanks, I… Wow. Thank you. I'll definitely give you a call."

"Good. Keep those grades up."

"I'll do that."

She reaches out and pats my shoulder. "Don't worry about all the media stuff. One glance at you on the court, and the world will forget it. We've got PR reps and stuff. You're history from today would disappear if you choose us."

My heart falls through the floor. She knows about the photos and, worse, thinks they are real.

"They're…" I stop myself. There's no use telling her they aren't real. It'll just look weak, like I'm lying to her. I don't want that to be her impression of me.

"Never mind," I say. "Thank you."

"I look forward to your phone call." She smiles as she steps away. I watch her walk through the main gym doors, my eyes passing over the south wall where the guys' basketball team hangs out. Well, everyone on the team but Justin and Alex.

Laura spins me around and I force a smile out, chatting with her and my parents, who are still clueless about the photos. *Thank God*. Eventually, I escape to the empty locker room. Finally alone, the pressure of keeping myself together isn't so strong. My phone taunts me. No texts from Justin for the last two hours. I debate whether or not I should call Mom to return and pick me up. My gorgeous car waits at home because I'm the idiot who believed her boyfriend would give her a ride.

I drag myself out the back door, pausing at the concrete wall that overlooks the soccer fields below. The only disruption to the night's darkness is a lone set of headlights coming up the hill. They grow larger, coming closer. The lights flash. Justin?

CHAPTER TWENTY

Justin

My lips press into her apple hair as I hold her. She hasn't said anything to me yet. "You okay?" I ask her again, rubbing her arms. Her breaths deepen, becoming steadier as she steps away.

"Where were you?" she finally says before her eyes drift from mine, studying the pavement.

"My dad and Paul held me up."

"Held you up? How?" Her tone has an edge, one I heard last summer a lot when she used to despise me. She's glaring at me now and I want to just shut down. I'm such an idiot. Why did I think Dad and Paul would be an excuse?

"You missed my game. You promised you'd be here."

"I…" My palm drifts to my hair. "Listen, I tried."

"You tried? Don't tell me that. If you tried, you would have been here."

"Lucy, it was a mess. I couldn't just disappear after what happened."

"You think you were in a mess? I was stuck here. Everyone calling me a slut!"

"Well how was I supposed to know that? You wouldn't text back."

"What was I supposed to say? What could I possibly say that would make anything that happened okay?" She covers her nose, turning her back to me. Her breath quickens. My gut sinks. Please, don't cry. I never imagined she'd be crying because she was mad at me.

I reach out, touching her shoulder. There. That should help. "It's okay."

She whirls around. "No, it's not. It's not okay. You weren't here. You don't know what it feels like to go through a whole day of school like that."

Her words are harsh and before I know it, I'm throwing some back. "And you don't know what it's like having your dad blame you for ruining everything he's ever worked toward his entire career."

"Fine." She picks up her bag, tossing it over her shoulder and begins walking back toward the gym.

No, this is not what I want. I'm better than this. I refuse to be the guy that takes my frustration out on my girlfriend.

"Lucy, I'm sorry I missed your game and wasn't there for you today." I carefully turn her around to face me. Her eyes find mine, red, swollen, and smudged with black. Here she is, this incredible person, that my situation as my father's son crushed. She'd never be in this situation if it wasn't for me. I failed her, not showing up when she needed me most.

"I made a mistake." The words are uncomfortable. I've always done the right thing. "My priorities got messed up. I should have been here. I should have left the inauguration."

"No, I wouldn't have wanted that. You needed to be at the inauguration." Her voice softens. "I know how hard your family has worked for that. And all the extra hours... No, I wasn't expecting you to miss that. I just..." she wipes away a streak of black from under her eyes. "I expected you at the game and when you weren't there, I fell apart."

"I'm sure you didn't fall apart."

"We lost the game, Justin. The season's done."

Lost? They had this game in the bag. "Listen," I extend my arms, hoping she won't reject me. She steps closer and I quickly pull her into a hug before she changes her mind. "I'm sorry I wasn't there. But losing a game isn't your fault. That happens."

"I know, I just..." She presses her head against my chest. "This day just sucked. What do we do? I can't imagine telling my parents, let alone proving the photos are fake when they look so real."

"Let's talk to your parents tonight. We'll be upfront about it and hope they understand."

"My dad is going to lose it. What if they ban you from seeing me?"

"We'll work through it. Somehow, we'll prove the photos are fake. My sister's lawyer is going to look into some things. Plus, there's always time. They can't keep me away from you forever."

She leans up, her lips pressing softly against mine. I press back, hating everything this day's held for us both.

"Lucy, I'm sorry. I won't get my priorities mixed up

again. I promise."

"Thanks, and I'll try to text back."

"It was pretty crappy of me to text in the first place. I should have been here with you."

She doesn't say anything, instead wrapping her fingers through mine. "We should probably get to my parents before they go online."

"Yeah." We walk down the hill hand-in-hand and I open the door for her. My stomach rolls as I cross behind the car to my side. Proving this to her parents will be near impossible. I've always felt confident in awkward situations, but this tops them all. We didn't do anything *wrong*, but we were making out alone in a bedroom at a party. No parent wants to know about that. Especially a dad.

I groan as I slide into the driver's seat.

He's going to kill me.

***

"Dad, Mom—as we said, they are fake. We wanted you to hear about it from us," Lucy says, resting her hand on her dad's arm. "It's not what it looks like."

Mr. Zwindler's face is Jim Gaffigan pale. I shift in my chair, filling his silence with an awkward creak.

"Well…" Her mom takes a deep breath but doesn't finish her sentence. Finally, she puts up her palms. "I have no grounds to stand on here. I lost my virginity when I was fifteen."

"MOM!" Lucy barks and I bite the inside of my cheek as my own face heats. "Why would you tell us that?"

"It's true." She sips her tea. "I was *experienced*."

"I'm not *experienced*, Mom."

"I'm not saying that. I was misguided. Wandering, you know? I had it all wrong."

"Sarah, is this really the time to share this?" Mr. Zwindler says, his tone clear.

"Yes, why not? I want them to know my past. This one time…"

"Sarah." Mr. Zwindler's eyes bulge as he interrupts.

"Okay. I'm only saying that knowing what I know now, I wouldn't advise my previous actions."

Lucy locks her fingers. "Mom. I really don't want to talk about this right now. Not in front of Justin. Please."

"Do not tell me what I can or can't share." The edge of her voice has me biting my tongue until the taste of iron seeps into my saliva. *Whoa.* So that's the tone Lucy's been talking about. She continues, "Even if you feel ready, you aren't. Not yet." Mrs. Zwindler's eyes meet mine and I nod, legitimately terrified. "You just… everything gets too serious, too fast. Trust me."

"Mom, the photos are fake though. We aren't doing that."

Mr. Zwindler shuts the laptop in front of him. "I'm sorry. I just…you have to understand, even if these are fake, being alone in a bedroom at a party isn't appropriate." He looks at me and it takes all of my strength to meet his eyes. "You went way too far."

"I understand, Mr. Zwindler. That situation won't happen again."

Her mom snorts through a laugh. "Everyone at this table knows that's an absurd promise."

"No, Mom. We aren't going to put ourselves in that situation again."

"Right…"

"Mr. and Mrs. Zwindler, the photos are fake. Please know that. Doing stuff like that isn't in our plans."

"Right now," her mom adds, making everything uncomfortable all over again, because she's right. I mean, sex does matter to me, but I want to wait and do it the right way. Not risk hurting Lucy in anyway. My dick can survive solitude if it means I protect her heart.

Lucy covers her face again while her dad coughs. "What do your parents think?" Mr. Zwindler changes the subject. Thank goodness.

"They believe they are real."

"We should probably speak with them about this. Do you mind giving me their number? I'd like to arrange a time where we can all get together to chat."

I enter my code into my phone and find Dad's contact info. "There you go." Mr. Zwindler's phone buzzes on the counter behind him with the text.

"Thank you," he says.

"Mom, Dad, do you believe us? That they are fake?"

Mr. Zwindler rubs his forehead. "I want more than anything to believe they are. But I don't know what to believe right now."

Her mom throws up her hands. "Again. No grounds for me to stand on here. The thing I'm curious about is who took this photo and why are they trying to ruin your lives?"

Mr. Zwindler clenches his fist. "You're right, Sarah. Whether these are fake or not, it's wrong the photo was taken. More could be coming."

The color drains from Lucy's face. "We won't be in that situation again, Dad."

"If these really are fake, they could edit anything

together to destroy your reputations."

"So you agree they are Photoshopped?" Lucy asks.

He shakes his head. "I'm not passing judgment on that yet. But we need to talk with Justin's parents. Soon."

I pull open my Google calendar on my phone and glance through Dad's meetings. "My father has an opening Wednesday night at six," I offer. "I'll write you in."

"Are you sure that won't be imposing?"

"He lives on a schedule. It's usually booked up months in advance."

"Is it always like that?" Mrs. Zwindler asks and I have the urge to squirm. For the first time, I'm realizing how abnormal it is. "Yeah," I say as I try to control the flush of my face. Labels fill his calendar, occasionally an orange family label pops up. But even then, those set aside times have been infringed upon a lot lately.

Mrs. Zwindler smiles and squeezes my hand. "I think Wednesday night will work great for us."

"Please invite them over for dinner. I'll make something good." Mr. Zwindler. "Not exactly how I imagined meeting your parents," he says. "But I like you, Justin. I do. So right now, I'm trusting you."

"Thank you." We shake hands. "I appreciate your confidence in me."

He smiles as he takes my glass. I shift in place, hating the truth that Mr. Zwindler trusts me more than my own dad. Mrs. Zwindler pats my arm. I want to bolt but I don't. They've got to know that something's up with me and my dad. What are they going to think about my parents? Mrs. Zwindler pats my hand again as Mr. Zwindler says, "Things will change with your parents, Justin. If they are anything like you, they'll come around."

"Thanks," I say before excusing myself to the restroom. Grasping the sink, my breath slowly fills my lungs with a spiraling, gray feeling. My parents were always solid to me. Lucy's parents were the ones I worried about, especially her mom. Her bluntness and her brash approach to life, unhindered by what others think, is so different than the politically correct nature my parents face the world with. It's refreshing. It's real. I love it.

I had been worried Mom and Dad wouldn't like Mrs. Zwindler. My reflection glares back at me, trying to kill the conceit I never knew I had. I hate myself for fearing Mrs. Zwindler would embarrass herself. No... embarrass me. How critical of me. How cruel. At least she's real. Can I say the same about my parents right now? No.

My fingers grasp my hair, but I refuse to pull. No balding for me.

The spiral of gray doesn't let up though. Now, all I want is for Lucy's parents to care about my own. Please don't let my parents mess this up and play it fake. The Zwindlers will see right through it.

Okay, time to get back into the kitchen. If I stay longer, they'll think I'm crapping and I really don't need that right now. I flush the toilet and wash my hands. This could go horrible on Wednesday. I replicate Dad's political game face, feigning confidence in myself as the gray spiral engulfs my lungs. I won't let this go bad. Lucy means too much to me. I'll find a way to make this work.

CHAPTER TWENTY-ONE

Lucy

This shouldn't be so terrifying. It's not like I have anything to apologize for. I tug at my sleeve, watching Marissa pass the front window of the coffee shop. The bell rings as she opens the door and glances at me. Her face is straight, solemn.

I wave back as she heads over to the counter to order something.

Everything in me screams for escape. Why would I listen to her after everything she put me through? But after that hour crying together in the janitor's closet and her direct approach to get me back on that basketball court, everything nags at me that I need to talk with her, get to the bottom of what she's trying to tell me with her eyes every time we pass in the hall.

Marissa smiles as she slides into the booth across from me. The strum of Ian's guitar and his pure tone fills the air.

"Wow," Marissa says. "He's good."

"Yeah, his name is Ian. He's cool."

"Right," she says as she turns back toward me. I wait for the assessment of his hotness or something more, but it doesn't come.

"So…" she sighs. "I don't really know how to ask this… it's embarrassing."

"Yeah?"

"Were you the one who brought me home? On New Year's?"

"I was." I take a sip from my Earl Grey Tea.

"Good. I mean, it's not good that you had to drag me home. But I'm thankful it was you and not someone else. Thank you."

"You're welcome." My eyes are stuck on her face, like she's some freak animal exhibit at a zoo. *Who are you?*

"Can I ask you another weird question?"

"You don't need to ask permission, Marissa. That's why I'm here."

"I know. I'm just trying to be different than before."

Her response twists around everything I know about her. "Oh, well…" My gosh. What do I say to that? "I appreciate that…" She smiles lightly and something in me eases. Maybe Marissa *has* changed. "So, what's on your mind?"

"Can you tell me why?" She leans in, eyes intense. "Why you helped me when you had every reason in the world to leave me or exploit me?"

The plastic of the booth squeaks as I shift. Whoa. That was not a question I was prepared for. "I don't know. I knew there was no way I could leave you like that. It wasn't fair."

"But it would have been fair. I was horrid to you. Wouldn't it have felt good to leave me there?"

"Maybe?" I shake my head. Would it? No, the guilt of leaving someone in need like that would have eaten me raw. "No. Honestly, it wouldn't have. There's no way I could leave you like that. No one deserves that."

"Even when I asked for it?"

My eyebrows peak. "You asked for those guys to take you to a room and take topless photos of you?"

"No, but I do remember feeling like it was fun."

"Was it?"

Her face pales. "No. It was horrid." She rubs her eyes. "I'm really messed up, Lucy."

Yeah. Totally.

"I'm sorry for trying to rule you. For manipulating you. For being jealous about Zach and stepping in, creating drama for fun." Her eyes drop from mine. "I'm a bad person."

An electric current slides over my skin as I respond, as I have no idea what I'm about to say. "You're not. You wouldn't be here if you were."

"I want to change, Lucy. I do. I just don't know how. I'm stuck at school. Everyone has already determined who I am. It's just easier to be that way than change."

"Easier paths are usually the wrong ones," I say, thinking about all of the foolish, hurtful battles I'd had with Mom. "I've taken that road way too many times. It doesn't work out."

"Was putting up with me as a friend an easier path?"

"Easier than being myself? Definitely."

"I'm sorry." She reaches out and touches my hand. "I want to change." Her voice is steady and soft, so different then her usual upbeat and pushy tone. If this is the real Marissa, it'd be damaging if I rejected her. She'd retreat forever. I know how much strength it takes to step out and be real for the first time.

A deep breath steadies me as I say the words I never thought I could. "You're forgiven."

"Thank you." She taps the table. "So, how do I change?"

Impressive. She's ready to move on. "I have no idea. Pretty sure that comes from within."

"Yeah. That's the hard part. There's not much in there."

"Yes there is. Trust me, I felt the same way about myself. There's way more to you than you know."

"Thanks," Marissa says lightly. "So, how's everything going for you after the photos? Is your mom freaking out?"

"Not really. I think she believes me."

"Seriously?" Her tone drifts toward her dramatic side. Her facial expression shifts. "Sorry, bad habit. Trying to change my impulses, I swear."

"Yeah. My mom and I communicate much better now," I add. "She's still…"

"Different?"

"Right. But I appreciate it now. She's there, that's what counts."

"Yeah…" Marissa gets a spacey look. Is she picturing her own mom passed out on the couch? She shakes her head clear. "So what's next?"

"My parents are meeting with Justin's tonight to discuss the situation."

"That's terrifying."

"You have no idea. I've been trying to picture our

parents sitting together for a long time. It's got this peasant family versus royalty feeling. Not that his parents make me feel that way about my family, it's just our parents are so different." My phone buzzes, Justin's call. I let it pass, not wanting to be rude. Then it buzzes again, with a text.

"Feel free to read and answer. No big deal," Marissa says, pulling out her own phone.

"Thanks." I glance at the text and my heart plummets.

Justin: There are new photos out. Give me a call when you can.

New photos? How? From where? When?… We haven't had a moment alone together since all of this shook out. And of all days, tonight? Our parents are supposed to meet.

"What's wrong?" Marissa asks.

"New photos," I say as I click on Justin's name.

"I'm on it," Marissa says, pulling open her browser.

Justin answers before the first ring finishes. "Lucy, I'm so sorry. I don't know why this is happening. Did you see the photos?"

"No," I glance at Marissa's fingers flying over her phone, tracking down the photos through her expertly navigated gossip sites, "but I will soon."

"I'm so sorry, Lucy."

"Don't be, it's not your fault. Or mine."

He pauses for a second. "My dad's pissed."

"Yeah, kind of dreading the conversation tonight. I was hoping a few days would give everyone time to cool off," I say as Marissa hands me her phone. "One sec, Marissa just found the photos."

The photos are at night, in back of the school, from when we chatted after the last game. A simple embrace after our first argument was edited to look like Justin had been tugging down the right side of my jeans, exposing my butt and a black thong. I don't even own a thong! Those things ride up my butt like crazy. The two I bought last year with Marissa ended up straight in the trash.

"That doesn't look good." Marissa taps my facial expression in the photo. It's pained, like I don't want him to touch me like that but he's doing it anyway. Like he's forcing himself on me. The truth? It's the look of devastation after realizing we have no idea how to stop the photos or why someone would do this to us.

Disgusting.

"You there?" Justin asks.

"Yeah. This looks really bad."

"I know." His voice drops.

"Our parents will believe us. They know you aren't like that."

"Yeah." There's a crack in the way he says it. Wait, does his dad really believe Justin would do this to me?

"It'll work out, I swear."

"I don't know. Dad's pissed. The media is bombarding his office. His public relations team has put me under house arrest. Someone showed up and pulled me out of our class review session this morning."

Marissa stands up, studying the photo on her cell in my hand. "Lucy," she whispers. "I can prove it's fake."

"Hold on, Justin," I say, covering the phone. "How?"

Marissa points to the inserted butt in the photo. "That's not your ass. We've shared too many dressing rooms. I know you tried to hide them, but I know about your scars. The ones from the locker room. Are they still there?"

Oh my gosh! She's right! The purple gashes from being shoved into the sharp locker handles... One on my hip, the other on my right butt cheek. They aren't there in this photo. But sharing them would mean telling Mom about what happened. Why I quit. Why I changed. Why I couldn't tell her… because I was afraid she'd break.

"Lucy, this is your out. It's time to give up the 'protecting my mom' act. She may be a bit looney, but she'll be okay. The only person that has to worry about those scars is Coach T and whoever the bastard is that keeps manipulating photos of you."

She's right. Why am I still trying to hide the past?

Because it's humiliating.

But it's also the key to the truth. I'm stronger than I was then. I have to share this. I pull the phone back up to my ear. "Justin, if you can get your parents to my house tonight, I can prove to everyone they are fake."

"Are you sure?" his voice raises.

"Yes. Without a doubt."

"Okay, I'm calling them. I'll see you at six?"

"Yup."

A text arrives from Mom the moment I end the call.

Mom: These new photos. Your father is going insane.

Me: Don't worry. This time I can PROVE they are fake.

Mom: I hope so. Justin should probably wear a hockey mask, just in case.

***

My face has got to be blue; I don't think I've taken a breath in three minutes. Mom pours the last glass of water at the table, and I catch Justin's eye. Other than formalities, no one has said anything since Justin's parents entered the kitchen. There's no food on the table. My parents were too frazzled to care. Apparently family members called all day, giving unwanted advice. It's been a minefield that I dodged at Laura's house, where Laura, Marissa, and I practiced what I'd say to them. Surprisingly, Laura was cool with including Marissa. I'm lucky to have a friend who's so relaxed and believes in change.

"Should I order a pizza?" I offer, breaking the awkward air.

"No thank you, Lucy," Mrs. Marshall says with a soft expression. Okay, at least she doesn't hate me. Good. That'll make mooning her a lot easier.

"We don't expect to stay very long," Mr. Marshall adds. My stomach clenches with the connotation of his words. Mrs. Marshall may not hate me, but he is definitely not a fan.

He leans in toward the table. "First, I'd like to say that I'm sorry about my son's behavior toward your daughter." He looks directly at Justin. "I'm ashamed."

Justin rubs his chin. "I've explained this, Dad. These photos aren't real."

Mr. Marshall looks back at Dad, Justin's words falling on deaf ears. "Mr. Zwindler, although you haven't yet voiced your concerns about Justin, I want you to know I understand. I promise that my son will be dealt with, harshly."

A vein pops out on the side of Dad's neck. I grasp the edge of the table. Oh crap, here we go. As he opens his mouth to speak, I cling to the table, making myself stay seated instead of flinging myself in front of Justin, protecting him from Dad's wrath.

"Mr. Marshall," Dad takes a deep breath, "I believe

your son."

Wait, what? He does?

"Justin has given me no reason to doubt his character," Dad looks at me, "and my daughter believes she can prove these photos are fake."

Mr. Marshall shifts in his seat. "I don't mean to be offensive, but it's going to take a lot more than trying to point out Photoshop blurring to convince me." He looks at Justin, who I assume tried to prove the first photos false that way.

"There's no Photoshop blurring involved," I assure him, standing up. "The proof is on me. Mrs. Marshall, would you mind stepping into the other room with me? Mom, you too?"

"No problem, dear." They stand together.

Mom leans in close as we walk out of the kitchen. "Do you have a tattoo?" she whispers harshly. I sigh, wishing that was the case. It'd be so much easier to deal with.

"No." I pull the living room curtains closed and turn to face them, looking at Mrs. Marshall. "Please know if this wasn't the only way to prove the photos are fake, that I would never in a million years do this."

One brow furrows, the other peaks.

"I have scars," I explain as I pull down the right side of my jeans and underwear, exposing my butt cheek.

Both Mom and Mrs. Marshall stare at the purple gash in the flesh of my butt and the one on my hip. Mom reaches out, touching the one on my hip.

"Are we good now?" I ask.

"Yes," Mrs. Marshall says. I quickly pull up my jeans.

"Lucy, what are those from?" Mom reaches out, trying to pull open the jeans to see the hip scar again, but I step away, buttoning my pants shut.

I take a deep breath. Okay, here it goes. "My freshman year of basketball."

"I don't understand," Mom says.

I wave toward the couch for Mom and Mrs. Marshall to sit down. I take a seat across from them on the coffee table.

"Mom, that's why I quit basketball." I take a deep breath and jump straight into my story. Mom's color drains as I describe the locker room bullying. Tears streak my face as she begins to shake. She's losing it. My heart tears open. *Please stay together, Mom.*

That's when Mrs. Marshall wraps her arm around Mom. "Sarah," she says, "it's always scary when we discover something about our children that hurt them that we didn't know about. It's okay." Mrs. Marshall looks at me. "Thank you for sharing this with me as well, Lucy. I had no idea this stuff happens at your school."

"Unfortunately, it does. It happens at a lot of schools."

"It's quite a wake-up call." She rubs Mom's shoulder.

"Lucy," Mom squeaks. "I'm sorry I wasn't there for you."

I slide off the coffee table, resting my hand on her knee. "I wouldn't let you be there for me. I didn't know how to deal with it at the time. I was too weak so I pushed you away."

"And to think of all those times I yelled at you…and you were dealing with this?" She shakes her head. "This can take years to recover from. No wonder you hid behind Marissa."

I nod. "Well, thankfully it didn't take that long. Justin helped me out a lot."

"Does he know about the scars?" Mrs. Marshall asks, her face pink.

"No." My face also heats as I debate the insinuation in her question. "But he's very perceptive. He knew I wasn't myself when we met and somehow drove me so crazy I couldn't be anyone but myself. It freed me. Thanks for raising a good guy."

Her eyes well with tears. "He's great. I can't believe we didn't believe him through all of this. He's never given us reason to doubt. Everything's been so chaotic, we figured he lost track of his priorities and morals with all the inauguration drama. We woke up wondering who our son had become and how we didn't notice his change."

"He's the same person. Amazing."

Mom closes her eyes for a moment then straightens up, miraculously pulling herself together. "It's difficult when the world is whispering lies in our ears, isn't it?"

"Yes." Mrs. Marshall wipes the wetness from under her eyes and stands up. "Okay, I need to get back into the kitchen before Jeff completely ruins everything."

As I stand back up, Mom wraps her arm around my waist. "I'm so sorry, honey."

I squeeze her in a sideways hug as we follow Mrs. Marshall to the kitchen. I'm still getting used to our relationship, now so much more affectionate than it was when I misunderstood her history of depression. So hugging her is weird. But it's nice too; it's starting to feel right.

Mrs. Marshall immediately goes to Justin, pulling him into an embrace. "I'm sorry I didn't believe you," she says to him. She turns to Mr. Marshall, whose mouth has dropped open. "Jeff, Lucy not only proved to me the photos are fake but also that we are wrong. We have not been listening to wise counsel. This is our *son*." She squeezes Justin's shoulder. "I'm ashamed I needed Lucy's proof to believe him."

Mr. Marshall looks at me. "What is the proof?"

Mrs. Marshall moves, standing between us. "I told you she's proved it. My word will be enough."

Justin's mouth parts and he shifts in his chair and stares at the floor. Clearly, his parents rarely argue. Especially around other people. I move next to him, resting my hand on his shoulder. This is good. There will be a breakthrough soon.

"Jeffery," Mrs. Marshall says. They look at one another for a moment, then finally Mr. Marshall breaks eye contact, tapping the table.

"Lucy, Mr. and Mrs. Zwindler, I apologize for not believing our children." Mr. Marshall says as he stands. He touches Justin's arm. "I'd like to talk with you at home, if that's okay."

"Right," Justin says, standing up from the table. "Thank you for having us over tonight."

"Our pleasure." Mom's voice cracks, her eyes still swollen from our conversation in the living room.

"Sarah? Are you okay?" Dad asks.

"Yes," she sighs, "but you better sit back down. Our family has more to talk about."

Justin raises an eyebrow at me. "I told our moms about my freshman year of basketball," I explain.

"Basketball?" Mr. Marshall says.

Mrs. Marshall taps his shoulder. "I'll explain on the ride home."

I follow Justin and his parents to the front door. Mrs. Marshall gives me an emotional goodbye. Justin hangs back after they go to the car. He tucks a loose strand of hair behind my ear. "What did you show my mom?"

"Some scars."

His brow furrows for a second and then he frowns. I look away, hating the scars and how ugly they are. An old fear resurfaces. What if someday the scars repulse him?

His finger tenderly lifts my chin and his lips meet mine. "I'm sure the scars are beautiful." He reaches out, touching my side and giving it a squeeze. "I'd love to see them someday," he adds with a forced chuckle.

I jump back to escape the playful attack. "Oh I'm sure you would."

Justin steps out the front door. "What? I can't help it, I'm a guy." There's something about the way he says it that isn't so fun anymore. He shoves his hands in his coat pockets as he turns and heads toward his parents' car. Shouldn't he be happier that our parents finally believe us? Now that I think about it, the bountiful, confident energy that usually embodies Justin in each movement is gone. His shoulders have been slumped like that since even before the photos. Since before election day.

How did I not notice that before?

I stand in the door, doing some stupid, over-the-top wave on my tiptoes as they pull out of the driveway. When I close the door, I brace myself as a thought hits me like a freight train.

What if Justin is changing because of me?

CHAPTER TWENTY-TWO

Justin

The way Mom's door slams when she gets out of the car shakes my spine. I follow her out. Dad's impossible to be around. He refused to speak with me before the Zwindlers' house. He didn't even give me a chance to explain what was really happening in that photo.

Mom tosses her purse on the counter, crossing her arms and staring down the door from the garage. Dad takes a few minutes before he finally walks through.

"Jeffery."

"Christy."

"*This* is what I've been talking about. You've been blind."

"You thought the photos were real too, Christy."

"No. I questioned them each time. But *you*...I can't

even…" She grabs a rag and starts rubbing the granite, then tosses it at the wall. "You aren't the man I married anymore. You aren't the man who was my hero when our son died. What happened to you?"

Holy crap. I step back. Clearly, I'm not the only one who has felt Dad turn to slime. I knew there was some friction there, but never this bad.

Dad tosses his hands up like Mom's insane. "Christy, you want to do this with Justin here? Fine." He glances at me. "Justin, can you please let your mother know who I am?" His question steals my breath. I've never been dragged into a fight like this before. He waits for me and gives me his political game face, and I feel his pull for me to agree.

No. Not happening anymore. I refuse to bend to that look again. I step next to Mom. If he wants to be immature and drag me into this, then fine. I'm eighteen. I can do immature.

"You've changed, Dad."

Dad grasps the back of his chair. "Justin, I've done what I've had to do to get this family where it is now. You need to understand that."

"This family didn't need to go *anywhere*. As long as we are together, we are a family," Mom says, her voice more solid than I've ever heard it.

"Come on, Christy, I led a family-centered campaign."

"I agree, you did." She places her hand on my shoulder. "But then you changed, taking for granted the people who were helping you most. Think of the time that Justin has given you." She glances at me and her eyes go glossy. "Time he's given us. We've taken away so much of his senior year, and we repay him by not believing him about these stupid photos."

"Justin? What do you have to say about that? You enjoyed helping, right?"

I rub my jaw as I contemplate what I'm about to do. I've always done whatever it took to please Dad. This won't please him though. If I don't tell the truth, he'll keep going down the road to being a political creep and I'll be sacrificing my own career to help him in his presidential campaign.

"I..." Shit. This is hard.

"Out with it," Dad snaps.

Oh, screw him!

"Do you hear yourself, Dad? Mom's right. I've given up so much to help you become governor. I was fine with it, until you changed."

"I still have the same policies and principals."

"Do you? You don't believe your own family! *Family-centered campaign* my ass. More like drive your family into the ground and then step on them because some weasel guy tells you to."

"Leave Paul out of this."

"Paul, *riiight.* You mean the guy who you've kept on staff despite the fact that he showed up on our family vacation in Hawaii with the contract for me to sign to be on that reality show?"

Mom gasps. "Jeffery. You didn't tell me about *that.*"

"Christy, Justin only told me about that after the trip, in the airport."

"And he's still one of your advisors?"

"It's complicated."

"No, Dad. It's not. Paul's a creep and he's turned you into one too."

"Paul comes highly recommended."

"From who? From people who've *won,* right? People who've gone on to presidential campaigns?" Mom says. "Shit, Jeff. We never wanted a presidential race, but now I overhear you talking about it with Paul all the time. You haven't even considered to speak with me."

Dad rolls his lips in for a mere second before recovering to his straight "I'm listening" political face.

"Dad. Who are you going to listen to, a guy who helps you win, or us?"

His face doesn't twitch.

"Come on, Dad," I say, sounding desperate. "This is your chance." I dig in then, using the knife I swore I'd never wield on anyone but myself. "What would Jackson say?"

I study him, waiting for some sign that he gets it. He blinks a few times, but that's it. Finally, he pulls his fingers through his hair like I do when I'm nervous. It's a gesture I haven't seen him do for a long time.

The front door squeaks open and someone clunks into our entryway. "Jeff? You in?"

"He has a key now?" Mom spits out.

Dad takes a deep breath, but doesn't answer Mom. Instead he yells, "We're in the kitchen, Paul." My heart tanks. Mom and I look at one another and she gives my palm a squeeze. I don't let go. If Dad's about to side with Paul, we need to be united.

Paul steps into the kitchen with his iPad. "Christy. Justin." He doesn't even bother to say hello. "Jeff, good news. I've set up a chat with the PR rep who turned Tantem's sex-tape scandal into a thriving career. I'm confident we can spin *this*," he eyes me, "with inside help."

"Paul," I take a deep breath, doing everything to not swear him into the ground. Mom squeezes my hand as I hear her breath catch in her throat. She looks at Dad.

His face changes then, the muscles in his cheek relax and there's that look in his eye that I've missed so much. Honesty. Comfort. Strength. Home.

Dad claps Paul on the back. "You're fired."

"Yes. I've got you scheduled to meet with him in three weeks. I think we can make it that long as long as no more photos come out."

Dad clears his throat. "Paul, did you hear me?" He takes the iPad out of Paul's hands. "You are fired."

"Excuse me?"

"Get out of my home."

Paul points at me. "You aren't listening to a kid's advice, are you, Jeff? If you want a presidential run…"

"I don't care about that right now. My son is telling the truth about the photos."

"You can't honestly believe that."

"Oh, I do."

"That'd take an extraordinary photographer with professional editing skills."

"Exactly. The type of person a producer from a reality show many know." I offer. "He's got reason to take me down. Take *you* down." I nod to Dad. "What did you think would happen, Paul, when I didn't sign that contract after he gave that crap load of money?"

Paul shifts in place and I swear a bead of sweat drops down his cheek.

"Why did you push the reality show?" Dad asks.

Paul wipes the sweat off his cheek. "This is ludicrous. You can't really believe Justin."

"Answer the question." Dad demands.

Paul's eyes dart to the floor.

"Was this the investment opportunity you mentioned last summer?" Paul doesn't react. Dad swears as he takes him by the arm and leads him from the kitchen. "You're fired. Never show up on this property again. If you do, I'm calling the police." He hands Paul his coat.

"Bad move, Marshall. Other people can hire me. Opponents. I know your weaknesses."

"His only weakness was you," I say, holding open the door.

"Goodbye, Paul," Dad says.

"I'm going to destroy you."

"I don't care. I've got what matters. You can't take that away."

Paul laughs like a freak as he steps out the door. "Don't even pretend you don't care about what others think about your term as governor. You'll never get re-elected without me."

"Re-election is the least of my concerns right now. *They* come first."

"I'm going to turn you into a fool."

"Well, good luck with that," Dad says as he closes the door in Paul's face. This should be where the crowd roars, but there's only Mom and me.

Dad rubs his face. When he uncovers it, his eyes are wet with tears. "To answer your question, Justin, a grown-up Jackson would have said 'Screw you' and stopped helping me long ago." He reaches for Mom's hand. "I am sorry that I couldn't see who I'd become." Mom starts to cry and he pulls her in. "I will fix this, Christy. I promise. I want to be your hero again."

I step away, letting them have their moment. "Justin," Dad calls when he realizes I'm down the hall. "Hold up."

He gives Mom's palms a squeeze and her cheek a kiss, leaving her crying in the entryway, and follows me down the hall. He puts both hands on my shoulders, looking me straight in the face. "I'm sorry for not believing you. I'm sorry for using you. And I'm sorry that I wasn't the example of who a man should be."

"Thanks," I say as he pulls me into a hug. "You're forgiven."

"Thank you for being such a man, son."

My eyes itch and I'm pretty sure I'm going to lose it if he says anything more. "I've got to go finish a paper."

"I understand. Let me know if you need help, okay?"

"I will."

"Sounds good," he says as he makes his way back to Mom.

***

Failure is worse than forty kicks to the balls.

Dear Mr. Marshall,

Thank you for your company's bid and proposal to paint the interior of the historic James. J. Hill Mansion. Although the proposal was researched thoroughly and within the MN Historic Society's budget, we unfortunately cannot commit to a company whose values do not reflect our own.

We appreciate the time and effort behind your proposal and wish you the best of luck in upcoming endeavors for Painting Purposeful Inc.

Sincerely,

The Minnesota Historic Society

"Son, you've got to stop reading that notice. It's not going to change anything," Dad offers from behind his laptop in the armchair next to mine. "Let me talk with them."

"No, this is my company. This is my battle." Unfortunately, it's one that's already lost. They won't understand until my name is cleared. The painting company was a way for me to escape Dad's political world, something just for me. The paper nearly folds itself along the well-worn crease as I return it to my wallet, next to Jackson's photo. My college fund and security rode on landing this gig. *Shit.*

This letter didn't surprise me though. Its arrival was inevitable. I stopped receiving updates from the board over a month ago. Since then, the photos that have surfaced are more incriminating than ever. What used to just be shots taken of me and Lucy have transitioned into me and any girl within a ten-foot radius. The miracle of Photoshop. Thankfully, no one from school has been implicated in any of the photos. But that's probably only because of my refusal to interact with any girls outside of school property or someone's home. I'm always sneaking into Lucy's house through the back basement door. Mr. Zwindler started leaving it unlocked for me, with the rule that I had to call ahead. I wish I could bring Lucy out to a movie like a normal boyfriend. But there's nothing normal about me anymore.

The weird thing is, at this point, I'm pretty sure I'm being set up for the shots. That one redhead from post-secondary who hunted me down in the parking lot to ask me a question about derivatives clearly had no idea what she was talking about. I should've left the moment she positioned herself between me and the door of the car, but I didn't want to be rude, in case her question was real. The photo of us together surfaced three hours later. I've scanned the lecture hall for her every day since. She's never there.

Dad closes his laptop, taking off his glasses and rubbing the bridge of his nose. "We'll get to the bottom of this and clear your name, Justin. I swear to you. I know you wouldn't be in this situation if it wasn't for my foolish decisions." He waves to the large oak room in the governor's mansion that he now calls an office. "It's not like I'm accomplishing much anyway."

"It's not your fault the house and senate have different majority rule. That's like asking oil and water to get along."

"They're impossible. I pursued this role to make a difference. Instead, I run up against brick walls. The only thing I've managed to accomplish is helping get that wretched girls' basketball coach fired." He sighs as he heaves himself out of the armchair. "How's Lucy?"

"She's glad he's gone but has hated the process. She's had to tell her story so many times. I hated watching her relive it. So many former students and players have stepped forward with their own stories about Coach T's ability to look the other way. She likes knowing she's not alone in her history anymore."

The iPad on the coffee table vibrates and Dad taps the screen. The pained expression on his face tells me everything I need to know.

"More photos?"

"Yup." He presses the screen a few more times, navigating somewhere new.

"Please tell me Lucy's not in them." It's so much easier to deal with the shots when she isn't involved. Her eyes are swollen for days after each release but she doesn't admit she's been crying. Not since that first photo a few months ago.

"Unfortunately, she is." He hands me the iPad. I study the photo which this website has censored with a blur over her chest. Again, I'm made to look like I just yanked and grabbed at her or something crude like that. "Where was this shot?"

"Yesterday in the school parking lot. I reached over her because she couldn't get her seatbelt unstuck." I shoot Lucy a text, giving her a heads up for the new photo.

"Photo on school property," he mutters as he types a new email to our investigator. When he finishes, he looks up at me. "How about you take the rest of the evening off? Go see Lucy? Believe it or not, I'd prefer to do your work this afternoon. Answering letters from students about how government functions is one of my favorite parts of this job."

"Thanks, I will." I scoop up my stuff as Dad looks at some of the drawings from the first graders. He pins a blue squiggle dog to the bulletin board behind him.

I duck out without a goodbye, phone to my ear. First order, calling Lucy.

When she answers her voice cracks and it's clear she just had one of those nasty snotty girl cries. "Hello?" she says again. "Justin, you there?" She sucks in a deep breath. "Justin?" she says again before she bursts back into tears.

That sound breaks my heart and, no matter how hard I try to fix the situation, I know there's nothing I can say to take away all the wounds it's caused. We've both canceled every social media account we own, but school makes everything worse. The way she ducks her head as she darts from class to class, it's killing me. It's like she's breaking all over again.

My fingers find End Call. Self-hatred follows the silence as I realize I chickened out. Hung up. Yet another epic Justin fail. I'm horrid. I don't know how to make it right though. No matter what I do, it gets worse. It's totally unfair.

I text her.

Me: Bad service. I'm on my way over. Are you okay?

A moment later she texts back.

Lucy: Yup. Just laughing over this foolish photo. Don't worry about me.

My insides burn knowing she's hiding her real reaction from me. Why is she so afraid to let me know how hard this is for her?

As I pull onto the highway, the answer is clear. She's trying to protect me from the truth.

That I should be protecting her.

There's heaviness in my gut that sucks all happiness away.

It's like I'm standing at the edge of a gorge, white rapids thrashing below. Lucy's head pops up and she calls my name before she's sucked under once more.

I'd jump without thinking about the rocks, the depth, and the rapids. I'd do anything to save her.

My knuckles have turned white from my grip on the steering wheel. I take a deep breath, knowing and hating what I have to do.

***

Her hair hangs wild, curling loosely as she greets me at the door. Those blue eyes are beautiful, even when they're bloodshot. My arms find their way around her, trying to memorize the feel of her. I breathe her in. My favorite smell will always be an apple.

"I'm sorry about the new photos, Lady." My heart sinks… Lady… My Lady. How did I let this happen to her? "I'm so sick of this."

Her face smashes into my chest. "Me too."

"You okay?"

"Yeah. I just want it to end, for both of us. It's not who we are." She looks over my shoulder at the driveway. "Where's your car?"

"I walked."

"From home?"

"Yeah, just needed to de-stress." Another lie. My car's around the block. A toy siren sounds from behind the kitchen door. "Is your family home?"

"Of course. After revealing the whole bullying thing, they barely leave me alone. It'd be nice to not have them hanging around every time you're here."

I nod, wishing they were gone too, but not for the same reason as Lucy. Her lips brush lightly against mine, and I force myself to keep still. Sensing my restraint, she ends the kiss quickly.

"Would you want to go for a walk?"

"Go outside with you? Really? Are our rules changing?" Lucy teases as she grabs her coat from the closet. My gut clenches. She has no idea how much the rules are about to change for us.

The current rules aren't working.

It's time for drastic measures if I'm going to keep her safe.

We walk hand-in-hand through the paths to a field. I

scan the trees, looking for a flash, a lens, or, I don't know, someone hanging out of a tree with a huge sign that says Camera Man. Who knows where the photographers are, but for once I'm relieved. This time, the photos will end up being a good thing.

"How's everything going with your dad?"

"Good. He's been much more himself since he fired Paul last month. We're spending a lot more time together. It's nice."

"That's great."

"Yeah." Ugh, lame response. Seriously, I have to make this believable.

"You okay?" Her question is my window of opportunity. Spinning her around to face me, I take both of her hands.

"No."

"What's wrong?" The depth of her blue eyes torture me. For a moment, I almost lose resolve and tell her all about the bid rejection on the James J. Hill House. Or tell her how much it kills me that she keeps hiding how much the photo scandal is affecting her. Instead, I rub the stubble on my jaw and step away from her. Time to play douchebag.

"Lucy, this isn't working." My eyes dart away from hers, both purposely so she'll think I'm immature and, more selfishly, because I'm not strong enough to watch her go through this.

"What do you mean?" Her voice is soft.

"Us," I say bluntly. "We aren't working out." I pull my hands through my hair, flexing under my sweater to be the egotistical guy she hated last summer.

It takes her a moment but, finally, she steps away from me. I glance up, watching the clouds reflect in her eyes. "But…" She hesitates and looks at me. Those blue eyes penetrate my heart. She reaches out, placing her hand on my heart. "Justin Marshall, don't you dare act like the hero right now."

Bullseye.

The weight of her hand is easy to remove. "I'm sorry, Lucy. I wish that was the case, but none of this feels right."

"Of course it doesn't, you fool. You're breaking up with me." There's fire behind her words and that's the only thing that gives me the strength to keep going. I've seen that fire before. She's strong enough to move on and away from me.

"It's been a long time coming," I lie.

"How so?"

"I don't know. We just don't mesh right. I can't explain it. We're rarely together anymore. I've had a lot of time alone. Time to think." Her brow arches. She's totally not buying it. Why didn't I plan this out? "The truth is, you're not my type. You're a bit too awkward and your family, well..." I can't say it. I can't actually throw her mom on the train tracks after knowing what they've been through.

Her lips part and her face drains of color. It's slight, but her shoulders slump.

I hate myself.

"It's time for me to move on." I barely get the words out.

"To the other girls?" she whispers, giving me an out that I'd only take if I was cruel. There's no way I can take it that far.

"There aren't any other girls." I take a quick breath, ready to make the final split. "Don't you dare insinuate I'd cheat on you. You know I'm not like that."

Her breath catches on her lip, hanging visible in the chilled air between us. Tears spill over her cheeks.

"I'm just not feeling it anymore, okay? Unfortunately, we aren't meant to be." I force annoyance into my tone, hating myself with each syllable. We stand, several feet apart, staring at the ground. I need to push it further. Give her a reason to hit me.

"But, listen," I begin, ignoring my heart screaming in the flames. "I'm open to benefits occasionally."

Her eyes fly to mine. "Benefits?"

I stretch out my shoulder to make myself look like a cock. "Yeah, you know—making out or whatever. Maybe next year in college, you can be my stress relief?" The words that fly out of my mouth bring a bit of bile with it. I swallow, not believing I know how to *play* this guy so well. It shouldn't come this easily.

She takes a step closer. "Excuse me?"

"Maybe if we're not together, we can actually get away with some of the stuff made up in the photos. Hands-on experience?"

With one step, her palms fly into my chest, throwing her weight at me. I fly backwards, taking the hit and landing dramatically in the snow. Grabbing my chest, I groan.

There's your photo, dude.

Lucy steps over me, a sob escaping as she rushes back to the path. Back to home, where her parents are waiting. Good parents that won't let me down in their love for her.

When she's out of sight, I brush the snow from my hair and flip off the tree-line. There. Happy now? I push myself up and out of the snow, walking along the tracks Lucy and I made together. Forward, I've got to move forward and get to my car that I conveniently parked around the corner.

With the door finally shut, I throw on my sunglasses, seeking safety from any lurking photographers. The pain comes then, that horrid break I knew would sever my soul. "Lucy," I whisper through quick breaths that fight back tears. It's no use though, the tears come, shaking my chest as the reality hits that I just forced away the only person in my life who feels right.

Lucy, the girl I'll love forever. My Lady.

CHAPTER TWENTY-THREE

Lucy

Mom grabs me as my knees crash into the kitchen floor.

"What's happening?" Dad's voice bounces through my head, but I can't get the words out past the sobs. Mom rubs my shoulders. "It'll be okay, Lucy."

"What will be okay? What's happened? More photos?" Dad rushes to the laptop.

"No," I gasp. "Yes. I…" Gagging takes over, a bowl lands in front of me just in time.

"Was she poisoned? Sarah, I'm calling the cops."

"No, Dan," Mom says softly. "It's not that. It's…"

"Justin," I whisper. "He…" But the words won't come out. Instead I fold in half, pressing myself into the floor harder with every new sob, wishing they'd swallow me whole.

"Oh." Dad's hands lift me from the floor. "Let's get you to your room, okay?"

"He doesn't love me."

Dad kisses my head as he leads me up the stairs, Mom right behind. Somehow, they get me to bed, turned toward the wall. Mom slides beside me, resting her hand on my back. Her hand is my constant as my body freaks out. Sobbing, gagging, gasping for breath.

Justin.

I know he's been keeping his distance since the photographs, but I still can't believe I missed his shift.

I'm such a fool.

He too easily tossed me aside. His love was never real.

CHAPTER TWENTY-FOUR

Justin

Nothing can prepare you for breaking two hearts at once. I'm an expert at filleting a heart. Every text I've ignored is me slicing into her and back into myself. At least the texts have stopped. It's been over two weeks since she's reached out. A full month of ignoring Lucy. But it worked; she's off the internet, out of the paper. Her last photo showed her shoving me to the ground. She came out with her reputation intact, looking confident and strong.

The C minus marked on the top of my assignment actually feels good, finally a punishment for hurting the love of my life. I grab my bag as the teacher stacks the essay tests up front. Jen leans over. "Where are you going?"

"Ditching class."

"Justin…" She grabs me, dragging me to her side.

"Don't you dare miss this essay. I can't cover for you right now."

"No need to try," I say, enjoying the burn of what my actions will surely bring me.

"You'll fail the class."

"I know. I'm cool with that." It feels good to brush past her after all of the lectures she's given me about breaking up with Lucy. She thinks I'm an ass, and maybe I am, but she's seriously getting annoying. The exit door at the top of the steps makes a giant creak as I yank it open. Nice angsty exit. No wonder people make stupid decisions. This rush is total freedom.

The wormy smell of spring hits me like oil-based paint as I step outside. March doesn't mean sunshine and flowers in Minnesota. It means filthy snow, heavy clouds, and a general feeling of being pissed off.

As I yank open my car door, I'm jolted sideways. What the hell? Ian stands behind me, holding me back from the car with the strap of my bag.

"What's up? We haven't talked in a while," Ian says, without his usual smile.

"I've been busy."

"Dude, you don't have to lie. I know you broke up with Lucy."

"Did she tell you?" The jealousy from those winter nights he spent with Lucy in a hotel resurfaces. "Did you mop up her tears, too?"

Ian takes a step away from me, dropping the strap of my bag. "Whoa, who the hell are you?" His words are a punch to my gut. That's a good question. I don't even know.

He turns to leave but pauses to say one more thing. "For the record, I did mop up her tears. I never thought they'd end, but they did."

"About time."

He stares at me for a second, then waves me away. "I was planning on asking your permission, but never mind. If I ask Lucy out, you obviously don't give a rip."

Dating Lucy?

What?

He leaves then, sliding into the rusty shell of what was once a Toyota Corolla. His engine chokes to life and he peels out of the parking lot, leaving me in the thickness of the gas fumes. My palm flies to my phone, opening it to read Lucy's last text one more time. The only text from all of her attempts to communicate that I refused to believe. Is it the truth?

Lucy: I'm over you now. I realize what we had wasn't real love. Goodbye.

My phone slides from my hand, bouncing on the pavement. The screen faces up at me, splintered like a spiderweb. Pretty sure my soul looks like that too. Why am I such an idiot? Here I've been going through self-destruction because of guilt and Lucy's already moved on.

I grab a pen and run back toward the building. Well, if she can't recognize what we had as true love, then maybe she never really loved me at all. The thought of her not loving me burns in my chest. My arrogance will forever be a battle for me. Losing her love never seemed like an option, even when I split things off.

The lecture door opens with another creak. All eyes stare at me as I walk down the steps to the front of the room. If Lucy can move forward, so can I. There'll be tons of girls to date at college. All those ice cream flavors to sample until I find the right one. Lucy was just a temporary distraction.

Blowing this essay is no longer an option. It's my ticket to moving on from the ache that's consuming me.

The professor lifts his eyes as I approach his desk. I bend down and offer one word of explanation under my breath. "Diarrhea."

CHAPTER TWENTY-FIVE

Lucy

The shards left in my heart make breathing hard. I move through life struggling to keep the sting of bitterness from my tongue. For once I'm thankful for my bullied year; it taught me how to power through hell.

Laura and Marissa hold the coffee shop door open for me. My coffee shop. Sure, Justin introduced me to the place, but it's not like we went here together more than a few times. He was always way too busy with that stupid calendar. Ian waves to us from the music corner while we order our drinks. Straight up, black coffee for me.

Laura's eyebrows bop toward Ian's corner. Marissa nudges me as he starts singing into the microphone. They're right, his voice is totally gorgeous. My face heats a bit and I bite my lip, embarrassed he invited me to come tonight.

He probably meant alone, but I had to bring Laura and Marissa with. After everything with Justin, I don't want to start anything new without girlfriend approval.

Marissa throws her hair up in a top bun and I can't help but smile. Her transformation has made my heartbreak bearable. Her eyeliner isn't as thick and her skirts aren't as short. Her real laugh is actually pleasing and cute, instead of that awful "man" attracting cackle she created long ago. The gross guys at school are finally leaving her alone, and the nice ones are starting to notice her. It's funny though, she's clueless when a real guy seems to actually be interested in her. Weird.

My body's turned, listening to Ian sing as I try to force out all thoughts of Justin. The How Did This Happen? Didn't He Love Me? He'll Come Around moments are always bombarding me. But this evening, I'm focusing on Ian.

Laura's right. He's really sweet, smart, and when he sings he's super hot. He's never asked me about the photos, but he has to know.

Instead, he spent the last month helping me with my homework on Saturday mornings or texting me songs to listen to and stupid jokes. His approach has been gentle and I appreciate that.

His eyes meet mine and my stomach tickles. That's good, right? What I had with Justin, my body's overwhelming chemical need to be near him, was only a product of lust.

Maybe a tiny tickle is how real love starts?

Ian's blue eyes have a way of smiling that I like. The last strum of his guitar comes sooner than I want. I shift uncomfortably, knowing tonight is different. Marissa leans over. "He's nice. Get a grip. This is no big deal."

Ian puts his guitar away and then joins the table, sliding in next to me without hesitation. I like that, it's natural.

"You were awesome," I say, forcing myself to give him a playful nudge. This is how flirting works, right? With Justin, these moments just happened. It's weird to try to create them now.

"Thanks, it was great of you guys to come. Want to play a game?"

"Yes! That sounds awesome! Luke is too wrapped up in March Madness to have any real fun. Can I pick?" Laura asks, not waiting for an answer and bounding from the booth to the shelf of games on the wall. I eye the cribbage board that's totally my thing with Ian now. If Laura wasn't here, Ian wouldn't have even asked. The board would arrive with his drink.

Laura returns with a bright pink and purple box. "Trivial Pursuit?"

"Sure," Ian says as Marissa groans. "Have you played before?" he asks with a light laugh.

"Nope, but come on. We all know I'm doomed."

"You never know. You may surprise yourself," Ian says as he opens the box to set up the game. The game begins and quickly I realize I'm horrible at this. Even though it's an updated version, I've spent the last few years so self-involved that I've been clueless about what's going on in the world. Laura kicks butt with the history category, I hold my own in science, and Marissa nails the entertainment questions.

Ian's pie fills in quickly. I lean over and whisper, "You're not in some crazy Trivial Pursuit homeschooling club, are you?"

He nudges me softly. "We have a monthly tournament." I smile back, totally not able to read if he's serious. Maybe he does? I don't want to insult him or something. Not that that would be lame. But… come on. It kind of would be, right?

Marissa finally lands on Arts and Literature and immediately she's biting her lip. Ian reads the question: "What potion does Professor Slughorn ask the class to make in Harry Potter and the Half-Blood Prince of which Harry first opts to use the scribbled advice of the Half-Blood prince?"

Laura laughs.

"Next," I say, mocking the words Marissa has used with every category but Entertainment. Marissa's laugh doesn't follow though. Instead, her head bobs, her eyes focused as her finger traces a scratch on the table. Finally, she looks up and takes a deep breath.

"Draught of the Living Death," she says.

"Correct!" Ian chimes, giving her a high-five.

"What?" Laura says. "Are you kidding me? You're a Harry Potter geek?"

Marissa shrugs. "They're awesome books. I have no problem with it." Awesome books? I've never seen anything with words in Marissa's hands but girly magazines!

Ian leans toward Marissa, putting down the card with a mischievous look in his eye. "When wizards travel by fireplace, what is that method of transportation called?"

She rolls her eyes. "The Floo Network. That wasn't even hard. Next," she says with a grin.

"What is the spell that protects Harry Potter from Voldemort?"

Marissa sighs as she sits back in the booth. I wait for her to take out her bun, toss her hair, do her laugh… something flirtatious. I mean, Ian's playing right into her but she doesn't budge. Instead, she crosses her arms. "That's the stupidest question ever. Everyone knows that Harry is protected not by a spell, but the oldest magic of all. *Love*."

Laura squeals. "Oh my gawd. I love when people turn my life upside down. You," she hugs Marissa, "…have just overhauled my concept of you and *I love it*! My little brother owns all the movies, want to come over and watch sometime?"

Marissa pulls her iPad from her purse and taps around a few times. "I've got the special editions on here if you want to see them with me?" The smile on Marissa's face is brilliant as she proudly passes around the iPad. Yup, they're all there. All eight movies. Wow.

Ian whistles. "Nice, Marissa. Very nice."

"Thanks," she says simply, dropping her eyes from his and taking a sip of her latte. Then she turns to Laura. "Do you want to check out the boutique across the street with me?"

"Yeah, that sounds fun. Those hats in the window are awesome." Laura snatches her purse and rises.

I suppress a groan. Clearly the old lady hats in the window across the street are everything but awesome. The place probably smells like cats. I doubt it's even open past eight on a Friday night. Ian and I stand up, giving them each brief hugs goodbye. Laura winks at me as she leaves. Ian chuckles so I know he saw it. Laura, seriously!

"Thanks for coming tonight," Ian says as we sit back down. "I love it when you're here when I play."

"You're really good."

"Lots of practice."

"Maybe, but there's natural talent there. That type of stuff can't be learned."

"Thanks," he says, shifting a bit closer to me. His breath quickens and I brace myself for what he's about to ask me. My heart throttles forward, trying to get me to run to the door. It's not ready for another guy. Clearly.

But I am. My heart just needs to get over the break. Move on. The pain of sulking in my memories of Justin's touch and smell, or… well… whatever he did to me, is killing me. I need new memories to cling to now.

"Lucy, would you like to go out to dinner sometime? Would that be of interest to you?"

Would that be of interest to you? I bite my lip, refusing to acknowledge the awkwardness of his homeschooled charm.

"That sounds nice," I say.

"Really?" He sounds a bit too eager, like Alex used to.

"Of course," I say, my words a bit forced. "We'll have fun."

"Great. Do you like Mexican food? I was thinking I could take you to this great place in Minneapolis next Saturday night. That is, if you're available."

Suddenly, my palms grow sweaty. Dinner, alone with Ian? What happens after the dinner, after the ride in the car? Do we make out? I still dream about Justin's lips every night. Will I only think about Justin if I kiss Ian? Oh my gosh. I'd be cheating on Ian without even trying… Cheating on him with a guy who would only want me around for benefits. That's absurd. I can't let this happen.

"Or we can just hang out here, if you want," Ian adds quickly.

"Uh…" I open my phone, looking for a way out. My face heats, worried he'll misinterpret the crash of my heart against my ribcage for lust. My calendar finally loads and a safer way to handle our first date stares back at me. The big spring break party at Watson's house. There'll be tons of people there. I won't actually be alone with him. He doesn't seem like the guy who'll make out in a public place. The party's perfect.

"Actually…" I point to the event on my calendar. "There's this spring break party I was hoping to go to that night. Want to come with me to that?"

"Yeah, that sounds solid."

"Great."

We sit silently for a moment and I pray the heat from my freak out isn't sending mixed signals. Please don't kiss me right now. He slides a micro-millimeter closer and that's when I launch into full freak out. Suddenly, I'm crawling over him, out of the booth. Sure, I probably just shoved my butt in his face but I need my space. "How about another game of cribbage?" I offer the moment I realize how awkward I'm being.

"Sure. Why not?"

"Awesome-sauce!" I say. Oh my gosh, seriously? Who am I? I grab the cribbage board and return to the booth, this time sliding in across from him. He smiles at me as he shuffles the deck.

"You should know that I've been studying techniques since you last beat me. You're going down."

I laugh, thankful that Ian transitioned our situation back to the friendship side of things. "We'll see about that," I say with a forced mischievous glance as he gives me my hand of cards. The numbers are like a punch to the gut though. Numbers always remind me of how good Justin is at Math.

CHAPTER TWENTY-SIX

Justin

Alex tosses me the ball and I square up. *Swish.* Seventh three-pointer in a row.

"You're on fire, man!"

"Thanks," I pant, receiving another toss, which I bank off the backboard.

"Eight!"

"I feel good," I say, wiping the sweat from my face. "Thanks for getting me out here." I square up for another shot, but he doesn't toss the rock. What the heck? I'm killing it here.

He palms the ball. "I want to talk."

"What about?"

"What do you think?"

"Listen, I'm sorry I didn't name you as captain of the

basketball team. You'll only be a sophomore next year. Don't worry about it. Your time will come."

"No, idiot. Not about that. About you. How are you, man?"

"I'm good. Fine." I slap my hands. "Now, toss me the rock." He does and I throw it back up. The ball ticks the rim. Crap. Streak's over.

"Sorry," Alex says. He picks up the ball and swishes the net with a simple hook shot. "Are you okay, though? I haven't seen you around school in ages."

"I only go for a few classes every other day now. Most everything's at the University now."

"Got it," Alex says. "How's the photo thing?"

"Still happening. I'm getting over it though." I force out a grin. "Actually, there are some benefits to it."

"How so?"

"Girls at the U recognize me. Prospects are everywhere." There's that nag to click my brain out of douchebag mode and remember the feeling of Lucy in my arms. I can't give into that though. It's not an option. I'm moving on. The world is at my fingertips… all that and more.

Alex laughs. "I don't think you've ever had the problem of prospects, dude, and you probably never will. You're freakin' Justin Marshall."

Yeah, I'm freakin' Justin Marshall!

"But," Alex says as he sits on the court to take off his Retro Air Jordan XIII's, switching to street shoes, "that's the thing. Are you?"

"Uh…" That slimy feeling returns to my gut. Like I haven't showered since I saw Lucy standing over me in the snow.

"Remember last week at dinner? When I went to the

bathroom at our big family meal? Okay, so don't hate me. But I kind of looked through your phone."

"*What?*"

"Sorry! I needed to know what was going on. You broke up with the love of your life and now you're awol. I was worried."

"Don't ever look at my phone again."

He holds up his hands as he stands up. "Dude. Calm down. I won't." He pulls on a pair of sweats over his shorts. "Justin, I've just got to know… why didn't you reply to all of Lucy's texts and calls? It's not like you." His words are venom to my soul.

"It was necessary," I say through gritted teeth.

"Whatever you say, man, but that's not the Justin I know."

I take the ball from him as we cross the parking lot. "People grow and change. It's okay."

He doesn't answer this time, instead biting his lip as we walk home. "No," he says finally. "I'm sorry, it's not okay. It's not okay at all. I saw that other pic on your phone too."

My gut crashes through to the pavement. Crap. The one of the blond in the blue bra? I thought I deleted that.

"Why is that there?"

"Girls send them to me now. Like they are auditioning for a cameo in these stupid photos. They have no idea they're fake."

"Your number is unlisted."

Okay, so maybe I've started handing out my number to girls after class, but I had no idea they'd be sending me selfies with puckered lips and way too much cleavage. Not that they're not attractive, it's just… so different. "They just find it."

"Right... So, are you dating again?"

"Not yet."

"Why not?"

"No one interesting enough, I guess?"

"Sure it's because they aren't Lucy?"

"Lucy's moved on, Alex."

He rolls his eyes. "You don't see her at school anymore. She walks through the motions but the life and spark in her step are gone. She's broken again, and it sucks."

Broken again?

"You're wrong. She's stronger than that."

"I don't know. Pretty sure she's just excellent at putting on a good show."

I kick the last of a mound of brown snow in the air as my heart breaks through the douchebag wall I've built. I'm total scum.

"You're not lying, Alex, are you? There's no way she can still like me after what I said to her."

"What did you say?"

I cringe.

"Come on, it can't be that bad."

"I told her that we could still have benefits…"

"What?" He punches me on the shoulder; the pain burrows deep. Frick. He's gotten strong. "For, Lucy," he says under his breath. He glares at me, the look of disappointment so thick in his eyes.

"Alex, it was the only way to make a clean break. I knew the benefits thing would be so insulting that she'd step away."

"But why were you trying to get her to leave? I thought you loved her."

"I do!"

"Then why the hell did you break up with her?"

"It's really hard to explain. The photos, they just took over everything. It was making her miserable. She deserved better than that."

"Honestly, the way she moves so lifelessly now, she had it better before." The truth of his words twist the knife that I shoved into my gut the moment I told Lucy I wanted to break up.

"Do you think she'd ever forgive me?"

"Justin, come on. Believe a little. You know love is stronger than that." He kicks snow at me, finally smiling again. "So are you done being a total fart now? The whole frat attitude is really getting old. Even Luke is getting sick of you. And the whole photo thing? Why isn't that over yet? Uncle Jeff is the frickin' governor. Just hire some photographer to follow you around when you're alone with a girl. The moment a scandalous photo surfaces, show the proof that you and the chick were dressed and eating ice cream."

His words hit me like a two-by-four. "Alex...holy crap! You're right!" We're wasting time investigating this reality show guy, when we could put a stop to the photos right away. When we stop the photos, we can continue with the investigation. Hell, I don't even care if we ever found out who did it. As long as the photos stopped, I'm thrilled.

"Really?"

"Yes!" I grab him by the back of the shirt and toss him in the car. "We're going to go tell my dad right now."

"Can you drop me at home? Uncle Jeff's not exactly a fan of me anymore."

"Alex, if he didn't like you, he wouldn't have sat you down on New Year's Day and lectured you like that."

"It sucked."

"Well, you deserved it. Plus, it's way better than your dad doing it, right?"

"For sure. Dad's pissed about my grades right now."

"Why? You showed them to me. You've done so much better so far. A couple A's and a few B's for midterm. Not bad at all."

Alex taps the back of his head against the seat. "You don't understand."

"Listen, I'm sick of you saying I don't understand what's happening in your life. I want to know what's going on with you. You're like my brother. Help me understand."

"Dad's pissed because I'm not..."

"Good at showering?"

He doesn't laugh, instead looking at the floor mat with the most solemn expression I've ever seen on him before. "Because I'm not you, Justin. He thinks I'm a fool."

Not me? Why the heck is Uncle Alex comparing Alex to me? I lost the James J. Hill House. I lost Lucy. I lost my frickin' sanity. But it's not like Uncle Alex knows any of this about me. Since the moment Jackson passed away, I've kept up with my act. My confidence, politeness, and brains all block everyone from seeing the truth: that I'm just as messed up as they are. In truth, trying to hide that fact may be the most messed up thing of all.

"Justin," Alex says, interrupting my self-loathing. "You've got to go get Lucy, man. I've heard of this thing called forgiveness. Pretty sure Lucy can do that."

"You think so?" The weight of one brick lifts from my chest and a want surfaces. No, a need. I need Lucy.

"She's back to being friends with Marissa now who, turns out, is actually pretty cool."

"Yeah, I noticed she's changing. Good for her."

"Yeah. So…? Are you going to get her?"

His question pours energy into my soul, giving it enough strength to throw off all the bricks I've used to burry my love for her. Suddenly, I'm needing and craving Lucy with more intensity than I've ever felt before.

"Dude. Are you going?"

"Am I? Yes. Should I? No. But I'm selfish, I need her back."

"Good for you, man!" That familiar bounce is back in his tone. It seems when I'm myself he's more himself too.

"Now I just need to figure out a plan. No, not a plan. An epic plan. A way to sweep her off her feet. She'll never see it coming. I bet I could get some of Dad's contacts to help me get an in at—"

"Don't plan it, idiot," Alex interrupts. "You don't have any time."

"What do you mean?"

"Lucy's bringing Ian—as a date—to Watson's party tonight."

CHAPTER TWENTY-SEVEN

Lucy

There's something magical about disappearing into a crowd. Ian looks back over his shoulder at me, eyes wide, as I leave for the bathroom. The moment I step away from his side, other girls pounce. He's cute as he smiles back at me, rolling his eyes. He's so not used to being the *hot new guy*. He'll be okay though, he's with Marissa. She'll fend the girls off for me.

It's crazy how confident I am in that. I shouldn't be with our history, but I trust her now. She hit rock bottom and has rebuilt in a way I have to respect, like the way she's held her head high through school with those New Year's Eve photos still floating around. I can't do that at all.

Who knew that Marissa could be so strong? In a non-witchy way?

260

I run downstairs to the bathrooms outside of Watson's home theatre. The line usually isn't that long down there. I only have to wait for three people before I get my chance at total escape.

I close the door, welcomed with the scent of vanilla bean. I sit on the floor, with my back against the door. No use looking in the mirror. There's no way my makeup is smudged after all the primer I put on. Thanks to Laura's hands and her super hairspray, my hair is Pinterest perfect tonight. It's actually a really cool bun wrap thing with a side braid, but I don't feel at all like myself. Maybe it's because every cell in my body is fully aware that any moment Justin may walk through Watson's front door. What if he brings a date? One of those girls from the photos? Laura said Luke saw him with a new brunette downtown. Seeing a girl on his arm would be almost as painful as the daily realization that I'll never feel his embrace again. Thankfully, he hasn't shown up and we've been here a while. Maybe he's given this territory over to me too?

Justin's rarely in school now, except for his elective art and cooking courses, which keeps him grounded in high school, allowing him to take a near full course load through post-secondary. He probably could have started college a year early, but this way he could still be captain of the basketball team and get free college courses.

It's good he's not there. If I had to see him every day, I'm pretty sure I'd just end up a puddle on the floor. Or suspended for yelling at him. Or expelled for punching him, if he seriously ever tried to take me up on *benefits*. What an ass.

God, there's so much I want to say to him. How could he yank the rug from underneath me like that? It's not like he gave me any hints it was coming… except for how stressed and sad he had become, but I did everything I could to protect him from my own added stress. Other than that one time, I never let him see me cry about the photos. I always held it together for him.

I worked so hard to keep things between us stable while he dealt with all the crap with his dad. It's not fair that he couldn't see that. That all he saw was a problem and he ran. There wasn't a problem. I made sure of it. It's almost like he snapped and became someone else.

Love. It was so solid, then fleeting. I know it was there, we had it. I know it. Nothing has ever felt so real to me. But then love shouldn't end so quickly. Love doesn't work like that. Right?

My heart jumps the moment my mind drifts to love. No, stupid soul. Don't you dare start loving him again. You deserve someone who will actually love you back.

I quickly pee, seizing the chance while the line isn't ridiculously long. Okay, it's time to go back out there. I blink a few times in the mirror, trying to brighten the blue of my eyes or something like that. I don't know? Look alive? What if Ian makes a move and I'm dead-faced. Or, worse, what if I kiss like a corpse?

Can heartbreak kill an ability to kiss?

My stomach twists. I really don't want to find out. Why am I doing this to myself? I'm not ready.

Someone knocks on the door. Right, time to face the night.

I step out to a large line. "Sorry," I say. "Had no idea people were waiting out here." My face flushes as I step away, thankful I didn't actually spend that time pooping. The vanilla bean smell should clue them in that I was just fixing my hair or something.

I dive back into the crowd, stopping briefly to chat with Jaclyn about the awesome prospect of a new coach. Anyone is better than Coach T. I excuse myself eventually to get back to Ian, not wanting to be rude. I duck under some idiot who's playing invisible table tennis.

Suddenly, there's a light palm on my hip that sends sparks up my spin. Another hand rests on the small of my back, its heat radiating in a way that makes me want to melt to the floor.

I freeze. Only one person on earth makes me feel this way. Justin.

He leans in, warm breath on my ear. "You shouldn't be here with him," he whispers.

"Oh?" I say after a few deep breaths.

"You belong with me."

His hand finds mine and he lightly tugs. My heart thrashes wildly inside my chest, it's taken over and soon I'm following him out the back door and out onto the abandoned back patio, out of the light, our breath visible in the air. Those strong, warm arms wrap around me, settling into their old place around my hips. "I've missed you, Lady," he whispers in my ear.

Lady? Warmth floods my chest. No, I'm stumbling into what he wants. This isn't how it works anymore. Lady? No, I'm sorry, his *Lady* is supposed to be the one he loves. What he did to me? That's not love.

I step quickly out of his embrace. "Excuse me? I'm not your lady anymore."

Justin reaches out. "Lucy, I'm sorry. God," he yanks his hands through his hair. "I miss you so much. I'm sorry. I was stupid."

"You call what you did stupid?" Laughter flies from my chest. I've shifted into total maniac mode. "No, Justin. You showed your true colors. I'm not playing your game."

"This isn't a game, Luce."

"You're serious?"

"Yes. Please." That look in his eyes hurts but I'm not an idiot. I know what he wants.

"I refuse to be a *benefit* when you feel like it. That's not how love works."

Justin groans. "Lucy, you don't honestly believe I meant that?"

Believe him?

"About the benefits?" He swears. "I said that to get you to hate me."

"Get me to hate you?" Why would he do that? I glare at him, adrenaline turning my blood sour. "Congratulations. It worked."

"Lucy, I love—"

"*Don't* say it." My chest burns with hope. The pain is too much. No. I refuse to go through this again. "I've moved on."

"Hear me out. I broke up with you to protect you, Lucy, from the photos. That's over now. News will break tomorrow, exposing all of the photos as false. My name will be cleared. It'll be easier now."

"Easier? Easier? Don't lecture me about easy, Justin. Breaking my heart was the right thing to do? I'm sorry. I don't call that easy at all."

"You must have known though, Lucy. I still love you. Haven't stopped."

I rub my temple. "Let me get this straight. You loved me, so you dumped me to protect me from the drama?"

"Exactly." He holds out his hands for me to come to him. Uh, no.

"Justin, I didn't even let you see the *drama*. I held it together for you."

"Right, and that was wrong too. I knew the photos were killing you, but you wouldn't share that with me at all. I heard you on the phone when I called you that afternoon. You were bawling your eyes out."

He heard me? Then why didn't he respond? He's demented. Instead of feeling loved, he's stirred an angry fire in my soul.

"So, you heard me cry? Then you pretended you didn't have service, texted, and came over to end everything."

He doesn't answer. Yeah, that's what I thought.

"Oh my God. Do you realize what a jerk you are? You can't honestly believe you broke up with me to protect me still, do you?"

"I did it because I love you."

I take a step closer to him now. "No," I whisper. "You broke up with me because you couldn't handle the situation. It wasn't perfect anymore."

"I was handling it fine."

"Were you? Instead of reaching out and welcoming my emotions, you broke up with me. I was *too much* for you. The photos made everything fall apart. The moment life didn't feel perfect anymore, you bolted." I step past him, ready to say goodbye forever. No, he doesn't even deserve a goodbye now, but I can't help but look back one last time.

"Your conceit and pride in perfection ruined us. Not those photos. Those photos were fake, what you did was real."

I slide open the back door, stepping back into the

crowd. My face feels wild but I don't care. I stomp up the stairs and find Ian in the corner. He's hanging out with Luke and Laura. Marissa's sitting a few feet away, swinging her legs on a bar stool.

"Long line?" she says.

"Something like that." I slide past her with a fake smile and take Ian's hand. He wraps his other hand around mine as he continues to talk to Luke about the logistics behind the latest Zombie film. Ian's hand is warm, the calluses from playing his guitar are thick on his fingertips.

Marissa's eyes smile at me as she climbs back on her stool. The last time I was here, she was dancing on tables. Now, she's the calm, relaxed girl. It's still odd to see her without a swarm of icky guys following her. I don't think they even recognize her anymore.

I study her as I try to push my confrontation with Justin from my mind. How come she isn't always so pissed at her life? Her mom's a drunk. Her dad's always absent, even when they're in the same room. She brings her camera to her face and snaps a few photos of the crowd. No wonder she's always loved photography. It's her only escape.

Occasionally, her eyes flicker my direction but they don't land on me. They land on Ian.

Oh my gosh.

Ian.

Why hadn't I thought of it before?

Does Marissa like him? She always takes the farthest seat away from him at the coffee shop. And she's quiet around him too, only adding to the conversation, never directing where it'll go.

Ian and Marissa? He's completely outside of her reputation. Yeah, he knows about her photos, too, but I'm certain he'll never look at them. He's way too respectable for that. Marissa would have a chance to start fresh with Ian. Oh my gosh, they should date! Ian's hand squeezes mine as if in confirmation of my thoughts.

I squeeze back before I let go, moving to Marissa's side. "Hey."

"Hey, having fun?"

"No. I spoke to Justin downstairs."

"Wow. How'd it go? Are you okay?"

I blow out a long breath. "It's definitely over. I got some closure." Total lie, but whatever. That's the closest to closure I'll ever get. I glance over at Ian. "He's cute, right?"

She doesn't even glance his way as she says, "One hundred percent hot, yup." Wow, she really does respect me now. Where she'd once drool and ogle, now she doesn't even look.

"You should go talk to him," I whisper.

"What?" she says, shifting down from the stool.

"Marissa, I can tell you like him. I…well, I mean, I like him but I'm not *into* him like you are. I don't think I'm ready to date, yet."

"Lucy, don't be insane. Ian's awesome."

"No, honestly. I'm not ready for this." A weight lifts from my shoulders and suddenly, it's easier to breathe. It's okay that I'm not ready. It's fine. I'll go at life and relationships at my own speed. Ian's not really the type of guy I'd ever fall for anyway. My type of guy is… well, other than Justin, I don't know. I'll have to figure that out. But Ian? Even that tickle I had around him last week is gone now. "Ian's not meant for me. Go hang out with him."

"Lucy, I'm not going to throw myself at him just because you say so."

"Right. No, of course not. I'm just saying feel free to start a friendship with him. Not that you need my permission—"

"No, I do after what I did to you," she says softly.

"Okay, well then, I'm giving it to you. Ian's fantastic. Become friends with him and see if it goes anywhere."

"I don't know."

"Why not?"

"That's terrifying, Lucy. Becoming friends with a guy and then risking it for a date or two?"

"Marissa, how else are you supposed to find love? Can you picture throwing yourself at him the way you used to?"

"No, he's too smart. Too Kind. Too..." She blushes. "He's so different then the other guys."

"See, that's why you should just start hanging out with him."

She nods. "We'll see."

"At least consider it. I'm telling Ian when we leave that we're not going to work out. He'll always be one of my good buddies but I can't really see myself making out with him, ya know?"

Marissa laughs. "No. I don't actually. I've been picturing making out with him since I first heard him sing. Seriously..." she flushes, "he's so frickin' hot."

"Then hang out with him, okay?"

"Okay, I'll see what happens. And, Lucy?" She tugs at my hand after I pull out of the hug. "Don't give up on Justin just yet."

"What do you mean?"

"Love is hard. Really hard. Not that I know...I mean, look at you and me. It took us a while but through the pain we found friendship. I'm glad the pain happened. Without it, I'd probably be on a beach somewhere posing for some Girls Gone Wild-ish video."

"So you're saying Justin dumping me is saving me from Girls Gone Wild?"

"Something like that." She squeezes my hand. "If the love is there, it'll work out."

"I had no idea you were so wise."

"I've been hiding lots."

"Why?"

"You know better than anyone—it's scary to be yourself."

Someone taps my shoulder and I jump. Justin again? I whip around, not ready, but I can't not look. Jen smiles back at me and gives me a hug. "I've missed you." Her words mean so much. We've seen each other a few times in groups but, with the breakup, I knew she'd stand with Justin after all the support he's given her. And that's okay. I'd never want to break their friendship up.

"I've missed you back," I say, hugging her. "What's new?"

Suddenly a girl with a pixie haircut slides into view. Trish. Jen reaches back, taking her hand. Here, at the party, in front of everyone.

"Hi, Lucy," Trish offers.

I don't know what to do. I want to yell at her for all of Jen's tears, but Jen smiles at me.

"We've been working things out," Jen explains.

"Right," I reach out, pulling Trish in for a brief hug. "Great to see you again, Trish. So, are you guys…"

"Together?" Jen offers. "Yup."

"Is this *out*?"

Jen laughs. "As of twenty minutes ago, yup. When

we walked in, Trish grabbed me and kissed me in front of everyone." She giggles. "I totally wasn't expecting that tonight."

"How'd I miss that?"

Marissa nudges me. "You were in the basement."

"Why didn't you tell me?"

"I did, babe. Remember? If the love is there, it'll work out."

"For real, wise one, could you be less cryptic next time?"

"Nah, I kind of like this route."

Ian smiles at me from the corner and my gut stirs. "Well, Jen and Trish, I'm happy you guys are back together."

"Thanks."

"Listen, I've got to get home. Curfew." We say goodbye, then I make my way back to Ian's side. "I'm sorry, but I've got to get home."

"Right, absolutely," he says to me, but I swear his eyes flicker above my shoulder, studying Marissa. Good. This won't be that hard.

In the car on the drive home, I'm honest. Totally straight forward. My breath catches as his head moves with my words, still studying the road. Finally, he responds, "That sounds fine to me. As long as we can still be friends. You're too cool to lose."

"Friends I can do. For sure."

"Great. Are we still on for the coffee shop Saturday morning so I can help you study for your ACT?"

"Yes, definitely."

I crawl out of his Toyota. "Do you mind if I bring a friend along?"

"No problem. I actually like teaching ACT tricks."

"Well, she's already taken her ACT. I'd be bringing her

for fun."

"Who?"

"Marissa?"

Then he smiles. Good, there's something there for him too. "That'd be great," he says. "She's fun, plus I can quiz her about Harry Potter."

"Right. I guess I'll see you tomorrow then?" I lean back into the car before I shut the door, giving him a brief kiss on the cheek. "Thanks for being a good guy, Ian."

He blushes a bit. "No problem."

CHAPTER TWENTY-EIGHT

Justin

Right about now, I'd take being run over by a heard of buffalo crushing my bones and defecating in my face over the pain of Lucy's rejection. Of course she wasn't going to jump into my arms with that stupid apology. I know better than that. Lucy's full of fire. I'd need a monsoon to sizzle her out before she'd listen to me. Not that I'd want that, her fierceness is what I need in my life—someone to see through my total bull crap.

I sink into the leather couch in the living room, thankful for the silence of the house. Mom and Dad are staying at the governor's mansion tonight. No interruptions. A chance to finally acknowledge how royally I've screwed up.

It's like a train of disaster is following me. No matter how hard I try, I can't keep everything going. I can't keep it all right. I've given up. Even my Google calendar is sending me reminders to plan events. If Google's noticing I'm falling behind, there's no way I can pull my shit together well enough for Lucy to take me back.

A pillow wedges uncomfortably behind my back. Stupid cylinder pillow. What type of home actually has this crap! The pillow soars from my hands, smashing into the wall. All the hanging photos crash to the hardwood floor.

Shit.

I haul myself off the couch and grab a broom. Yet another awesome Justin Marshall moment. Just as I pick up the first photo out of the pile of glass, the garage door opens. Awesome. Goodbye, night to myself.

Dad walks in. His eyes widen as he takes in the scene. I catch my reflection in the mirror over the fireplace. It's been a while since I've had a haircut and with all the hair yanking I've been doing, I've got some crazy ass scientist hair. Dad must think I've gone nuts. He walks carefully into the room, eyebrow raised. Smart father. Beware of rabid son. His eyes don't leave mine as he reaches down, plucking a photo from the ground.

"You remind me so much of him like that," he says, touching my hair.

"Who?"

"Jackson," he smiles, glancing down at the photo in his hand. "Remember how funny he was? He used to do this weird act in the living room, making his hair stand up just like that."

"Vaguely." There's a flash of Jackson jumping off the couch into a pile of cushions, his hair all over the place.

"Jackson." Dad shakes his head as he takes a seat on the coffee table. "That kid. Man."

"He was great," I launch into his speech for him.

Dad laughs, coughing a little. "Actually, I was going to say that he drove me nuts."

"What? Jackson was a saint."

Dad laughs. "No, he was all over the place. If I turned around, he'd be climbing the counters. He figured out how to climb the walls when he was three. Three!"

"He was an amazing athlete."

"He was a kid with a great heart, but a total headache." He pulls out his wallet and hands me a photo. Jackson's got a huge smirk on his face, standing way too close to a cliff with his hands on his hips. "He refused to walk away from the edge until we took this picture at the Grand Canyon. That kid got in so much trouble pulling that stunt. I swore I'd never let him out of the car again."

"Weird, I don't remember Jackson like that."

"Of course you don't. He was your big brother, purely amazing in your eyes. You two were great together. I loved watching you play. Jackson's saving grace was how much he cared for you. He thought you were the world, wanted to teach you everything."

"Yeah, that's the Jackson I know. He knew how to do everything right. He was perfect."

"Jackson was fantastic, but far from perfect. He almost burned down our house once!"

"He probably didn't know what he was doing."

"No, he knew. He managed it while he was home on Hospice, a few weeks before he passed away. He was eight. He knew how fire worked."

"Then why'd he do it?"

"He was angry he was going to die," Dad says, taking the photo back and carefully putting it in his wallet. "The thing is, even in those moments, he was fantastic. Before he got sick, I used to research ways to raise a challenging child." He rubs the bridge of his nose. "I bought so many books. Nothing worked. Jackson did his thing and, thankfully, his heart was good. But man, did he love to screw things up.

"After he got sick, I saw him more clearly. How fantastic Jackson was for thinking outside of the box, for pushing the limits. It's what made him so great. He fought for what he wanted, hard. He never gave up. Even his last breath was strong."

"How come you're sharing this with me now?"

"I don't know. The whole photo scandal reminds me of something that would've happened to Jackson if he was here. That frustration… I wasn't used to feeling that toward you. After raising Jackson and it ending the way it did, I wanted everything to go right for you."

"Dad, Jackson didn't get leukemia and die because of anything you did, you know that, right?"

"Yes, I know, but the reasoning behind my hopes for your life is real. I wanted you to have it all. You did. You do."

"Weird…"

"What?"

"I always wanted to have it all because of Jackson. Wanted to be the perfect son and make up for what you guys were missing with him gone. Jackson's behind so many of my decisions. He always seemed to have the right answer."

"For you, he did. But in reality, he made mistakes. We all make mistakes. That's okay. Listen," he taps my knee. "I'm sorry if I ever made you feel like you had to be perfect just because I wanted you to have it all."

"You didn't ever drive perfection into me. That's my own deal."

"Based off of trying to be a replacement for Jackson for me and your mother?"

My nose starts to burn as I look away from him. Whoa. I didn't see this conversation coming, ever.

"Let it all go. Fight fiercely for what you want. If that means some plates come crashing down, I'll help you clean up the mess." He eyes the broken photos on the floor. "We'll always love you. No matter what. This year seriously messed me up. Actually, that's why I came home tonight."

"Why?" Did he and Mom get in another fight? Things have seemed better between them since he fired Paul.

"To tell you about a decision I made with your mom tonight." A light, relaxed smile spreads across his face. "After firing Paul, Mom and I revisited if we really did want to start down the track toward presidential candidacy. We agreed it's something that we don't want. I do still want to be Minnesota's Governor, so I'll run another term. If I lose though, it's okay. Mom and I are planning to start up a non-profit in our retirement. Something local and involving education. The idea's still a baby, but we are passionate about making it a reality."

"Wow, that's great. No, it's awesome. I didn't want you to become president either."

"Yeah. That path in life isn't for me. It's not for my family either." He takes off his sport coat. "It feels amazing to not have 'presidential candidate' on my radar anymore."

"I bet."

"So," he stands, grabbing the broom from the floor. "Why are the photos smashed on the floor?"

"Eh, I'm…"

"Oh, just spill it."

"I asked Lucy to take me back tonight and she rejected me. So I threw the pillow." My face burns as I bend down with the dustpan, keeping it still while Dad sweeps into it.

"That sucks."

"Yeah."

"What are you going to do about it?"

"I don't know."

He puts down the broom. "Why wouldn't she take you back?"

I reach down, mulling it over as I pick up the last photo. Jackson holding a baby. Me. His smile is crooked and there's a wild look in his eye. Dad's right, he did have that mischievous look. And there I am, sleeping peacefully in his arms. Being perfect.

That's it.

Oh my gosh. Lucy was right. Of course she's right! She's the smartest wise ass I know.

I'm obsessed with perfection. Just because it doesn't feel correct doesn't mean it's wrong. Unknowingly, I've gone through life as a critical asshole. I thought I was just striving to do good, but the moment things got too overwhelming, I fled. I couldn't handle things being real. My pursuit of perfection kept me from learning how to cope. No wonder Lucy kept her feelings from me. She was trying to keep our relationship easy, *perfect*, for me. She knew I needed it. She did what she could to hold us together. She's able to roll with the punches, even when they hurt, and I couldn't. I freaked out.

"There it is," Dad says. "Did you figure it out?"

"Yeah, I think I did. Perfect doesn't mean right."

"Love isn't perfect, Justin. It's a terrifying, messy thing

that requires the strength to not only believe in it but fight for it. Work on it. Love is hard. The hardest thing I've ever done and the greatest thing I'll ever do." He picks up a photo of Mom. "I'll fight for her the rest of my life. I want you to know that."

"I do. Thanks. She deserves it."

"She does." He takes the photo out of the shattered glass. "So, what's next for you?"

His words freeze me in place. Terror doesn't even begin to describe what I think I'm about to do.

"Go to Lucy. Live with your heart, not your head." He grabs the broom and smacks my leg with the bristles. "Let me clean up this mess."

CHAPTER TWENTY-NINE

Lucy

The shower runs cold. The transition stings my scalp, making my bones shift. Okay, okay. The hot shower obviously didn't work and this, well, *this* just sucks. I climb out, wrapping in a towel before dressing in my favorite pair of yoga pants and racer-back tank top. My breathing is still rapid, despite the steamy room.

Justin.

Why did he have to come back? Assuming I'd just jump back into his arms. Hell no. Not with that attitude. He hurt me so much. He's never going to understand it. Screw him. I was finally able to walk around without a thousand pounds weighing down my heart. Move through life, with just nine hundred and ninety-nine pounds weighing me down. But with that one pound gone, I got through. I moved on. But then why does everything feel so fresh? The way Justin held me tonight, for that moment in his arms. God. My skin still burns with his touch. It felt so good, but I can't let it happen again. Never again.

My heart flips and plunges, my toes curl. Instinct drives my heart, willing it to escape through the floor. This. Pain. Sucks. This isn't fair. I thought I'd moved on. He shouldn't be able to have this effect on me. Not anymore.

My phone vibrates on the counter. Surely, it's Laura's play-by-play of what I missed at the party after I left. Probably some stuff about Jen and Trish and how people are reacting. I pick it up, hoping that whatever people said to them was kind.

Instead, Justin's name is branded across my screen.

Justin: Can we talk? Please?

My breath catches in my throat. No. There's no way I'm talking to him. He ignored my texts forever. Enjoy how it feels, buddy.

I walk away, setting the phone back down as I go into my bedroom. Our team photo from this year hangs askew on the wall, so I reach over and tweak it. Better. On the desk below, two picture frames are turned over. My finger flips it over before I catch myself. Justin stares back at me, his hands wrapped around my waist, smiling as he brushes white paint on my face.

Pressing the photo back into the desk, I walk away. No need to flip over the other photo of us after homecoming and torture myself.

The phone vibrates again on the counter. And again. And again. Seriously? Get a clue. I pace the room with each vibration. The buzzing goes crazy. Oh my gosh. Is he seriously calling me? We haven't spoken on the phone since the day we broke up.

I crawl into bed, propping pillows on my lap. A lame attempt at self-restraint to keep me from running into that bathroom and answering the phone. I can do this. I can stay away from Justin. I will not fall into his arms just because he's finally calling me. That's not how this works.

Suddenly, something *clinks* against my window. Weird. The forecast said rainstorm but no hail. The clinks keep coming, but only on that window, and in rhythmic form. Maybe I should look? There's always been that crazy part of me that's wanted the guy throwing pebbles. But, no. I won't go.

But what if it's Ian? What if he's being all cute and romantic, trying to show he really is into me and I should give him another chance? I mean, yeah, that'd be creepy, but he's homeschooled. That's what guys do in the movies. It's already raining lightly. If he was stuck waiting out in that and got sick because of me, I'd feel horrible.

Okay. I move the pillows away. I'll check, just in case it's him.

I peel back the curtain and try to see through the branches of the tree blocking my window to the ground below. Dad's right. This thing needs to come down before it crushes me in my sleep during a storm. It's way too close. Another clink hits the window, right at nose level.

What the heck?

I focus in on the only place where a direct hit like that could come from. The tree trunk. Justin's wrapped around it, his hair wildly curly in the rain. The brightness of his green eyes startles me. I jump back, knocking over my desk chair.

"Open the window!" Justin screams. Oh my god! My

parents are going to hear him!

I yank open the window and lean out. "Justin Marshall. What are you doing? My parents are still awake in the kitchen. They are going to hear you."

"I don't care. I don't care if the whole world hears me, as long as you hear me."

I glare at him. He's insane. "Not happening. I've said all I needed to say to you." I slam the window shut and yank the curtains closed. Holy crap. He's in my tree.

"Lucy!"

And he's yelling again at the top of his lungs. I lunge again, opening the curtains and yanking open the window. "I'm not kidding. You need to stop. You're going to get me in trouble."

"I'm not kidding either. I'll yell until they call the cops. I don't care." He opens his mouth again to shout my name but I throw up my hand.

"Fine," I say.

"Can I come in?"

"Hell, no," I say as I remove the screen. I fling my leg over the windowsill, grabbing the branch above me and letting my feet dangle, finding the one below. My arms lift me and I tiptoe on the branch until the two come closer together. The bark is slippery from the mist. My toes slide and I scramble to find footing.

"Shit, Lucy." Justin reaches out, pulling me around the waist toward the thicker part of the branch and the trunk. He holds me for a moment, with heavy breath. My skin screams for him. Must find distance. I reach above, pulling myself to another branch, giving myself the space I need from his amazing touch.

"Are you crazy?" Justin says, a scold to his voice I've

never heard before.

"You're the one who wanted to talk," I snap back.

"Not out here."

"Then why the hell did you climb my tree?"

"You wouldn't answer the phone. Your light was on…I don't know. I needed to talk to you!" He pulls his hands through his hair before he stabilizes on the branches. He lets go of the trunk, pulling his hoodie over his head, so he's just wearing his gray v-neck undershirt. He steps out toward me and I tremble, realizing how horrible I'd feel if he fell. He hands me the hoodie. "Take it. I don't want you getting sick."

The hair on my skin is already standing on end, goosebumps becoming more pronounced with each shiver.

"Take it," he insists and I do. I pull it over my head and the smell—oh God—the warm smell of Justin wraps itself around me. The sensation overwhelms me and I struggle to maintain composure. His smell will not send me to tears.

"Why did you come here?" I ask as he reaches up to steady himself on the branch above me.

"To say I'm stupid."

"Yeah, you are," I spit back. The tears start. He *is* stupid!

"I should've never let you go. Take me back."

"Why? Why would I ever do that?" I scoot farther away on the branch, but he's there, climbing with me.

"Because you were right and I was wrong. I wanted everything to be perfect for you. But here's the truth, Lucy: I'm not perfect… I'm a mess. I can't promise perfection and I was a fool to believe I could keep things like that. Turns out, I don't *want* perfection. I want a *real* relationship." He reaches out, touching my cheek. "I want to know when you cry, so I can dry your tears and share your pain. I never want you to hold back how you feel because you're afraid it'll stress me out. I can handle it now, because I'm a mess. Because I know it's okay. It's life."

His words are like hydrogen peroxide to my wounds.

"You weren't happy with me. It got hard. Really hard," I say between shaky breaths. Crap, I don't even know what I'm saying. With Justin so close and his smell all around me, it's impossible to know what I want. My head's gone and my emotional pendulum is swinging on turbo mode.

"It's not always going to be easy. Look at your parents, look at your friendships. Not easy. That honeymoon stage was awesome, but we'd be foolish to think it lasts like that always. Heck, I don't want it to. Challenges are coming. I want to meet life's challenges *with* you. The best part will be growing together, changing. It's going to be the hardest thing I've ever done. But I want it. All of it." He leans down toward me, his mouth hovering only a few inches from my own. "All the kisses. All the fights. All the tears." I blink as his finger gently wipes away the tears that somehow made it onto my cheek. "Be with me," he says with bated breath.

I gaze at him as my heart plays wrecking ball inside the cage where I shoved it when he left me. "You can't show up and apologize for breaking my heart and expect everything to be fine." My adrenaline kicks in, fighting back against his ability to make me swoon. Words need to be said, right now.

He laughs wildly then, his hair crazy and his shirt soaking wet. "Believe it or not, I don't want everything to always be fine. I lived like that for a long time and it sucked. Who knows what the future holds? All I know is I want to tackle it with you." He reaches again for my arm. "Lucy, you're the love of my life. I need you in it, if you'll have me."

My pulse throbs in my ears. I reach out, wanting to shake some sense into him. Why is he doing this to me? It hurts so much. But just as my hand reaches his chest, he shifts positions and suddenly, he's falling forward out of the tree.

Oh no! My heart stops as I watch the fall and only beats again as he lands on his feet. Thank God he's so athletic. He turns around and glares up at me, his face all screwed up. Whoa. I don't think I've ever seen Justin pissed off before.

The rain picks up strength. He shields his face as he looks up toward me. "Don't you dare end things like that," he yells up to me. "I'm here, loving every part of you. Take it."

"It's not that easy!" I shout back over the now downpour.

"It can be though. How else do you take a risk? Sometimes you've just got to leap."

I cling to the tree. If I jump, will he think I'm all in? Because…oh God. Yes, I am. But, no…this is such a mess still!

"Get your butt down here and let's finish this conversation. For better or worse." His pissed off look does something then that I never expected. It proves he's not just perfect, he's human. Somehow, being pissed at me is one of the best things he's ever done.

I swing my legs, antagonizing him. "It's not going to end well."

"I don't care. Either come down or I'm coming back up."

I jump then, bracing my ankles to take the impact of the landing. Suddenly, he steps in front of my landing spot, catching me at the hip. He holds me above him, pressing me against his chest as he slowly lowers me to his eye level.

I push against him. "Put me down!" How dare he hold me right now.

"Is that what you really want?" His voice is husky, the intensity sends warmth up my spine. "Me to let you go?"

I hesitate, feeling the thump of his heart against my own. Our hearts reach out for one another, mingling in rhythm and song. This, this is... whoa. *Whoa.* Every cell in my body aligns, finally feeling right where I belong.

"I thought so," he says after I don't answer him. He still holds me as the skies open and sheets of rain fall. "I'll never let you go, Lucy. Unless you want me to. But, please," he says, "don't ever ask me to do that."

His lips find my jawline. So soft against my skin. A sigh of longing follows. "I love everything about you. Please, let me back into your life. I want you. All of you. Always."

As I try to breathe through the power of his kiss, my eyes catch the silhouette of my parents in the window. They're putting away dishes, still clueless I'm out here. The image of them together makes everything click. My parents only made it through Mom's depression because they fought for one another, worked hard, and believed in love. They had no idea they'd be handling that when they started dating. Life isn't an exclusively lovely road. It'd be naive of me to think that's what love is. Hell, I don't want a love that shallow. I want a love that will last a lifetime, like theirs.

"Please, be with me?" Justin asks one more time. His voice melts my steely resolve. My hands find his hair, my lips scorch against his. I wrap my legs around him as I abandon the idea of *perfect* love, instead, embracing real love. A love that's shaking me to my bones.

"Yes."

"Yes?"

I lean into him once more, answering with my lips again. Our bodies tremble together as we explore one another in an intensity we've never experienced before. "I love you," I say.

Real, raw, terrifying love.

A complete mess. Perfect.

EPILOGUE

My breath stills as I lean back, delighting in the early summer warmth on my cheek. God, it feels so good to be back at the pool. I shift on the bench, enjoying another deep breath. The pool gate creaks back and forth as I eavesdrop on people talking about their plans for Watson's Kick-Off Summer party tonight.

I can't help but laugh, remembering what happened a year ago on this exact bench. I was weak, lost, and pissed off. So incredibly pissed off at the guy who thought he was wise and knew how I should be living my life.

Suddenly, a hand rests on my shoulder and, instead of jumping, my muscles relax.

"Hey, Lady," he whispers before his lips press into my cheek, that five o'clock stubble tickling me. "What are you thinking about?" He takes my hand as he crosses to the front of the bench, sliding next to me and smiling.

That strong jaw and always there five o'clock shadow still makes my heart trip. I lean in, kissing it lightly before I tell him everything.

The End

ACKNOWLEDGEMENTS

First, I must thank my readers for loving *Effortless With You* enough to give me the opportunity to share more of Justin and Lucy's story in *Perfectly Messy*. Every word of praise and encouragement has meant the world to me. Thank you.

To my husband, Greg, thank you for fighting daily to have a real relationship with me. You're my warrior and I love you.

To Evelyn, Penelope, and Owen, thank you for making me a better and stronger person. Being your mother is the best thing that's ever happened to me. I look at you and know I can do it, because I do it for you. It's always for you.

Also, thank you to my parents and siblings for their love and support. A special shout out to David Wirt for lending a guy's perspective and picking out a great pair of basketball shoes.

To my first readers, Rebecca Froehle and Rose Froehle, your enthusiasm for *Primer* gave me the courage to step out there and take a chance on my dream. Thank you.

To Elissa Lucier, thank you for dealing with me frantically throwing plot twists at you over the phone. Your insight as a youth pastor was invaluable! Katie Stano, thank you for watching my children so this book could actually make it into readers' hands.

To my wonderful critique partners, Fiona McLaren, Katrina Sincek, Cassie Mae, Rebecca Yarros and Nikki Urang, thank you for diving in and helping me bring the next step of Justin and Lucy's relationship to life. To my supportive author groups, The Off Beats and Beta Book Peeps, thank you for your endless encouragement and love.

This book also wouldn't exist without the support of my amazing agent, Dr. Jamie Bodnar Drowley. Thank you for being a woman of great character.

Thank you to Mandy Schoen, my incredible editor, for "getting" me and dealing with my create-a-word vocabulary. More than anyone, you've always understood the heart of each story. Working with you is a joy.

Thank you also to Georgia McBride and the team at Swoon Romance for all they have done to help this series become a reality.

LIZZY CHARLES

Lizzy Charles lives in the Twin Cities and is a graduate of the University of Minnesota. When she isn't raising her three children or caring for premature and sick babies as a neonatal intensive care nurse, she's seeking refuge with her laptop, sparkling water, and dark chocolate. She married her high school sweetheart, a swoon-worthy musician, so it's no surprise she's fallen in love with writing contemporary YA romance novels.

Preview more great YA titles from Swoon Romance.

Visit **www.myswoonromance.com**

EFFORTLESS *with* YOU

A NOVEL

LIZZY CHARLES

HOW TO DATE

A

N E R D

Bestselling Author of *Reasons I Fell*
For The Funny Fat Friend

CASSIE MAE

HOW TO SEDUCE
A
BAND
GEEK

From Amazon Bestselling Author
CASSIE MAE

HOW TO HOOK A
BOOK WORM

From Amazon Bestselling Author
CASSIE MAE

Teaching bores to
score since 2013!

the ROMEO club

REBEKAH L. PURDY

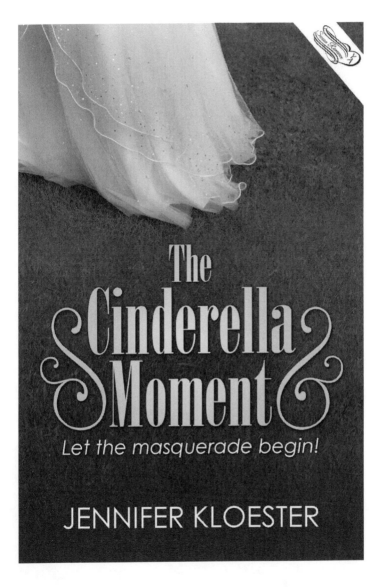

The
Cinderella
Moment

Let the masquerade begin!

JENNIFER KLOESTER

14833098R00186

Made in the USA
San Bernardino, CA
06 September 2014